She could hear the pain in his voice, see the wounded expression of his eyes, which told her so much more than his words. His wife had left behind scars. Watching the muscle twitch at his jaw she sensed that he still hadn't gotten over being rejected. Even though Jesse wanted to push him into revealing more, the frown on his face stopped her. Instead, she allowed herself to imagine for a moment what it would be like to be married to him. She couldn't speculate on what the days would be like, but she had already experienced a night first hand. She couldn't stop the ripple of pleasure that escalated up her body.

DEDICATION

To Willie Mae Rogers and Eleanor Daniels. Where would the world be without grandmothers like you?

ACKNOWLEDGMENTS

To the hundreds of readers who have taken the time to write me and share their positive feedback about my books. Thank you so much!

PROLOGUE

"Jesse James."

At the sound of the low raspy voice, the nineteen-year-old college student swung around. Her eyes roamed the crowd of people flooding the quadrangle, in search of a familiar face. She found several. However, the only person trying to get her attention was an old lady standing behind a booth at the edge of the carnival.

"Chile, you hear me talkin' to ya?"

Jesse removed a pair of sunglasses perched on her short straight nose. Gazing across the green grass, her eyes narrowed suspiciously. "How do you know my name?"

A secretive smile formed on the old woman's lips. "I'm supposed to know."

Yeah, right. The teenager didn't believe that for one moment, but decided to leave well enough alone, for now.

Jesse took a quick glance at the sign over the booth: Ms. Persia, Fortune-Teller. *You've got to be kidding.* She'd never been superstitious and thought psychics to be a lot of bull.

"Come on over here, chile." The frail turban-wearing woman crooked an index finger and signaled the teenager to move closer. She obviously sensed Jesse's hesitation because she added, "You don't have to believe, just listen to what the crystal ball has to say."

Frowning, Jesse looked around. Students were everywhere. But where was Chanelle? She mumbled a string of choice words under her breath. Her best friend had to be behind this. Ever since she had come out from using the port-a-potty, Chanelle had been nowhere to be found. Jesse could bet she was somewhere close by, watching and laughing.

Jesse turned her attention back to the woman waiting anxiously for her response. *Okay, I'll play along.* "Alright, how much is this going to cost?" she asked as she strolled forward.

"Five dollars."

Jesse grumbled as she placed her glasses in her purse and removed a five-dollar bill. Five dollars was a lot for a struggling college student. The least Chanelle could have done was prepay the woman. Unlike most of her friends at the University of Illinois-Chicago, UIC, her parents weren't paying her way. She was fortunate enough to have earned a full-scholarship. Even then, she still worked a part-time job to cover her daily living expenses. "Okay."

As Ms. Persia's long thin fingers caressed the crystal, Jesse fixed her eyes on the woman's exotic features. Her mahogany complexion was pulled taunt over high cheekbones. She had a long nose, big lips and slanted eyes that were as dark as blackberries. The only signs of aging were her wrinkled hands and bony fingers.

The rays of the sun cast marvelous green shadows on the ball and to her surprise, Jesse found the object fascinating. Shifting her gaze back to the fortune-teller, Jesse discovered Ms. Persia staring intensely at the beautiful object, as if she were peeking through a window.

"I see the word *Will*."

Jesse arched a sweeping, curved eyebrow. "Will?"

"Maybe Wayne…no, it's Will. He will change your life forever," she predicted with a decisive nod of the head.

Whatever. No man was ever going to change her life. Her last two boyfriends had destroyed any fantasy she might have had about finding her soul mate. She and the male gender didn't mix. And as far as Jesse was concerned, a man was the last thing she needed. Without another word, she thanked the woman for wasting her time and walked away.

"There will also be a baby," Ms. Persia called after her.

Jesse stopped in her tracks, then spun on the heels of her sneakers. "A baby? Me?"

"Yes, a baby boy," she replied with a nod.

"Lady, you're crazy!" Jesse was cracking up as she turned and moved into the thick of the crowd. Having a baby required the help of a man. Both were the farthest things from her mind.

CHAPTER ONE

Six years later

"Why haven't you started remodeling the other two guest rooms?"

Pace Delaney sneered at Jesse, his eyes openly speculative. "Because I felt replacing the carpet in the living room was more important."

Jesse leaned across her desk and glared at him. In the past week alone, she had found Pace undermining her authority on several occasions. He obviously needed to be reminded who the boss was. "You are aware all decisions are to be approved by me?"

"Your father never seemed to mind," he drawled.

She slammed her palms on the desk, then rose. "I'm not my father."

"No…you're not." Pace looked thoroughly in control of himself and of the situation. "Your father had confidence in my ability. Too bad *you* can't say the same."

Jesse groaned inwardly. He never let up. Pace was a pompous ass. Unfortunately, Delaney Construction was all she could afford and Pace was the foreman. If he left, the renovations would cease and she couldn't have that. Only eight weeks remained before the tourist season began and Katherine's Bed and Breakfast wasn't even close to being ready for reopening.

Jesse glanced up at Pace's fat nose and thick lips. Despite the fact that he was barely ten years her senior, his hair had long since departed. He had both hands planted in his pockets, parting his windbreaker at the waist, giving her a clear view of his large, protruding stomach.

"Maybe I haven't made myself clear. This is *my* house, not yours. *I* run things here, not you," she said rapidly. "If you have a problem with that, then I suggest that you and your crew pack up and get the hell off my property."

There was a tense moment of silence and for a split second Jesse almost believed she might have gone too far. Then Pace finally spoke again.

"I still can't understand why you're wasting your money trying to repair this rundown old house, especially since in a year this establishment will belong to someone else…perhaps even me." Pace took one sweeping look at her, then sneered again with as much malice as he was capable of, "Unless you've found yourself a husband."

Jesse's breath caught in her throat. However, she refused to let Pace know his comment hurt. It was bad enough her father had named her after a boy; it was even worse that she looked like one.

With as much dignity as she could muster, she replied in a voice with an icy twist, "I'm here to stay, so get used to it." Lowering back into her seat, Jesse added, "I hope this is the last time we have this discussion. You may go now." She then emphasized her meaning with a dismissive wave of the hand. It wasn't until the door shut that she slumped back in her seat.

Why did I come back? Life in Chicago was so much simpler. She had been home two months, long enough to discover that nothing was the same.

The only thing she and Pace seemed to agree on was that the bed and breakfast was rundown. She'd had no idea things were as bad as they were. If she had only known, she wouldn't have stayed away so long.

Jesse had attended The University of Illinois-Chicago, majoring in hotel management. She had been determined to prove to her father that she was just as capable of running the family-owned establishment as she would have been if she were male. After graduation, she had taken a job managing a small hotel chain, learning everything she could for three years, determined to return to Delaware and take hold of the reins. Now, after years of trying to prove herself to her father she was finally in charge. Only it hadn't turned out the way she had hoped.

Her pulse began to throb at her temple. Jesse reached into the top drawer of the large old desk for a bottle of ibuprofen. As soon as she had gotten word that her father had been rushed to the hospital, she had returned home. Only it had been too late.

Jesse felt old memories come to life. Happier times when her father was vibrant, alive. Why had God taken him away so soon? He'd died of kidney failure, two months before her twenty-fifth birthday. Closing her eyes, she allowed sorrow to push to the surface. His death had been too soon. Not only had she lost the father she loved, but she hadn't been given enough time to prove to him that she was ready to follow in his footsteps.

Jesse removed the bottle cap and slid two tablets into the palm of her hand, then washed them down with a swig of bottled water. Sighing, she leaned back in her chair and closed her eyes again. Deep down inside she knew all her years of education and training still wouldn't have made a bit of difference to Jesse James, Senior.

Though she had tried for years to prove to her father that she was prepared to be his successor, he had never taken her seriously. However, she had been confident that the next time they talked she would make him listen and see things differently. But she hadn't had that opportunity. If they'd had that talk, he might not have tied her hands the way he had, forcing her to do something she would never have dreamed of doing.

Jesse had loved Jesse James, or Ole Man as he was called by everyone, including his daughter. The big burly man with an ill temper and chauvinistic views was all she'd ever had. Elizabeth James, who had been twenty years his junior, had walked out on them when Jesse was only two years old and never looked back. As a child, Jesse had fantasized about her mother's return but as the years progressed and at her father's insistence, she had finally given up hope.

Now that her father was gone, Jesse realized she had paid for her mother's mistake. Ole Man had never gotten over his wife leaving him and as a result had turned into a cold and bitter man, who distrusted all women. Despite the fact that Jesse had done everything in her power to prove him wrong, in the end it hadn't mattered. Under the terms of her father's will, she could lose her legacy, Katherine's Bed and

Breakfast, which had been in her family for generations, if she didn't meet certain stipulations: She either had to be married or have given birth to a male child before her twenty-sixth birthday.

Ole Man was an old-fashioned type of guy, who believed a woman's place was in the kitchen. He truly believed that if he had put his foot down with his wife, things would have been different. And when it came to his daughter, Ole Man had wanted Jesse to marry well and spend her life having babies and devoting her time to her man.

When Jesse was offered a full scholarship to UIC, her father fought her, but in the end, Jesse had won. In her freshman year she discovered what freedom really was. She hadn't known how smothering a life she had lived until she went away to school for four years. Finally she had been allowed to think for herself. She had been able to breathe. She didn't want another man dictating her life the way her father had.

Only now, her hands were tied.

Jesse ran a frustrated hand through her unruly curls. She kept her reddish brown hair cut short, almost a man's hairstyle, so that she could simply run a comb through it. Cosmetics were something she knew nothing about and she had a nervous habit of biting her nails. Her wardrobe proved that fashion was not her thing. She had always worn clothes two sizes too big to hide the wide hips she had inherited from her mother and the flat chest she had gotten from her father's side of the family. Whenever she wore a dress, it was because she was attending a wedding or funeral. It was no wonder that men didn't look twice at her. Now, however, looking feminine was mandatory because she couldn't stand the thought of someone else running Katherine's Bed and Breakfast. She had to push forward, not drag her feet. *Where there's a will, there's a way.* That was the motto she'd governed her life by, but now it took on a whole new meaning.

The fortune-teller had been right. A will would change her life forever. The irony was that it came in the form of a sheet of paper instead of a man.

Lowering her head to her hands, Jesse groaned aloud. She had paid some fancy lawyer in Wilmington, Delaware, to examine the will.

Apparently, her father had also hired a high-priced lawyer to draw up the terms because there were no loopholes: The document was iron-clad, so her lawyer said.

"Damn you, Ole Man!"

What was she going to do? Let someone like Pace step in and steal her future? No way! She had never been a quitter.

So, she either had to marry or get pregnant. Marriage wasn't a consideration. She could just see some man walking in and taking over. But a baby? Maybe. The fortune-teller had told her that she would give birth to a son. He would be all she needed.

One thing for certain, she was going to save the bed and breakfast even if she had to lose her virginity to do it.

CHAPTER TWO

Jesse stepped into Kuttin' Up hair salon before she lost her nerve. What she really wanted to do was run back to her car, start the engine and zoom away.

The nauseating scents of chemical relaxers and hair spray greeted her at the door. WJKS 101.7 FM and women's chatter filled the air. The full service salon was in full swing. All of the stylists had customers in their chairs and more were sitting in the cozy waiting area, watching Jerry Springer.

"May I help you?" the receptionist cordially asked.

Jesse's throat was suddenly dry. Nervously, she moistened her lips. "Uh…I have a ten-thirty appointment with Bernice."

The young ebony woman briefly glanced down at her calendar. Nodding, she glanced up again with a warm smile. "Welcome, Jesse. Have a seat. She'll be with you shortly."

Jesse nodded and moved to the only available seat on a faux leather couch to the far right of the big-screen TV. It was barely ten o'clock. However, Jesse figured with as much work as she required, she had better get an early start.

Her best friend, Chanelle Carpenter, had made the appointment with the salon; first with her stylist, next with a nail technician. Afterward she would go to Chanelle's house to continue her makeover. Jesse had never been any good at any feminine things, not even make-up. She'd never felt the necessity. *Until now.*

She blew out a long breath as she thought about the quest at hand. Though she wasn't sure any amount of grooming would help, at this point she was desperate enough to try just about anything.

Today would be the first day since her return to Delaware she had taken a day off. There was no telling what decisions Pace would make while she was away. She had known him all her life, but he'd changed into a bitter man after the death of his parents. If Pace had his way, he would drag his feet until he destroyed everything her father had created. Damn him. If only she had the money to hire a real crew.

Slumping comfortably on the couch, Jesse listened as some hillbilly on the screen told his wife he was leaving her and their six kids for his sixty-five-year-old mother-in-law. Jesse shook her head. She'd never understood how people could watch the trash that came on daytime television.

To pass the time, she picked up a new issue of *Essence* from a small table and flipped through the magazine while she waited.

"Jesse?"

Tilting her head at an angle, she glanced up at a busty, caramel-skinned woman. Ample cleavage peeked from beneath her green smock.

"I'm Bernice. Follow me."

Jesse rose from the couch and followed her lead to a chair at the back of the room. It was a nice salon. Although she hadn't been in many salons in her lifetime, she knew a nice one when she saw it.

The floor was covered with green and white marble tile. The walls were a striking white and were hung with pictures of hair designs and mirrors. The workstations were spaced far enough apart so that a patron didn't feel cramped. All of the employees wore green smocks and had hairdos that were out of this world. Jesse could swear a dark chick in the corner had a pineapple on her head. Another's hair was almost the same shade as her smock, and two had bleached blonde hair.

Jesse nibbled nervously on her bottom lip and wondered if maybe coming here wasn't such a good idea. There was no way in hell she was going to leave the salon looking like one of them. If the staff represented the type of services provided, maybe she needed to hightail it out of there as quickly as possible. Some of the customers in their chairs, however, looked fantastic.

Once Jesse was seated in the chair, Bernice shifted the chair from side to side as she examined her. Finally, she gave Jesse a funny look, then asked, "What do you have in mind?"

Jesse shrugged without even considering the question. "I don't have the slightest idea. As long as I don't have to use a curling iron or tie my hair up at night I'm game for just about anything."

Nodding, Bernice draped a black cape around her shoulders, secured it with a single snap, and reached for a comb. She raked it through Jesse's curly hair several times, determining the length and texture, then said, "May I make a suggestion?"

"Sure, anything," Jesse said, looking at Bernice's reflection in the mirror.

"How about adding some highlights to your color, then giving you a cut that is a bit more…feminine?" she suggested.

Jesse glared at the woman and was tempted to ask her what she was trying to imply, then decided against it. Chanelle had told her Bernice was one of the best in the city. The last thing she wanted to do was upset her. Besides, a feminine look was what she so desperately needed.

"Fine," she mumbled as she slumped down in the chair with a dejected look. "Whatever you think will work."

"Don't worry, you're gonna love it," Bernice said with complete confidence as she reached for a pair of scissors.

If the smell didn't kill her, Jesse was certain wasting what felt like an entire day, moving from one chair to the next, would. She couldn't understand how women endured it month after month. She was shuffled from one chair to the next while having to listen to all of the neighborhood gossip. Jesse was thankful for the hum of the hairdryer just to drown out all the laughter. You would have thought she was at a town meeting.

She was only seconds from falling asleep when Bernice signaled for her to return to her chair. Jesse lifted the dryer head and dragged herself over. How much longer? she asked herself. As Bernice reached for a pair of trimmers, Jesse closed her eyes and tried to ignore the doubt in the back of her mind. Earlier, she had made the mistake of looking down at the floor at the locks of her hair. She had been on edge ever since. If she already looked like a boy, wouldn't cutting her hair even shorter make her look more so? She cringed at the idea of having to wear a baseball cap until her hair grew out again.

Ten minutes later, Bernice swung her around in the chair and handed her a mirror. "Well, what do you think?"

Jesse curled her fingers around the handle and stared at her reflection. She was stunned, speechless. Was the lovely woman staring at her really her?

Her naturally curly hair had gold highlights and had a cut that accentuated her delicate peanut butter-colored face.

A satisfied smile curved her strong mouth. Everything was going to be okay.

Jesse pulled her beat-up Buick into the charming community of Dogwood Lane. A beautiful pond sat at the entrance, surrounded by white and red dogwoods. With the beginning of spring, the flowering trees were in full bloom. Chanelle's custom built two-story home of stone and stucco was at the end of the lane. She pulled in behind her candy apple red Mercedes and climbed out.

Moving up the steps, Jesse patted her hair, to make sure there wasn't a strand out of place before she rang the doorbell. She didn't have to wait long before she heard slippers sliding across the floor.

"Jesse, you look fabulous, girl," Chanelle enthused, wrapping her in a tight hug. She stepped back to assess her friend and shook her head in amazement. "I knew that beneath that wild hair there was a beautiful woman just waiting to come out."

Jesse and Chanelle had been best friends since high school. They'd grown up on the same street, attended the same school, and shared the same friends.

While Jesse had hoped to follow in her family's footsteps, Chanelle had always wanted to be an author. But after marrying a professional basketball player and giving birth to a beautiful little girl, she'd put her own dreams aside and focused on her family. It wasn't until after she went through a bitter divorce that she finally decided to buy a computer and pursue her first love. She was now the author of three best-selling novels and had just completed her fourth manuscript.

While Jesse was stubborn, explosive and tactless, Chanelle was fun loving, wild and carefree. Jesse truly admired her friend. Even though they bumped heads quite a bit on different issues, mainly men, there had always been a part of her that wished she could be more like Chanelle.

Jesse took in her friend's appearance. She had a way of making loose fitting jeans and a short-sleeved, red turtleneck sweater look good. She was a size seven with a flawless cinnamon-toned complexion that Jesse had always envied.

"I'll let that beautiful woman comment pass," Jesse said in greeting as she stepped into the foyer.

"Girl, puhleeze. I bet men were hanging out their cars trying to get a good look at you," Chanelle teased as she followed her into a spacious living room. "I told you Bernice could work wonders with your hair." She laughed again and plopped down on the couch. "And it's about time." She had been trying for years to convince Jesse to do something about her hair and had been shocked when Jesse had made the suggestion herself.

Jesse took a seat in the recliner and looked around in the elegant room with its vaulted ceiling, Berber carpet, and carefully chosen contemporary furnishings. She hoped to someday have a home of her own. Right now, she was grateful for the meager suite on the first level of the bed and breakfast.

An old grandfather clock in the corner chimed three o'clock, drawing her attention.

"Where's my goddaughter?"

"She's with her father for the weekend. He drove down this morning."

She saw the look on Chanelle's face at the mention of Cecil. He was a point guard for the Philadelphia Sixers. Even after a bitter divorce, she had a strong suspicion Chanelle still had her heart set on reconciling.

"How is Cecil?"

"Now that they are out of the playoffs he has plenty of time on his hands to spend with Chante *and* Amber." She scrunched her lips at the mention of the woman. She was bitter that not only had he left her but had left her for a woman with blonde hair and blue eyes.

As Chanelle tipped her head to look at Jesse, her chemically relaxed, shoulder length hair flowed to one shoulder. "Not that I'm complaining, but why the sudden need to change your appearance?"

Jesse looked pointedly at her, making sure she had Chanelle's attention. "I need to find a man."

Chanelle laughed lightly. "Girl, don't we all."

She shook her head and decided to try a different approach. "You don't understand. I want to have a baby."

Chanelle's mouth dropped open and for the first time in all the years Jesse had known her, her best friend was speechless.

"Did you hear what I said?" Jesse asked after an awkward moment of silence passed between them.

Chanelle closed her mouth, her amber eyes wide with disbelief. "You're kidding me, right?" she finally muttered.

She shook her head. "No. I'm not."

"Girl, you don't even have time for a man." She waved her hand in dismissal. "You couldn't possibly want to be tied down with a child."

"I have to have a baby before I turn twenty-six. I don't have a choice."

Chanelle frowned and shook her head to clear it. "Girl, you still have another ten years to find a husband and get married before your biological clock starts to tick."

"No. I'm afraid I don't." She then explained her father's will.

Chanelle gasped. "Why didn't you tell me this before?"

Her lips were pressed firmly together and Jesse could tell Chanelle was hurt that she had not shared the information sooner. "I was hoping to find a lawyer who could overturn it."

"Unbelievable."

"I know. I can hardy believe it myself."

Chanelle crossed her long legs and impatiently tapped a manicured nail against her thigh. "You couldn't possibly be considering marriage?"

"No. I'm considering finding a man to impregnate me."

Chanelle's neck snapped back. "Please tell me you're joking."

Jesse took an exasperated breath and rose. "No, Chanelle, I'm not. I really don't have much of a choice. As soon as I produce a birth certificate for a son, my father's lawyer will hand over the deed and a check for two hundred and fifty thousand dollars."

"This is crazy! You can't just meet a man and have sex with him. Besides, there is no guarantee you'd have a son. And what about all the diseases going around? Are you really willing to take that chance?" she challenged.

"Yes, damn it, I am. I'll do whatever it takes to save the bed and breakfast."

Chanelle was quiet as she contemplated her options. "And how do you plan to pull this off?"

Suddenly the wind went out of her sails. "That's where you come in."

Chanelle simply arched a perfect eyebrow.

Jesse shrugged. "I need your expertise."

She pursed her lips. "Uh-huh, I'm listening."

"I need you to take me to one of those nightclubs you hang out at on the weekends."

Chanelle was quiet for several seconds before she released a heavy breath and said, "Are you sure about this?"

Jesse nodded.

"Alright, I'll help you, but first we need to make a trip to the mall. We need to find you something sexy to wear for tonight, then stop by the cosmetic counter. Mauve would look great on your face."

"Uh-uh."

Chanelle rose from her relaxed position on the couch. "Let me grab my purse. We've got to start at Victoria's Secret. Then we have to find a knock-out dress, then some shoes and…"

Jesse blew out a breath as she reached for her purse. What had she gotten herself into?

CHAPTER THREE

"I look like a slut!" Jesse bellowed as she tugged at the hemline of the little black dress Chanelle had talked her in to buying.

Chanelle gave her a reassuring smile. "No you don't. You look fabulous. In fact, you've got everybody looking at you."

"That's the problem," she groaned. Every dog in the house had his tongue hanging out of his mouth, gawking at her as if she were a ham bone. Nevertheless, despite her dismay, the dress was a necessary costume for the role she had to play tonight.

They had only been at Spencer's for about twenty minutes. The Philadelphia lounge was bustling with a happy hour crew anxious to start their weekend.

The two-hour drive from Rehoboth Beach, Delaware had been her idea. With what she had planned, Jesse wanted to be as far away from home as possible.

Heart pumping, palms sweating, Jesse chewed her lip and studied the stream of people dressed in suits and ties. Somewhere among those men had to be her baby's daddy.

They were sitting at a quiet booth in the corner of the lounge where she was able to get a clear view of everyone who came through the door. She picked up her glass of tequila, sipped and swallowed, trying to ease her dry mouth. She was incredibly nervous. Never before in her life had she ever thought of doing something so bold. Her heartbeat thundered like an on-coming train, nearly deafening her. Glancing wistfully at the door, she took a shuddery breath, trying to relax her body and mind.

"There are definitely some fine brothas in here tonight," she heard Chanelle say.

Jesse nodded. Indeed, there were several attractive men standing around the bar but no one had piqued her interest quite yet. Her mission required a good-looking brother who looked desperate enough to sleep with her without thinking about asking her for her last name or phone number.

Crossing her bare legs underneath the table, Jesse thought about the way, unlike her friend, she had managed to stay away from the singles scene.

Nightclubs had never fascinated her. Even during college, partying never seemed to matter much to her. True, it wasn't as if the boys had been beating down her door. With a flat chest and a baseball cap on her head, she had often been mistaken as a boy. Not that she had cared. After dating one jerk after another, Jesse had come to the conclusion that a relationship wasn't in the cards for her and had decided to focus on her education. In doing so, she had managed to graduate at the top of her class. Since then she had dated only occasionally.

Tonight she needed to think and act like man. Sweet talk him into her bed, then be on her way. A one night stand. Nothing more. It shouldn't be too hard. She hoped.

A voice with deep sensual timbre cut through her thoughts. She gazed toward the stage and saw two men standing about twenty feet away.

They must be the band, she thought. Spencer's had live entertainment every Saturday night. The flyers posted around the lounge had read that the group scheduled to perform today was from Maryland.

The one with the bedroom voice was laughing along with another guy while setting up the sound system. She couldn't see his face but the sound of his voice sent a shiver of pure longing careening through her. She shook it off and took in his appearance. His broad shoulders were encased in a black shirt. When he reached for a box, the muscles in his forearm and biceps flexed. She swallowed thickly, then allowed her eyes to travel down to a pair of snug black slacks. All those muscles were wrapped so snuggly, the slacks looked as if they had been poured over his sexy body.

Three more guys also dressed in black arrived and assisted in setting up the equipment.

"I guess I don't have to ask who you are looking at."

Jesse was annoyed that Chanelle had caught her staring. She shrugged and reached for her almost empty glass. "One of them might do."

Her best friend snorted. "I think you've already got your sights set on that one in the middle. Sexy eyes, full lips and a helluva body. I think he would probably make a beautiful baby."

"Would you please shut up before he hears you?" Jesse hissed between her teeth as her eyes darted right, then left.

"You want to get his attention, right?"

Jesse gave a nonchalant shrug. "I haven't decided yet." She sat back and shifted her focus upward just as the man's eyes brushed across the crowd and collided with hers. Jesse's breath hitched, then released in one long rush.

A shiver of desire tore through her. His handsome face could have jumped straight out of her fantasies. Large, dark eyes. Sharp, confident angles. A broad nose and high cheekbones. His coal black shoulder length locs framed his sable face.

He was definitely a pretty boy. He had the look that left a woman's mind spinning and her body overheating. The cocky smile on his face was a clear indication that he knew it too. A disconcerting heat rushed through Jesse. Certainly not him. Whoever he was, he was definitely wrong. He had her emotions running wild. She needed a man that she could easily forget and she'd bet Sexy wasn't easily intimidated.

Jesse finally managed to break eye contact and glanced at each of the other band members until her eyes landed on the tallest and youngest of the bunch. He looked naïve, like a little brother. She bet he was still wet behind the ears. If she was lucky, he was very inexperienced. Now, that was the kind of guy she needed. Someone eager for attention and easy to manipulate.

When a dorky-looking guy standing next to her prospect caught her staring and nudged him on the shoulder, Mr. Naïve glanced her way. Jesse gave him a sensual smile. He returned it with a wobbly smile of his own before looking away.

Bingo! Jesse smirked ferociously. He was blushing. Excellent!

She didn't have long to indulge in her discovery before out the corner of her eyes she found Sexy watching her. He was looking at her with curious intensity, his heavy, smooth eyebrows raised and his succulent lips slightly parted with the tip of his tongue in view. For an unsettling moment, her heart thumped against her rib cage as she realized the cocky stranger would be more than willing to warm her bed.

Feeling uncomfortable, she looked away to find Chanelle grinning from ear to ear. "I see the two of you have made eye contact. Girl, he can't take his eyes off you."

"Which one?" Jesse pretended she didn't know who Chanelle was talking about.

"You know which one. The one with the dreads. He looks like that fine brotha from the soap opera."

Frowning, Jesse replied, "I was actually considering the tall one on the left."

"That bony little boy?" She chuckled. "Girl, he barely looks out of high school."

Jesse drew in a deep breath. "That's what makes him perfect."

Chanelle smiled, waving off her words with her hand. "You need a real man, not a boy."

That was where Chanelle was wrong. What she needed was somebody that she could easily forget.

After making certain she was no longer being watched, she glanced over at the stage, then pulled in a deep breath.

The handsome stranger had his back to her. It was now or never. The moment had finally arrived. Jesse's heart thumped. She had to do this. She had to. Summoning up much needed courage, she rose.

"Where are you going?" Chanelle asked.

"To meet my baby's daddy." She tossed the glass up and finished it, then placed it back down on the table and sashayed towards the stage. She couldn't get cold feet now. Her future depended on her.

Jesse slowed her pace and worked to maintain her composure as she admired the handsome stranger's butt and shook her head. No man should look that good. Whoever he was, he was definitely not the type of man she was looking for tonight, regardless of how gorgeous he was.

Remember what's at stake. Remember the mission. You can do this, she told herself soothingly. The bed and breakfast meant too much to her to lose track of what was most important.

Jesse set her jaw, then thrust her shoulders back. Taking a deep breath to settle the feeling of butterflies in her stomach, she moved closer to the stage. She was going to introduce herself to the youngest-looking man.

A rueful smile twisted Will's lips. *William Jones, you're getting too old for this business.* The gorgeous woman sitting across the room had barely spared him one glance from her wide eyes. She'd been too busy flirting with Chris Calhoun. Hell, she looked old enough to be Chris's big sister. Chris was barely the legal age to drink and wouldn't know what to do with a woman like her. Now him…that was an entirely different story.

Glancing over his shoulder, he spotted the woman heading towards Chris. She looked like a woman with an agenda. The question was, what? Chris was entirely too gullible when it came to women. The last one had taken him back to his hotel room and had cleaned out his wallet. Chris didn't know how to act when a woman found him attractive. *It looks as if history is about to repeat itself.* Will blew out a frustrated breath and stepped from behind his keyboard. Women like this woman knew how to strip a man of everything. Although Will didn't have the time or the patience to deal with the situation, he didn't feel he could ignore it. He moved to intercept the woman who seemed determined to make resistance next to impossible.

Physically she was different than the type of women he was usually attracted to. Petite, probably no more than five-three, she had a small waist that flared out into wide shapely hips. His brothers liked their women thick with plenty of meat on their bones, but Will preferred his tall and thin with long cascading curls. Nevertheless, he was attracted to this petite woman who was almost the complete opposite.

Short curls framed an angelic face with slanted dark brown eyes. Her peanut butter coloring appeared smooth and creamy. Despite the fact that she wasn't his type, it bothered him more than he cared to admit that she looked straight past him and locked onto Chris's back.

The fierce concentration on her features surprised him. What was she up to? Since he was Chris's self-appointed guardian, it was his job to find out. He stepped into her path.

"Hey, cutie. Can I help you?"

She sent him a pointed, narrow-eyed message that he chose to ignore. "No, you can not."

She tried to step around him but Will blocked her path again. When she rolled her eyes and tried moving to the left, Will slid to the right, blocking her. She moved again and then again and each time he countered.

The woman looked at him with sudden bewilderment. Then their eyes locked and held, pulling him into what felt like a whirlwind.

"Get out of my way," she finally said and though the spell was broken, his gaze never strayed from her face. Her supple lips were painted a muted shade of rose that would have tempted him if they weren't pressed so firmly together.

"Move."

"Can't let you up here." *Damn, she was fine.* Will took a minute to savor her sweetly curved form, working his way from the hand on her small waist to her eyes which were shooting sparks. He couldn't help noticing that the dress clung to curves and teased him with what it revealed and hid. There'd been a time when he'd let himself be distracted by a beautiful body, but not anymore. Her kind spelled trouble. He crossed his arms in the way that let her know he wasn't easily intimidated.

She inhaled sharply. "I just want to ask that guy a question."

Will followed her eyes, dark and veiled by sweeping lashes, directed at Chris, who was grinning in their direction. That boy had gotten them in enough trouble. This was one trip when he was setting the rules. "What is it you need to ask him?"

Her mouth curved slightly and one eyebrow lifted, challenging him. "I don't think that's any of your business."

He rubbed his chin wryly. "I'm afraid it is my business. This is my band and we don't need any groupies hanging around the stage."

"I'm not a groupie. I'm a grown woman."

Yes you are. "Sorry but you'll have to wait until after we perform." That would give him plenty of time to send Chris off to his room, where he would be safe from mischief.

Her face flushed and her chin lifted. "Look, buster, why don't you move before you get hurt?"

He narrowed his dark eyes on her for a moment, then leaned his head back and laughed. "Either you return to your seat or I'll be forced to carry you myself."

Jesse fought the urge to squirm beneath the challenging stare. However, something in his eyes told her he meant every word.

You'll have plenty of time to meet him after the performance.

With a dramatic roll of her eyes, she turned and walked back to her seat.

"How did it go?" Chanelle asked before she had even reached their booth.

"It didn't." Jesse flopped down onto the bench and folded her arms across her chest.

Thanks to the man who'd run interference, she'd missed her chance to meet the potential father of her baby. "That big bozo was cock blocking. I couldn't get two words in."

Chanelle shook her head. "I don't know what you see in that little kid. He looks too inexperienced. You'd probably have to show him all the right moves."

"Chanelle, for what I need, that's A-OK," she shot back.

"What you need is that man right ova' there." She wagged a brow toward the stage.

Despite every effort, Jesse's eyes glanced in the direction of Mr. Wrong and when their eyes collided, the air sizzled between them.

Something about him held her attention. Maybe it was that quality of male assurance that not many women could easily ignore or forget. Something told her to get out of her seat and get as far away from that man as she possibly could, but her feet wouldn't move. She couldn't seem to break free of the devil's spell. All she could do was sit and stare. Jesse blamed it on the way he kept licking his supple lips like LL Cool J. For the first time in her life, a man had evoked an immediate response from her. As if she were a fish on a hook, he was slowly reeling her in.

Remember the mission.

He isn't what you need tonight or any other night for that matter, she told herself. She was physically attracted to him and that made him all wrong. With her lips pressed tightly, she looked away.

She needed a man who was easy to forget. All she needed was thirty minutes of his time.

She was grateful when Chanelle ordered a round of margaritas. She would have to be drunk to pull off her stunt tonight.

CHAPTER FOUR

Jesse sipped her drink while considering her next move. All too soon, the lights dimmed and the band came onto the stage. The drummer clicked his sticks and the serenade began. A large woman moved to the microphone and bellowed out Phyllis Hyman songs.

Jesse sat back in her seat and crossed her legs. Although she tried to concentrate on baby boy, her gaze kept drifting to Mr. Wrong in the back. Her stomach lurched and she struggled to pull air past the knot in her throat. Again, she had the strongest urge to bolt out the lounge. Instead, she gripped her glass for dear life.

When she felt him watching her, Jesse experienced an unfamiliar curling sensation inside her. She acknowledged it with a shiver of excitement. Attraction, pure but not so simple. The man had sex appeal oozing from every pore and it had struck her on a primitive level. Her senses had responded by setting every nerve in her body tingling. Given his physical attractiveness, she wasn't surprised that her body would respond, but she was surprised by the strength of her response. The man had something and whatever it was, her senses liked it. Liked it a lot. And that's what made him all wrong for her.

As the performance continued, she found herself forgetting about the mission at hand and instead allowing her body to relax to the soothing tunes. She signaled for another round of drinks and sipped slowly while she watched. Before she knew it, the performance was over and the band was clearing the stage.

"That was nice," Chanelle said, breaking the silence at the table.

Jesse simply nodded in agreement.

The deejay resumed his post and slowed the music down. A guy with a tie that looked as if it were cutting off his air supply came over and asked Chanelle to dance. With a smile, Jesse watched him lead her onto the dance floor.

"Care to join them?"

Before she turned around, Jesse caught his scent, felt his presence pulsating around her. Looking up, she found Mr. Wrong standing beside her.

His silky voice stirred something elemental in her blood. Despite the fact his invitation was tempting, she couldn't. When she caught Chanelle's gaze, the message clearly said, *Isn't that the reason why we are here?*

"No."

He snorted, then said, "Too bad."

Before she could protest further, he grabbed hold of her arm, and led her onto the dance floor. She wanted to be annoyed by his arrogance but the moment he touched her, she lost the will to resist and instead found the physical contact arousing. He pulled her gently into the circle of his arms and the heat of his body coursed down the length of hers.

One dance, she told herself as she wrapped her arms loosely around his waist. One dance and then she could continue her mission.

The deejay had put on a slow number by Jaheim. She was very aware of the warm gentle imprint of his fingers on her bare back when they began to move to the music. As his hands moved gently along her back, the shiver coursing up her spine had nothing to do with the temperature of the room.

He pulled back slightly, his eyes studying her face. "You're trembling. Are you cold?" he asked. The warmth of his breath fanned her lips and the heat spread quickly through her body.

"No, she replied, not liking the effect he had on her.

She was inexperienced when it came to sexual attraction, but she was smart enough to know game when she heard it. Mr. Wrong had a magnetism that had no doubt won a lot of women's hearts, not to mention their beds, she thought. If he thought it was going to work on her, though, he was in for a rude awakening.

A glance to her left verified that Chanelle was on the other side of the dance floor watching her and grinning from ear-to-ear. Like a stubborn child, she stuck out her tongue, then turned away.

"How come you didn't want to dance with me?"

Jesse tipped her head to study him. "Why do you ask? You're not used to women saying no?"

"Honestly, no," he replied with a slow smile, taunting her.

She pretended not to notice his full, supple lips. "Then there's a first time for every thing."

He chuckled. "I can tell you're something else."

"I can tell you're full of yourself," Jesse replied, rolling her eyes and glancing across the room in an attempt to mask her attraction.

He shook his head and smiled. "I can also tell by the shape of your lips that you're one hell of a kisser."

She pulled back, her eyes wide with alarm. Mr. Wrong tipped his head back and roared with laughter.

"My bad. I just couldn't resist." The humor in his eyes contained a sensuous flame.

She didn't bother to comment. He didn't speak again until the song changed.

"Can you at least tell me your name?" he asked as they continued to move to the beat of the music.

"Jesse."

"Jesse what?" His warm, moist breath feathered over her nose.

"Just Jesse," she said, being purposely evasive.

"Well, Just Jesse, I'm William Jones, but my friends all call me Will." When she didn't comment, he added while staring intensely at her, "I hope by the end of the evening I can consider you a friend."

She snorted. "I doubt it, *William*."

"Why not, *Jess*?"

She scowled, hating the way people she didn't know shortened her name. "Because you're not my type."

He pressed his hips closer to hers. "What is your type? My boy Chris?"

She tried to pull free of his arousing heat but he held her tight.

"That's none of your business."

"Oh it's my business when an attractive woman wants a boy when she can have a man."

Her body stiffened and she was quiet until the end of the song. "I'd like to return to my seat now."

"Not yet. Please dance one more with me." He glanced down at her, noting her indecisiveness.

She heaved an enormous sigh, then heard herself say, "Alright."

Her body relaxed and this time she rested her cheek against his chest. The softness of her body cut through Will's body like a high voltage shock searing through his veins. Although he was holding her close, it wasn't close enough. The small space separating their bodies aroused him in the worse way. His instinctive response to her was so powerful it was mind-boggling. Very few women had ever ignited such a strong reaction.

Jesse's face was both delicacy and strength. Her beautiful eyes reflected stubbornness. But in them, he had also seen unspoken hints of pain alive and glowing. Something was on her mind and it definitely wasn't him.

As his arms drew her even closer to his body, his warmth made Jesse's heart pound out an erratic rhythm. *The last thing you need is another man messing with your mind. You have enough sense to see this guy is trouble,* she tried to remind herself.

Will rested his cheek on top of her head. Engulfed in his arms, swaying together to the slow beat of the music, he made her feel alive and feminine. The heat of his breath in her hair as he murmured the words of the love song made her heart pound harder and her brain go fuzzy. She drew in a deep breath and released it slowly, but it did nothing to reduce the tension winding tighter and tighter in her.

His scent was drugging her senses, sending her mind into a scattered frenzy. Will Jones was not at all what she needed. With that in mind, she decided that holding a polite conversation would be the best way to keep from being drawn to his potent charm. "So you're a musician?"

"Yes, Jess, I am."

This time a shiver of want raced through her at the sound of her nickname rolling off his tongue. His voice was deeper than before, huskier, like that of a satisfied lover.

She took a deep, calming breath. "What made you decide to play the piano?"

"I've been playing since grammar school."

This time she pulled back and looked deeply into his eyes. "You don't look like a musician."

His laugh was warm and rich. "What's a musician supposed to look like?"

The probing question whipped a red tint to her cheeks. "What I mean is…that you aren't at all what I expected a piano player to look like. I would have guessed you to play the sax," she replied, proud of her quick thinking. There was no way she would tell him what she actually thought, that he looked like a body builder.

A sensuous smile curled his lips. "I once played the clarinet but was never any good at it."

"You made the right choice. Your solo performance was captivating."

Will grinned, his teeth strikingly white against his rich dark skin. "Thank you. May I ask what you do?" he murmured huskily.

"I run a bed and breakfast," she heard herself say.

"Really? That's an unusual profession for a sista."

"It's a family business, three generations. I can't imagine doing anything else."

It was amazing but for the first time Jesse gave him a smile that Will felt was genuine. It made her face change…soften. He doubted she had any idea how her dark brown eyes glowed when she smiled. The transformation made her more dangerously attractive than she already was.

"I wish I could say the same. I thought music was my life but lately I find that I yearn for stability. I'm considering applying to graduate school, maybe teaching music at an elementary school.

Jesse looked up at him. The deep emotion in his voice had got her attention. Stability, all the more reason he was wrong for her.

When he released her as the music came to an end, she felt an odd sense of loss.

"Thanks for the dance, Jesse."

He led her from the dance floor. The pressure of his hand on her back was light, but his long masculine fingers seemed to burn hot against her sensitive skin.

"You care to join me at my table?"

Jesse glanced over her shoulder at him. Getting through a dance with him had been tough enough. An entire evening in his company was not part of the mission. Not now, not ever. "No thank you."

A probing query came into his eyes. "Can I at least buy you a drink?"

She smiled, inwardly doubting that many women turned him down for anything but knowing if she didn't, she'd never get rid of him.

She shook her head. "I'm fine, really."

He reached out and caressed her cheek. "Then promise me you'll save me another slow dance."

At the intensity of his touch, Jesse jerked away, then cleared her throat. "I don't want to make any promises. If you'll excuse me, I need to talk to my girlfriend about something." She walked off, feeling the heat of Will's intense gaze on her back.

"Back so soon? I thought the two of you were hitting it off quite nicely."

Jesse gave Chanelle a glare. "Girl, please. Don't even think it. We danced, that's it. End of story."

"I thought you were going through with your plan?" Chanelle's eyes narrowed slightly. It was a look she used whenever she didn't approve of something.

"I am, but not with him."

Their waitress arrived, bringing a brief end to their conversation. Purposely avoiding the side of the room where Will stood, Jesse scanned the room for another possibility. Chris was no longer an option. He and Will were too closely joined at the hip.

Chanelle cleared her throat noisily. Jesse glanced over at her and frowned when she found a silly smirk on her best friend's face.

"Don't look now but your baby's daddy is watching you."

Sure enough, Will was making it no secret that he was staring. With his eyes locked upon her, the rest of the world faded away. Suddenly there was nothing between them but an expression of totally unwanted attraction shimmering across the room for anyone happening by to see. Jesse's throat went dry. Sliding her glass close to her, she dropped her eyes, and quickly slurped her margarita through the straw.

Just then, a short chocolate brother with an outdated fade strolled over to the table.

"How are you ladies tonight?" he said, although his attention was on Jesse.

"We're fine and you?" Chanelle said with a bittersweet smile.

A grin curved his mouth and crinkled his eyes. "Very good, now that I've met the two of you."

Jesse didn't miss his obvious interest. Quickly she scanned his expensive gray suit and wing-tip shoes, then looked back up at his face again.

He had average features—gentle brown eyes, a wide mouth and a stern nose. As he stared at her, she felt absolutely nothing, which made him a perfect candidate.

Jesse had pulled a chair out, ready to offer him a seat, when a hand came to rest on her shoulder. It was Will.

"Sweetheart, thanks for saving me a seat."

At the endearment, Jesse's delicate jaw dropped. She then glanced at Chanelle, who gave her a pointed look. Mr. Average quickly excused himself and scrambled away.

Jesse chased away the lump in her throat with a swig from her glass.

Without waiting for an invitation, Will slid in beside her then gestured for the guitar player to sit down on the bench next to Chanelle. After a quick round of introductions, she learned the cutie admiring her best friend was named Jamar.

Chanelle scooted to her left on the U-shaped bench, crunching Jesse against Will's hard thigh. He then draped his arm along the back of the booth, brushing lightly against her bare skin. A shiver raced through her. She tried to shift away but another bump from Chanelle hemmed her in.

Jesse glared at Will, then hissed, "Give me some room."

He smiled, teeth straight and pearly white. Powerful as a caress, his gaze drifted from her eyes to her lips, to her cleavage, displayed by her Wonderbra. She decided not to make a big deal about it. She refused to let him know how much he affected her.

She inhaled slowly, hoping to calm her racing pulse. The scent of his cologne was just as sexy as the rest of him, she thought as she tried to arch away as far as possible. There was no way she would allow her attraction to him distract her from her mission.

Jesse leaned forward, resting her elbows on the table. All the men in this building and she was stuck with Mr. Wrong and no way to get away. Dang, unless she could find a way out, the night would be a total loss. She glanced over at Chanelle. To her dismay, she seemed to be enjoying Jamar's attention. *Doesn't she realize I'm supposed to be the one receiving the attention tonight? Has she forgotten I'm supposed to be looking for my baby's daddy?*

The waitress appeared and nodded towards the empty glasses. "Want another?"

Before she could answer, Will cut in. "Order whatever you want. Drinks are on me."

Chanelle asked for another margarita. As much as Jesse needed the courage of something strong, she wouldn't be able to accomplish her mission tonight if she drank anything else. "A Coke for me please."

Will frowned at her request, then turned back to the waitress. "Why don't you bring me a pitcher of beer?"

The waitress nodded, then retrieved the empty glasses. She leaned over low enough that anyone could tell she wasn't wearing a bra.

Jesse rolled her eyes upward. The woman was flirting. *She's got some nerve. What if Will was my man? Well, he isn't, so why do you care?*

Will's arm brushed against the fine hairs at the back of her neck. Jesse stiffened to stop the pleasure tremor racing down her spine, started to lean away from the contact, then changed her mind. The frown on the waitress's face was too good to pass up.

What the heck are you doing? Remember the mission.

"How long have the two of you been playing together?" Chanelle asked after the waitress left.

Jamar twisted in his seat, giving her his undivided attention. "About five years. Right, Will?"

He nodded. "Yep, just about. Five long years."

Chanelle gave him a direct stare. "You sound like you don't like your job."

Jesse tilted her head and looked up at him, finding herself curious about his answer.

Will leaned back and linked his fingers behind his head. "I like it. I'm just ready to do something else."

Jamar snorted. "He's trying to bail out."

Will chuckled, the sound deep, warm, and loud. "Don't listen to my boy. He's known for almost three months that I'll be leaving at the end of this tour."

A smile of admiration curved Jamar's lips. "I know. I'm just giving you a hard time. We wish you the best in whatever you do."

Resting her elbows on the table, Chanelle laced her fingers together. "What are you planning to do now?"

Will shrugged a broad shoulder. "Buy a business, go back to school. I haven't quite decided yet."

The waitress returned and distributed their drink orders.

Jamar filled his glass with the frosty beverage and raised it high. "Let me make a toast. Here's to another fabulous show."

Jesse raised her glass and clicked it against the others.

Jamar hailed another member standing across the room. He joined the group, squeezing into the booth. The gap she'd tried to put between her and Will vanished. To make matters worse, Will dropped his hand to her knee and squeezed. Jesse held her breath, fighting the tingle.

Distracted by the strength of the hand cupping her knee, Jesse couldn't follow the conversation bouncing around the table. What a mess! Her bed and breakfast was on the line and her hormones were in an uproar for the wrong man. She tried to push his hand away.

Will gave her knee another squeeze. "What's wrong? You're much too quiet."

Her traitorous spine nearly melted. "That's because your company isn't welcome." Jesse lifted her glass to her lips, then set it back to the table. On second thought, with Will sitting so close, there was no way she was going to be able to survive this night without something stronger to drink.

"What can I do to make it up to you?"

Jesse opened her mouth but couldn't get any words out. He was so doggone handsome she found it next to impossible to control her emotions. Finally she found her voice and said, "How about ordering me something stronger?"

"Your wish is my command. What would you like?" he asked, with an expectant gleam in his eyes.

She couldn't think straight with him looking at her that way. Jesse swallowed. "Surprise me."

He signaled for the waitress. "Give this beautiful woman a Thug Passion."

A what? Jesse looked up at him, startled.

The waitress chuckled. "Coming right up," she said as she walked away.

Glancing to her right, Jesse could have sworn Chanelle was trying not to laugh.

"What's a Thug Passion?" she asked.

"A little more than you can handle," Chanelle chuckled. "Hennessy and Alizé.

Eyes wide, Jesse looked to Will who gave her a challenging smile. Being the stubborn person that she was, she couldn't let him know she wasn't as strong as she appeared. She would just have to sip it slowly.

"I can't wait," she mumbled.

Conversation traveled around the table. Looking to her right, she noticed the drummer watching her with interest. He wasn't particularly what she was looking for in a baby's daddy; he was short and thin, but then what really was she looking for?

A man.

At this point it didn't matter. She would love her son regardless.

Will squeezed her closer and her stomach churned.

No way, no how. Will was definitely not what she was looking for.

When her drink arrived, she took cautious sips. She shifted her attention to the drummer again and smiled but couldn't draw his full attention. She bet he was under the impression that she and Will were a couple. Since his arm was draped across the bench and they were sitting so close, it was understandable. If she wanted to get away and find a sperm donor, she needed to put the drummer in line quickly.

"I'm sorry, I didn't get your name," she told the drummer.

"Eduardo."

She gave him a smile that she hoped looked provocative. "Nice to meet you. I'm—"

"Ed, this is my girl, Jess," Will interrupted.

He glanced from Will to Jesse and back to Will again. "Man, I didn't know you had a girl in Philly."

Will pulled her closer and said with a wicked smile, "That's because I don't kiss and tell."

Jesse choked on her drink and wheezed. Will patted, then stroked her back. The fire creeping up her spine had nothing whatsoever to do with the liquid she'd consumed.

Stunned, Jesse swiveled. In the bat of an eyelid, he had just ruined everything "You...I..." A stirring at the pit of her stomach erased whatever she'd been trying to say. She closed her eyes.

"I'm sorry, baby. I know we agreed we would keep our relationship private." He reached up and stroked a calloused finger over her cheek, causing a stirring at the pit of her stomach. What was it about him that did this to her?

Less than five minutes later, Eduardo excused himself and joined a table of women.

Will continued to sit there, stroking her cheek, his intense eyes never leaving her face. He looked supremely male, confident. *Sexy.*

Jesse stifled the urge to dump the rest of her drink in his lap and pressed the cold glass to the fire he'd caused in her cheek. If he'd wanted to spoil her chances with another man, he couldn't have chosen a better way. Even if she could ditch this irritating jerk, she no longer stood a chance with Eduardo or any other man in the lounge, except for maybe the homely looking guy watching her from the corner. She grimaced, then downed the remainder of her drink. She might be desperate but she wasn't that desperate. The liquid hit the back of her throat and she wheezed and coughed, trying to catch her breath. How in the world could people drink stuff like that? With her head spinning, she felt she didn't have the energy to fight his advances any more. However, she had never been one to give up easily and she decided suddenly that she wasn't putting up with this a second longer. "I want to talk to you in private," she said after swatting his hand away.

"What did I do?" Will asked, pretending innocence.

"You'll find out soon enough," she said through gritted teeth.

"I can't wait," he purred with a triumphant smile on his lips.

Anger warmed her veins. Awareness made it difficult to think. Damn him! She shoved him hard and the contact with his muscular arm sent heat through her hand all the way to her toes. She glared at him and murmured, "Hurry up and move." She then turned to face Chanelle's amused expression. "I'll see you upstairs."

As soon as Will stood to his full height of six-three, she slid off the bench. Cursing him under her breath, Jesse stalked out of the lounge in the direction of the hotel lobby. She was drunk and she was mad. Her head spun and before she reached the lobby, she stumbled. Will, who was right behind her, scooped Jesse into his arms and moved toward the bank of elevators. She gasped and was ready to give him a piece of her mind when a wave of nausea hit her. Will stepped inside the elevator and pressed the button. Had she given him her room number? She closed her eyes, too drunk to care. All she wanted to do was to lay her head down.

The doors opened and Will stepped out and continued to carry her. She set her lips to tell him that her keycard was in her purse but he opened the door before she had a chance. Had she already given it to him? She wasn't sure of anything right about now.

Will lowered her to the floor. Opening her eyes, she found him standing too close, drowning her in his scent, his heat. She was about to put him out of her room but another wave of nausea hit her and she raced past him and straight to the bathroom.

CHAPTER FIVE

Will stood in the middle of the room, unable to move. All he could do was stand and watch her sway those delectable curves into the bathroom.

He knew he was pushing his luck but Jesse was up to something and until he figured out what it was, he planned to keep her by his side.

The bathroom door opened and Jesse strolled back into the room. Her chest rose and fell swiftly, drawing his attention to her small bosom. She parked her clenched fists on her hips. "You ruined my evening."

Will gazed down at her angry expression, her cold, unfriendly eyes. Did she realize how sexy she looked when she was mad? "Who, me?"

She shot him a frustrated look. "Yes, you. How could you do that to me?"

Just like that her anger turned to something far different and her eyes began to water. Will's heart twisted. He couldn't stand a woman crying. "Boo, I—"

"I'm not your boo! Nor is my name Jess!" she spat. "I can't believe you did that. I...I...just get out of my room!" she demanded as tears streaked mascara down her cheeks.

"Listen..." She looked so pitiful, Will wanted to pull her into his arms, hold her, kiss her. "Jess, I'm sorry. It was just a joke."

"A joke?" She wiped a hand across her face, smearing the makeup across her cheek. "Why?"

He looked down at his shoes, unable to face what he was about to admit. "Because I was jealous. You were trying to get my boy's attention while ignoring me in the process. I'm not used to that kind of rejection."

She glared at him. "Why in the world would you be jealous? You don't even know anything about me," she said angrily.

There was a slight hesitation before he spoke. "You're right. I don't."

Jesse released a windy breath. Catching a glimpse of her face in the mirror, she sighed, then turned to face him again.

She shook her head sadly. "I had something I needed to do tonight and you ruined everything," she mumbled in a sad, faraway voice. Sinking onto the edge of the bed, she buried her face in her hands. "Do me a favor and go away."

Will studied the defeated sag of her shoulders. "I can't."

She snatched her head up. "Why is that?"

His lips curled in a sad half-smile. "Because it's my room."

For the first time, Jesse glanced around and noticed that the personal belongings thrown across a chair near a window weren't hers. Yet, instead of making a mad dash for the door, as he thought she would, she simply buried her head in her hands again.

Puzzled by her behavior, Will took a seat beside her on the bed. Her scent stirred a primitive response in him. Normally he ignored such feelings. He wouldn't have made it as far as he had if he hadn't. Only this time he was failing miserably.

He stared at her, fighting the hard throb of his body and the knowledge that women like this knew how to strip a man of everything, especially their wallets.

"I guess I better be going." Jesse jumped up from the bed with unshed tears glistening in her eyes.

Will reached out and gently encircled her wrist with one hand. "Stay." He rose to stand before her.

She looked directly up at him and swallowed as if she were pondering his request. He was having a hard time thinking with her sweet erotic breath sweeping across his chin, evoking a passion that thrilled him like no other in his previous experience. Will wanted to blame it on the alcohol he'd had in the lounge, but he'd drunk twice as much on any given weekend with little effect. For whatever reason, he wanted to feel her lips on his more than he'd wanted anything in a long time.

"I should leave," Jesse whispered, her eyes focused on his mouth.

Will's lips tingled, anticipating the kiss he couldn't do without. He traced a path from her slender wrist to her silky shoulder with a surprisingly unsteady hand.

"What if I don't want you to?" His thumb delicately stroked across her bottom lip.

She drew back and studied him for several unblinking moments.

Seeing the pain reflected in her big brown eyes, Will felt an overwhelming need to protect her, and to do whatever was in his power to take that pain away.

He couldn't tell who moved first. All he knew was that by the time their lips touched, he had an erection that wasn't going away. She felt so good, tasted so good. Following a moan, her lips parted, inviting a deeper share of the intimacy crackling between them. Their tongues met, taking their kiss to a new and dangerous level. She tasted of sweet liquor and secrets never told. Never had he thought a simple kiss could have such an undisputed impact on his senses. In fact, his reaction was so intense he was already addicted to the taste of her. He had to be out of his mind because there was no way he was letting her leave.

"You taste delicious," he whispered as his tongue traced the fullness of her lips and his hand roamed freely over her bottom.

If he had any sense he'd get her the hell out of here. But his good sense wasn't listening. "You know what I want, don't you, Jesse?" He crushed her against him just so she'd know how aroused he was. He then leaned back to look down into her startled eyes, allowed his gaze to trail down her face to her mouth and back up again.

Then he looked her directly in the eyes, searching the depth of her soul. She wanted him; he'd seen the desire in her expression, heard it in the way her breath caught when he touched her.

"I want to make love to you. I want to taste every inch of you, starting right here." Will nipped her earlobe. Jesse pulled in a shuddery breath, then exhaled a sigh. Pulling back, he stroked his palm across her smooth cheek, and as he had hoped, she nuzzled into it. "You want that, too?"

She nodded and moistened her lips. "Yes."

The eagerness in her voice was his undoing. When he noticed a fire burning behind her eyes, the thought that she was up to something no longer mattered. She wanted him and that knowledge sent a shiver of pure desire echoing through him. He should ask her how much it was going to cost. He knew this was going to cost him but right now he was willing to give her his entire paycheck if he had to.

Her mouth opened, then closed, as if she'd had something to say and had changed her mind. As if an afterthought, she slipped a hand beneath his shirt. Will forgot all reason and molded her body against every inch of his, making sure she felt the strain within his zipper.

Jesse gave herself over to the sensation, wrapping her arms around Will's neck and opening her mouth. He drew her nearer, caging her within his arms.

His hand sought her breasts, arousing a frantic ache deep within her. And even as her mind screamed that this was stupid and wrong, her body quivered with longing. She was suddenly alive, as if something inside her had been waiting for this moment to happen. She leaned into him, enjoying his fingertips as they lightly caressed her left nipple through her dress.

Will overwhelmed her with his kisses. The thrust of his tongue was growing more demanding and hungry. Jesse thought she'd turn into a blazing inferno. Alarmed by her body's eager response, Jesse pushed him away and stared at him. *What are you doing?* she scolded herself as she stood there trembling. She shouldn't enjoy it this much but the way he made her feel was incredible. He was so gentle and yet his hunger for her was unmistakable. She should have been pleased that she had attracted his attention. But something told her he would be much too hard to forget. Before she had a chance to protest, Will reached for her, then lowered his lips and nibbled on her collarbone.

Breathless, Jesse grasped for sanity, for control. When his tongue traced a path up to the sensitive spot behind her ear, her reasons for resisting toppled like a house of cards. Then his mouth crushed hers and wild incredible pleasure surged through her body and settled between her thighs. She forgot about holding back. Instead she arched her back and held him close. "Oh…Will."

"What, boo?" he asked as he pressed his kisses across her cheek and neck.

"You're driving me crazy," she crooned.

"You ain't seen nothing yet," he whispered. On that note, he caught the fabric of her dress in between his teeth and tugged it down over her shoulders to reveal a strapless lace bra. Before she had time to feel embarrassed, he caught her wrists and pulled her even closer.

He rubbed his cheek against her hair and whispered, "I need to touch you, Jess."

Jesse hesitated but the desire blazing through her body convinced her to relax as his hands crept up her spine to unhook her bra. She felt peculiar, as if every nerve ending she possessed hungered for his touch.

Then to her delight, he satisfied her yearning as he took her breast in his palm, caressing the tip with his thumb. She whimpered, unprepared for the rush of pleasure that radiated through her. Jesse closed her eyes and let her head fall back. The man had magical hands. He had her body begging to be touched.

He lowered her onto the bedspread and captured a nipple in his mouth, suckling, making her anxious for more. Lying beside her, Will transferred his attention to her other breast. All at once Jesse wanted it to go on. She hoped she would survive the intense pleasure that she knew was only the beginning. Crying out, she buried her fingers in his hair, arching her back to get closer. When his lips left her flesh to slide the dress down her hips, she nearly cried. Then the dress was gone and she lay before him in nothing but a black thong and high heels.

Jesse's heart pounded as he lay there, taking it all in. He made her feel beautiful, desirable. Her body responded to his gaze, silently begging to be touched. After what felt like forever, Will finally slid a hand between her thighs. Her breath came fast as he stroked his index finger across the silk crotch. Her every nerve seemed to vibrate under the pressure of his touch.

"You like that, don't you?" he murmured.

He didn't know the half of it. Never had a man touched her this way. Not even in her wildest dreams. As his fingers continued to tease her through the thin material, she shivered and her legs began to tremble.

"Please, Will," she begged.

"Tell me what you want," he urged.

Jesse couldn't think, instead allowed her body to take the lead, which wasn't hard to do since it seemed to have a mind of its own.

As she tried to think straight and form words, Will's fingers slipped beneath the material and slid inside her hot wet core. In response, she lifted her hips up to meet each thrust of his finger. "Ooh! That feels so good," she cooed. Hungrily, she reached for his mouth for a deep taunting kiss, but it wasn't enough. Her need for him was coming out in small gasps.

Will must have sensed she was nearing the edge because he rose from the bed and quickly began removing his clothes. When his hands fell to his belt buckle, Jesse closed her eyes. Watching the man undress was more than she could bear.

Her mouth watered. Her skin tingled. Anticipation of what he'd do to her next left her panting. *You shouldn't be enjoying this.* But she was.

Returning to the bed, Will removed her shoes and thong, then gently eased her thighs apart and lowered on top of her. With one quick thrust, he filled her. Jesse arched off the bed at the unexpected stab of pain.

Will bolted back and stared down at her in surprise. "You're a virgin."

Ignoring his curious expression, Jesse closed her eyes, then replied, "Not anymore." On that final note, she lifted her hips at the exact same moment she placed both hands on his buttocks and pushed him deeper inside of her. When he hesitated further, she began to wiggle her hips.

On the verge of losing control, Will somehow managed to restrain himself. "Am I hurting you?" he asked, searching her eyes.

Without answering, Jesse raised her mouth to his.

As they kissed, Will tried to be as gentle as he could manage. He moved slowly at first, pulling only slightly out of her, then pushing back in. When her legs began to relax and the muscles around his hardened flesh began to ease, he took each stroke deeper until they found their own rhythm.

Reaching their peak was exquisite torture as each movement brought them closer to sweet release. He could no longer hold on, the pleasure was too much. Liquid pulsed through his body and stole all thoughts except for the woman beneath him. He felt himself drain into her body and he shuddered as he felt the last wave come crashing down around him.

Will rolled to her side, enjoying the warm soft pressure of Jesse's curvy backside snuggled against him. He draped one arm across her waist as he whispered into her ear, "Boo, you are something else." He then fell asleep with a smile on his lips.

Head pounding, mouth dry, Jesse considered lying there until Chanelle insisted that it was time to leave. However, her best friend had never been an early riser, and if Jesse left it up to her, they wouldn't leave until check-out time.

Jesse rolled over and felt something warm beside her. Startled, her eyes opened and she found a man lying next to her.

Oh no!

Then the memories hit her, causing her head to spin. She had done it. Blinking her eyes several times, she tried to remember her partner's name. Will somebody and she was in his room. *Oh my God!* She had to escape before she had to face him.

Carefully, she eased away from him and rose. Reaching for her undergarments, she slipped them on, all the time her gaze never leaving him.

Will was sleeping soundly. Her pace slowed as she took in his muscular chest and the sheet around his waist. He was a beautiful man and the things he'd done to her, the way he had made her feel, would be forever embedded in her brain. For that she would never forget him.

She'd had every intention of returning to her room last night but Will had changed her mind. Her stomach clenched as she thought about the things he had taught her. She had given up her virginity to save the bed and breakfast and surprisingly enjoyed every minute. Her one night stand had been beautiful.

She had to leave before Will awoke. She was embarrassed and knew she couldn't face him. What she'd done last night contradicted everything her father had taught her. She had shared her body with a stranger.

As she slid into her dress, she wondered how she could have enjoyed it so much. How could she have forgotten even for one second why she was doing what she'd done?

Couples didn't make love because it was something to do, at least that was what she had been raised to believe. Couples made love to express love and she was certainly not in love with Will. Further, she had no intention of seeing him again after today.

Jesse felt a moment's regret for what might have been had they met under other circumstances. But no, she didn't want to give a man control of her life again. She'd learned the hard way that nothing was more important than independence.

Other than the couple of hours she had spent in the lounge, Will was a total stranger. She had never felt like that with a man before and something told her she never would again. If only… No, she wasn't even going to think about what ifs. She had fought too long and hard to even consider giving her independence up now. Still, she felt guilty for using him. Men used women all the time. Yet, somehow that didn't make it right.

Reaching for her purse, she pulled out a scrap of paper and scribbled a brief yet necessary note. Jesse tiptoed into the bathroom, left the note in a spot he couldn't miss, then returned to the room in search of her shoes. The note was the least she could do although she doubted he would even remember she had been there. A man like Will probably had a woman in every city and probably wouldn't even remember her name. It should have made her using him easier to digest, but instead it saddened her.

With her shoes in hand, Jesse tiptoed across the room and quietly out the door.

Will woke with the sting of sunlight on his eyelids and a smile on his face. Feeling the space beside him, he discovered it was empty. Had it all been a dream? If it was, it had been one hell of a way to spend a night. He snuggled deeper into the pillow. The sweet scent of vanilla confirmed that it had been a reality. Scenes played in his head of him burying himself deep inside of her, of hearing her moan his name. Suddenly he froze and quickly opened his eyes. Where was she now? He listened quietly for some movement in the bathroom and heard nothing. Rolling towards the edge, he swung back the covers and climbed out of the bed. Taking a quick sweep of the room, he realized the sexy dress and high heel shoes were gone.

Damn!

He rushed over to his discarded pants that were thrown across a chair and reached in his pocket for his wallet. Quickly counting the bills, he was relieved to find his money all there.

Will lowered himself to the edge of the bed. He knew he should feel relief that she had left, saving them from an awkward morning, but he didn't. He was disappointed. He wouldn't have minded ordering room service, then spending until checkout trying out several different positions. Instead, she had snuck out like a thief in the night. But why? he wondered as he lowered his head to his hands.

Closing his eyes, memories of their meeting came rushing back. From the beginning, Jesse had behaved like a woman on a mission. He had seen the determination in her eyes, the tension of her shoulders. Yet one look at the enticing sway of her voluptuous hips and he let his guard down and allowed her to wrap him around her finger. She had made him do something he prided himself in avoiding. He'd had unprotected sex. Now there were unpleasant possibilities, not the least of which was pregnancy.

Stupid, stupid!

How could he have been so weak? He had been disease free all his life and now...

His head shot up in recollection. Jesse had been a virgin. He had been drunk but not so drunk that he couldn't remember the feel of her snug around him. Feeling a stirring in his loins, he rose and moved away from the bed. Why had she done it?

It frustrated him to know he had been used and for what purpose? Did she know she could now be pregnant with his child?

He struggled to pull air past the knot in his throat. A baby? No, it couldn't be, but he wouldn't be able to rest until he found out for sure.

Pacing back and forth, he realized he didn't even know her last name. All he knew was that she ran a bed and breakfast. At the time it didn't dawn on him that she was being so evasive, but now he knew why. Jesse didn't want to be found.

Damn!

He was too old fashioned to just ignore the incident. But he also knew trying to find her was going to be like finding a needle in a haystack.

Going into the bathroom to splash water onto his face, he noticed a sheet of paper at the corner of the mirror.

Thanks, Jess.

Anger brewed. What the hell was she thanking him for? For assisting her in losing her virginity?

Will snatched the note out of the corner, analyzing her fine penmanship. Flipping it over, a smile crept to his lips as he realized her mistake. Jesse had just blown her calculated attempt to not be found. She had scribbled the note on the back of a gas receipt. The address was that of a Shore Stop gas station down at Rehoboth Beach.

Jesse had just narrowed down his search. It was only a matter of time before he found her.

CHAPTER SIX

Will pulled his Escalade off at the Rehoboth Beach exit. It had been a long three weeks. He'd had several gigs in several cities on the Eastern Shore and was bone tired. However, his mind wasn't on work. It was on the woman who had made him lower his guard.

Finding Jesse had been easier than he expected. There were twelve bed and breakfasts at the beach, but a woman named Jesse had been easy to track down. Now the only thing he needed an answer to was the why of it all.

He glanced down at his directions, which indicated he needed to make a left at the next corner. Lowering the paper to the seat beside him, he tightened his fingers around the steering wheel.

It irritated him that he hadn't figured out what game Jesse was playing before seeing her again. Now he just wanted to have closure before he began his month-long vacation until the weekend of Memorial Day.

Had she been as caught up in their lovemaking as he'd been and simply forgotten to use protection? Or had she purposely tried to get pregnant? Will scowled at that thought. She wouldn't be the first female to try that trick. Because of his past experiences, he should have known better.

He'd never been careless before. Ever since he was a teenager he had always practiced safe sex. What he had done was sloppy and it was now his responsibility to clean up the mess. He'd be damned before he'd have a little Jones running around he knew nothing about. The family values his parents had instilled in him were too strong for that. What a mess he could be in. Now was not the time to be thinking about starting a family with anyone. Not when he was planning to temporarily store away his keyboard and further his education.

The degree in business he already had had been his father's idea so that he would someday work alongside him and his three brothers in the home improvement business. However, even though Will was talented, remodeling and all that went with it was his second love, not his first. His passion was music. It always had been, regardless of how much his dad complained. When Sheon, Clayton and Wayne all followed in his father's footsteps, Will had hoped there were enough Joneses already in the business to relieve him of his family obligation. Instead, he had received increased pressure to join the clan. Being the rebellious child that he was, he had refused to join the business until he graduated from college, and wouldn't have won that fight if it hadn't been for Hattie Jones.

His mother had always had a way of getting William Sr. to do what she wanted when she wanted, and what she wanted was for at least one of her children to get a college education. So after she put her foot down, his father agreed to pay for Will's education as long as he agreed to join the business immediately after graduation.

True to his word, he joined a week after graduation. While Will handled the administrative side of the business, his brothers handled the field work. Then he had met Ebony and thought he was ready for the white picket fence and children. The marriage lasted six months before she filed for divorce. As soon as he was granted his freedom, he yanked off his tie and quit the business and joined a local band that he had already been playing with occasionally on the weekends.

Now here he was quitting again. After five years of traveling and living out of a suitcase, he was ready for a place to call his own. But until he had that, until he received his master's and started a career as a music teacher, he didn't need anyone in his life claiming he was the father of their child.

He blew out a frustrated breath. The last thing he needed was child support enforcement tracking him down and garnishing his check just because of one careless night.

One carelessly memorable night. His traitorous loins throbbed with remembered passion. If Jesse was carrying his child, he was going to take care of his responsibilities as a father.

Will pulled off the main road onto a small winding road that led up an incline. Tucked into the hillside, hiding behind flowering pear trees, he found a large house. Will frowned. The two-story federal style home had seen better days. The clapboards that wrapped the house were loose and badly in need of a fresh coat of white paint, while the black shutters that framed the windows and doors were hanging off their hinges. A covered veranda extended along three sides of the house. Looking past the cobblestone walkway to the porch, he noticed that several spindles were missing and the stairs leading up to the door were badly in need of repair.

Will pulled into the circular driveway. The house was surrounded by a once white picket fence. A sign in the yard that read Katherine's Bed and Breakfast confirmed he was in the right place.

What was she doing at this dump? he wondered. There was only one way to find out. He turned off the engine and climbed out his SUV.

Jesse carried in another can of paint. At the rate she was going, she would have the stairwell leading to the second floor painted before nightfall. She sighed. Tomorrow she would begin painting the upstairs hallway.

She halted abruptly at the sight of Pace sitting in the living room with his dirty work boots on her great-grandmother's coffee table. Anger brewed. Obviously, he had no intention of finishing the parquet floor in the foyer today. "Is there a problem?"

He looked up and sneered. "No problem. I'm just taking a break."

Jesse set the can down in the corner. With her fists planted at her hips, she stepped towards him. The constant power struggle between them all week had driven her pretty close to a mental breakdown. "You were taking a break when I left for the hardware store an hour ago."

He rose in one fluid motion. "Now I'm taking another."

She didn't miss the challenge in his voice or the smell of his bad breath. Rumor had it he was a heavy drinker. He had come to work with liquor on his breath on more than one occasion. Most people in town were leery of using him. "You either get back to work now or you're fired," she replied in a low, composed voice even though calm was the last thing she was feeling.

Pace had the audacity to start laughing. "You can't afford to fire me."

"Then do as the lady said and get back to work."

Jesse spun toward the rich timbre voice and sucked in a quick gasp of shock. It couldn't be! She had been evasive with her personal information. So there was no way he could have found her. She briefly closed her eyes, hoping he was just a figment of her imagination. But when she opened them, William Jones was standing less than twelve feet away.

"I don't know who you are, but this is between Jesse and me." Pace's tone was as stiff as his stance.

Will gazed over at the angry foreman. Pace's cold narrowed eyes, locked jaw and firmly pressed lips said he didn't like him. Good. Will didn't like him either. "That's where you are wrong. For the next couple of days anything that happens to this lady *is* my business. So, let me repeat myself…either you get back to work or else…" He purposely allowed his voice to trail off for added emphasis.

Pace stepped forward. "Or else what?" he challenged.

Jesse noticed his fists were balled and quickly snapped out of her haze to stand between the two.

"Pace, break's over," she said in a stern voice.

Pace's face darkened. With his lips compressed, he paused long enough to glare at the man standing behind her and gave him a look that said, "This ain't over," before turning on his heels and storming out the door.

It wasn't until Jesse heard the screen door slam shut that she swung around and glared at Will. As she tried to regain her normal rhythm of breathing, she allowed her eyes to roam over him.

His dark green T-shirt stretched across a pair of powerful shoulders and pecs that made her want to reach out and touch them. She remembered feeling the strength of his chest when her head was pressed firmly against it and her stomach knotted. Quickly, she snapped her gaze to his face.

The expression on Will's face told her he wanted answers and she couldn't blame him. She had left like a thief in the night. That he had found her obviously meant that he was determined to hear some kind of explanation.

"Hello, Jess. I bet you never expected to see me again," he commented with a grim smile. The glint in his eyes told her he wanted answers.

She backed away as if he had a gun pointed at her chest. Although she tried to speak, she couldn't because she just didn't know what to say. Besides, she was certain he wasn't really asking a question but instead was stating a fact and he was right. She hadn't had any intention of ever seeing the musician again.

She swallowed the lump in her throat. "What brings you to my neck of the woods?" Her voice was tight as if someone were squeezing her neck, affecting her vocal cords.

He looked her up and down as if searching for some kind of explanation. "I think you already know the answer to that question."

Glancing up, Jesse spotted two of Pace's men working at the top of the stairs. What they needed to discuss needed to be done in private. "Come with me."

A moment of pure male appreciation snagged Will as he followed Jesse down a narrow hall. His eyes were drawn to the enticing, seductive sway of her round hips. Damn she made a pair of dingy overalls look good! Memory of the way each buttock felt in the palm of his hands was leading him back to their one sensual night. In order to keep his anger in place what he needed to do was to focus on how she had used him.

Pulling his eyes away from her, he noticed the inside of the house needed repairs almost as desperately as the outside. The walls in the hallway needed a second coat of paint. The carpet in the living room was worn. The only thing that looked new was the wood flooring in the foyer and even that wasn't complete.

Jesse opened a door at the end of the hallway and Will followed her into the room.

"You can pull that chair over." Jesse pointed toward a brown over-stuffed chair facing a window that offered a picturesque view of a private beach in back.

He reached for the chair. Carrying the chair over near a large wooden desk, he lowered it with a loud thump.

Will sat in the badly worn chair and to his surprise found it extremely comfortable. Leaning back, he glanced at Jesse, who was sitting in a large swivel chair at an oak desk with her elbows resting on a stack of unopened mail.

Looking past her angry expression, he focused on her beautiful mouth with its appealing half-smile, full unpainted lips and…

Resenting her effect on him, he cleared his throat three times, then straightened in the chair.

"Why are you here?" Jesse finally asked.

Will could see the uneasiness in her eyes, but this time he wasn't falling for it. "Why did you leave?"

She gave a sound that was a cross between a chuckle and a snort. "Isn't that what usually happens after a one-night stand?"

Will gave her a wry look. He didn't know why but it annoyed him that she thought of their night together as nothing more than a one-night stand, even though that was all it was supposed to have been. Except that she had been a virgin and he had been too stupid to remember to use a condom.

"Yes, in most cases," he began, "only your situation is different. You had never been with a man before. Should I also assume you weren't taking any form of birth control either?"

He watched a muscle at her jaw quiver. Her gaze lowered to her desk and with her shoulders rounded, she looked like a kid who had just been caught with her hand in the cookie jar. She was guilty of something and he was determined to find out what it was.

"Are you pregnant?" he blurted out.

Her gaze shot up and he met her eyes and saw the look of guilt in them and knew.

"I'm not sure," she whispered.

"What the hell is that supposed to mean?" he demanded.

She swallowed convulsively, then lowered her face into the palms of her hands. "It means I should know for sure in a couple of days."

Her words hit him like a ton of bricks. Although Will had considered the possibility, he had hoped against hope that she would respond to his question with absurd laughter, then announce that she had been taking the pill and all his worrying had been for nothing. Anything but what she had just admitted—that there was a possibility she might be pregnant. "Did you plan it?"

She looked up again, her eyes unfocused. The lines of her mouth tightened in annoyance as she leaned back in the chair. "Do we ever plan anything that happens in life?"

He stared across the desk at her. "You didn't answer my question."

She glanced at him, her gaze unwavering and her fear apparent, but he wouldn't let himself feel sorry for her.

On the way over he had hoped to discover he was wrong. He had hoped she would tell him it had been one big misunderstanding. He had hoped that for once in his life someone wasn't trying to use him for their own personal gain. For once he had wanted to discover there was a woman who was different from all of the others.

Staring at her, he waited patiently for her to deny everything. Only as the seconds passed, she sat there, quiet and still, looking guilty as sin.

Jesse finally let out a deep breath and said, "Yes, I planned it."

Her words struck him like a blow to the chest. He released a disgusted whoosh of air, shaking his head in disbelief. "What game are you playing?" he demanded in a harsh, accusing tone.

Jesse flinched, appearing stunned by his words. "I'm not playing any games."

Anger flashed through his entire body at the thought of what she had done. "Then what would you call it?" When was he going to learn to never underestimate a woman? He should have been smarter than that. He had fallen for the oldest trick in the book, tears. Hadn't he learned anything from his ex-wife? Women lied and used their God-given assets to charm and manipulate men. They always had a reason and it usually had something to do with money.

Jesse leaned forward, resting her elbows on the desk. "Listen, this is really none of your business."

"That's where you are wrong. If you are carrying my child, it has everything to do with me."

She straightened her spine. "No, it doesn't. I'm not looking for a father for my child."

"Then you should have thought about that before you got me involved," he replied in an irritated tone as his intense eyes held her gaze.

She shook her head with dismay, then muttered, "This wasn't the way it was supposed to happen. You weren't supposed to know. I wasn't supposed to ever see you again."

He glared across at her. "I don't walk away from my responsibilities. If you are pregnant, you better believe I plan to be a part of my child's life."

She sat tongue-tied and stunned by his bluntness.

Annoyed, Will rose to his feet and crossed the room to a large picture window. Looking out, he found comfort in the serenity that comes with staring out at deep blue water. The winds catching the waves called out to him. It was several seconds before he was aware of the silence of the room. Only a clock ticked.

He turned to face her again and watched as she looked away briefly. Returning his gaze, she stared straight into his eyes. "I wouldn't have imagined you as the paternal type."

Will looked at her, surprised at how pale her peanut butter-colored face had become. His eyes blazed with anger. "I guess you figured wrong."

Jesse raised her chin and met his glare with one of her own. "I'm sure everything is going to turn out just fine. I'll call you in a couple of days and let you know for certain."

"I'm not going anywhere until I know for certain you're not carrying my child." He'd never been around kids much. He had nieces, but with his schedule, he rarely got to see them except on holidays. However, if Jesse was carrying his child, he was just going to have to learn in a hurry. He would never abandon his child. Never.

He returned to his seat, clenching and unclenching his fists in his lap. Jesse no longer looked like she was ready to insist that he leave. Instead, she looked sad, almost defeated. He wasn't going to be sympathetic. The woman had used him in the worse way.

Jesse sighed. "I guess I do owe you an explanation."

He cocked a lazy eyebrow, not feeling her statement justified an answer.

"Would you like something to drink?" she offered.

"No, just an explanation." He saw her flinch and realized he'd elevated his voice. Rubbing a hand across his brow, he took a deep breath and said in a softer tone. "I want to know why you're trying to get pregnant."

He expected her to tell him to go to hell. Instead, her gaze dropped, then rose again. She then shrugged, her face moody. "I'm not getting any younger and I wanted to start a family."

Will threw his head back and laughed. "Girl, who are you trying to fool? You still have the smell of Enfamil on your breath."

Jesse tried not to appear moved by his comment. "Don't try to act like I'm the first woman you've ever taken back to a hotel room."

His jaws tightened. "No, but you're the first virgin."

Will watched her as she tried to maintain a straight face to keep him from knowing his words had affected her. Only the quiver of her sensual lower lip gave away her uneasiness. He had said that only to see what kind of reaction he would get, but the wide-eyed expression that crossed her face aroused his curiosity even more.

Jesse shrugged a shoulder. "Consider it a sperm donation." She then slid up her sleeve and made a show of checking her watch. "Now if you'd excuse me, I've got work to do." She rose from her chair.

Will was growing tired of her evasive behavior. "We haven't finished our discussion."

"We'll talk later," she said in a tone that communicated she was done talking. Then she turned and headed for the door.

"You got any vacant rooms in this joint?" he asked, even though the answer was quite apparent. Taking in the condition of the bed and breakfast, Jesse obviously hadn't had any guests in quite some time.

She turned around and gave him a look that said, "Very funny," before folding her arms belligerently beneath her breasts.

"Why?" she dared to ask.

He strolled toward her. "Because I plan to stick around until I have some answers."

She placed a hand to her hip. "I don't need you in my way. If you leave me a forwarding address or phone number, I'll be glad to get back with you when I know for sure."

"Nope. I think I'll just stick around. You should know something within the week, right?" he punctuated the question with a razor-sharp smile.

She swallowed, then nodded her head. If her period was on time, she would have an answer in a matter of days.

"Then I'm going to stick around and make myself useful." He crossed the room to stand in front of her. "I know enough about remodeling to know with that lazy-looking crew you have out front, you need my help."

"I don't need your help," she countered defensively.

"Yes, you do. Otherwise you'd have never pulled that stunt in Philly."

Whatever she'd planned on saying died on her lips. There was a brief pause before Jesse said, "Take the room at the top of the stairs on the right." With that she pivoted on her heels and hurried out of the room.

Will inhaled, letting his breath hiss out between his teeth. What kind of game was that girl trying to play with him? She still hadn't given him a clue and he had resisted the urge to wangle it out of her. Whatever it was, he planned to stick around long enough to find out.

He glanced around the room that she called her office. The walls of the small room were covered in outdated walnut paneling. The rust-colored carpet covering the floor was old and worn and the room reeked of cheap cigars. Jesse had given no indication that she smoked, so either she had had an early visitor who did or the room belonged to someone else.

He moved to a small wooden table in the far right corner and turned off a coffee pot that smelled as if the coffee had been brewed the day before. Even though it probably tasted terrible, he reached for a mug on the table and after wiping it off with his shirt, poured the dark liquid into the mug and followed it with three sugar cubes. Stirring it with his finger, he moved toward the window behind her desk. As he brought the mug to his lips, he gazed out.

The grass was so high in parts of the backyard that it would require a weed whacker to knock it down. The bushes had grown wild and there was a layer of green slime floating on what someone might call an in-ground swimming pool. What had happened to this place? he wondered, not that it was any of his business. His only concern was the child that might be growing inside her womb.

Turning away from the window, he took another sip from his mug and cringed at the taste. It tasted almost as bad as the coffee his father used to make.

When he took a seat in the chair Jesse had earlier occupied, the springs creaked with the weight of his body. Glancing down, he noticed several pink slips on the desk and an electric bill that had "FINAL NOTICE" stamped across it. Remembering her verbal confrontation with her foreman, he felt a tender spot for her. Why would such a young pretty woman want to run a place like this? As his thoughts continued, he also asked himself why she would give up her virginity and not only that, risk the chance of getting pregnant. It didn't appear she could even afford to take care of herself, let alone a child. From the looks of things, Jesse was in way over her head.

He rose from the chair. Taking one last swallow, he finished the coffee and returned the mug to the table. Spotting several photos on a small shelf in the corner, he moved over to relieve his curiosity. He lifted one frame and blew off heavy dust to discover a photograph of a beautiful little girl. It didn't take a rocket scientist to know the little girl was Jesse. Her curly reddish brown hair was all over her head. She was swinging from a tree in the backyard. The next photo was of her and a man who had to be her father. Her arms were curled tightly around his neck. Will felt a great deal of love emanating from the photo. Love was something that he had always possessed in his life. The only exception had been his failed marriage. Now the only love he needed was that of his family. He would never risk giving his heart to another woman again.

He shook his head, wondering why he was even thinking about love and family when the only thing that should be on his mind was Jesse and the possibility of an unborn child. Feeling a return of frustrations, he headed for the door and went in search of a lawnmower.

CHAPTER SEVEN

Jesse was sitting in her bedroom when she heard the hum of a lawnmower. She dashed from the chair to peer out the window. It couldn't possibly be one of her employees. That bunch of lazy jerks barely did what she asked them to do. Pushing the curtain aside, she saw Will clearing the overgrown grass in the backyard. Why? She didn't need his charity. She folded her arms across her chest and swung away from the window. Why couldn't he just leave!

She couldn't get over finding him in her home. She had never expected to see him again except in her dreams. And that's exactly where he had been for the last three weeks. Memory of the way he had made her feel haunted her. That one night of passion, though, would have to last her for all eternity. He had been her first but she didn't need another lover to know it could never be that good with anyone else. The two of them had meshed perfectly. It had been too perfect and that was why it could never happen again. She shook her head as if to shake off the thought.

Glancing through the window again, she watched his movements, the muscles in his arms, the way he squinted his eyes as he faced the sun, and was more than a bit confused at how it made her insides churn.

Resenting him for his perfection, she closed the curtain, then paced around the room like a caged animal. She didn't need Will or his help. Everything was going to work out, she was certain of that. Her period was already two days late. And if she was pregnant with a boy, she was home free. Now all she had to do was find a way to get rid of Will without him finding out the truth.

The lawnmower stopped and she strolled over to the window and peered out, taking extra care not to be spotted. Luckily, Will was nowhere to be seen. He had cleared a nice path. She could almost see the swimming pool, not that it was a pretty sight. She frowned. The pool needed to be drained and cleaned, and she didn't know how she was going to afford it. The bed and breakfast hadn't been occupied by tourists in over two years. They had never made a lot of money but she had never imagined things had been as bad as they apparently had been. For some unknown reason, her father had stopped caring. Now there was only enough money to hire Pace to get the renovations done. And without the bed and breakfast up and running at full capacity, there was no way to tackle the bills that were beginning to pile up or to save the house.

Glancing out the window, she saw Will return, carrying a bottle of water. The bottle of water she had left in the refrigerator this morning? She scowled. He had already made himself at home in the kitchen.

With one yank of the cord, he started the engine and began cutting the grass again. She stamped her foot. She didn't need his help. She could cut her own grass and had planned to so as soon as she found the time. He hadn't even asked. Will was trying to take over and she wasn't going to have it. She valued her independence. That was why she had no intention of ever marrying.

Out the corner of her eye she saw Pace and his crew moving to the picnic area. The spot had somehow become their designated smoking area. Today, however, it appeared they planned to spend more time smoking than working.

"Well, I'm not having it," she mumbled under her breath as she proceeded out of her room and down the hall. She'd had it with men trying to take over.

Will turned off the lawnmower long enough to take a swig of water from the bottle. While mopping sweat from his brow, he noticed Pace and two of his crew sitting at the picnic table, smoking and laughing.

He didn't like what his senses were telling him. It was plain as day the crew was taking advantage of Jesse.

With long strides he moved to where they were sitting and stopped in front of the foreman. "You couldn't possibly be finished with that floor."

The cocky man snarled up at him. "Nope. Just started but we don't have enough supplies so I'm waiting for one of my crew to return from Lowe's."

"I assume you're officially off the clock."

"What's it to you?"

Will glared at him. "Ms. James is not paying you for your breaks. Instead of cackling like a bunch of hyenas, the three of you could be clearing the shingles on that roof."

Pace chuckled rudely and the other two joined in. He then rose from his seat and stood eye to eye with Will. "The only person I take orders from is me."

Although Will didn't want to appear weak in front of the man, he staggered back slightly at the stink of stale beer on the man's breath.

Will clenched and unclenched his hands at his sides, battling for control. "Well, guess what? I plan on being around for a while and while I'm here I plan to watch you and your crew closely. I have years of experience in construction so don't even think for a minute you are going to put one over on Ms. James by using cheap materials or inflating prices."

The two were glaring at each other when Jesse came across the yard.

"What are the two of you doing?" she yelled.

Still glaring at Will, Pace replied, "This here pretty boy thinks he's running things."

"The only one that is running things is me. Why aren't you working?" Jesse demanded as she moved swiftly across the grass and joined the group.

"I decided to take a little break."

"Well, I'm not paying for breaks. You guys either get back to work or I'm going to start docking you for all of your idle time."

Pace was practically foaming at the mouth he was so angry. "We'll see about that," he muttered, then turned to his crew. "Come on, boys. Let's get back to work." The two rose and they walked back into the house.

"You need to watch your back, Jesse," Will warned as he watched the crew leave. "That man is trying to take advantage of you."

"Tell me something I don't already know." She stepped around him and headed over to the clearing he had made. "What are you doing?"

"I thought I'd cut your grass."

"I didn't ask you to do that," she pointed out.

"I know, but I wanted to do it," Will told her.

She regarded him with distrust. "I don't need your help."

"Yes you do. Now quit being so stubborn."

She was sounding like a whining kid but she couldn't help it. She also knew she should just turn around and leave, but as usual, her stubborn pride wouldn't let her just walk away. Will was making her feel like a child who needed someone to hold her hand.

"I told you I planned to stick around for awhile. So since I am here you might as well use my expertise. The first thing you need to do is fire that crew and hire someone more qualified."

She shook her head in dismay. Her voice was shaking and she hated the tears that sprang to her eyes. "I can't do that."

"Why the hell not?"

"Because I can't afford it!" She stumped past him and headed toward the house.

Will followed her into the kitchen and took a seat at a small wooden table. Despite the appearance of the rest of the house, the kitchen was in fairly good condition.

"You want some iced tea?" she asked.

A chill remained in her gaze, a distant polite smile on her lips. "Sure. I would love a glass."

She poured them each a glass, then reached for a package of deli ham, cheddar cheese and Miracle Whip. Then she took the seat across from him. Grabbing a knife, she busied herself making sandwiches.

"Things just haven't been the same around here since my father died."

The sadness in her voice touched him. "I'm sorry."

Her shoulders sagged, the stress of the last couple of months weighing them down. "So am I. It's been three months but I have learned to cope."

"Does this have anything to do with what happened in Philly?"

She studied her sandwich as if the answer to her problems resided in the grains of the bread. "He didn't think I could run the business because I'm a woman," she said very calmly.

He simply nodded, encouraging her to continue.

"This house has been in our family for three generations, passing from one son to the next. My dad wanted a son so bad that he named me after himself." She reached for her sandwich and took a bite. "I couldn't understand him sometimes. Instead of buying me dolls, he bought me trucks. He taught me how to play every sport there was. I can hit a homerun. I can even slam dunk a ball."

She tapped a small delicate hand on the table. Those long slender fingers had stroked his back. A flush of heat rushed through his veins. Will shifted so quickly in his seat that she noticed.

"You want a sandwich?" she asked.

Will simply reached for the bread and began preparing his own while she spoke.

"I watched him run this place for years. Whenever the maid or the cook was on vacation, I filled in," she began in a faraway voice. "Even with a master's in hotel management he didn't think I could manage this place."

His brow quirked. Beauty and brains. "You have a master's?"

"Yeah, last year I completed an accelerated, weekend master's program while managing a hotel during the week," she answered with a nonchalant shrug. "It seemed only natural that I would fill his shoes. I just knew that he was going to leave me this house. I would never have imagined…" She shook her head and gave a frustrated sigh.

Will bit into his sandwich, allowing her time to pull her words together. When she looked at him again, her gaze cooled as she focused on the present.

"I have to either be married or have given birth to a son within the year or the property will be sold."

As she explained the stipulations of her father's will, Will stopped chewing and lowered his sandwich to the plate. Everything was starting to make sense. Jesse had been willing to give up her virginity to save her family legacy. She had preferred having a child to being tied down. The thought of his child growing inside her made something unfamiliar flutter inside him. "It takes nine months to have a baby. What happens if you're not pregnant or if you have a girl?"

Jesse's hands trembled until she clasped them tight around her frosty glass. "I guess I'd have to find me a husband."

Her answer irritated him. "Is this place worth it? You're willing to have a baby by a perfect stranger just to get your hands on this rundown old house?"

She crossed her arms over her chest guardedly before saying, "You made your feelings clear in Philly. I would never call you, Will. You don't want to be married. Well, neither do I." She paused to roll her eyes at him. "This house might not look like much but at one time it was the most popular spot at the beach. And it will be again." She jabbed a thumb to her chest. "With me in charge."

"As for the baby…" Her face and voice softened. "Boy or girl, I'm going to love it and try to be the best mother possible."

Will noted the tears in her eyes before she blinked them away. He had to fight the urge to take her in his arms. No point in weakening now.

He reached for his sandwich and took another bite before he spoke again. "Jesse, this place is falling apart. From what I've seen you don't have any rooms ready. The front porch looks ready to cave in with the first gust of wind. You have boards and roofing that need replacing and everything needs a fresh coat of paint. Do you have the cash for that?"

Jesse lowered her elbows to the table. "I barely have enough to pay the utilities. I have an alcoholic and a trio of ex-cons remodeling my home because I can't afford anyone else. Pace is a pain in the ass but I've known him all my life. At one time he loved this house as much as I do." She bit her lip, looking as if she regretted telling him her problems. However, the stress of everything had finally taken its toll. "If I could just get two of the rooms ready, I could at least generate some income."

"You're talking about a great deal of renovation and construction, which will require a hell of a lot of money. At the rate that crew is moving, it will be time for you to move into a nursing home before this house is ready."

She looked impressed. "You sound like you know something about renovation."

Will simply shrugged. "I grew up in construction. My father owns a business that does everything from dry walling to roofing. I think he bought me my first hammer when I was barely out of diapers. I spent many years working by his side before I started my music career. Jess, it's not easy nor is it cheap. How do you plan to do this all by yourself?"

She squared her shoulders. Will had to admire her determination even if she was ignoring the obvious.

"I'll manage."

"No, you can't. You've got to pick up the pace around here and the only way you can do that is if you can get a bank loan."

She shook her head. "I already tried. No such luck."

"Then let me help," He heard the words leave his mouth and wondered if he'd lost his freaking mind.

"No," she barked without even taking a moment to think things through.

His brow rose with surprise. "Why not? You obviously need the help."

"I don't want a man doing anything for me."

"Unless he's serving your purpose."

Her cheeks flared and he knew she knew what he was talking about.

"If I wanted help I would just get married. Then I would have the money I needed."

His eyes narrowed quizzically. "How is that?"

"If I marry, my father's lawyer will hand over a check for two hundred and fifty thousand dollars."

He shook his head. This girl was not making any sense to him at all. "So why wait nine months when you obviously need the money now?"

He watched her contemplate her answer before speaking again. "Because the check would be made payable to my husband." The tears began to flow and resignation settled over Jesse's features.

He took in the sadness of her eyes and suddenly understood what she was feeling. She felt betrayed by her father. The same way he had felt betrayed by his wife when she walked away and left him with nothing.

"So why don't you marry me?" he suggested, not taking his gaze from her.

Surprise flared in her eyes. "What did you just say?"

"You heard me." What was he doing? He'd sworn that he would never settle down with another woman. Women used men.

Jesse looked as if she too doubted his sanity. He didn't think it possible for her to look any more surprised. She swallowed deeply and looked at him for a long moment, then said, "What if I'm not pregnant?"

At that moment it didn't even matter. Pregnant or not, the idea of having her back in his bed for any amount of time was too appealing to pass up. For some reason Jesse got to him in a way no other woman had. He shrugged. "You said you'd inherit if you got married."

She nodded hesitantly. A single tear slid from a corner of her eye.

"Then marry me. I'll give the check to you and you can use it to fix this place up," he said, his warm breath tickling her ear.

A strained moment passed between them.

"I don't want to get married," she protested as she rose and moved away from the table.

Determined to convince her, Will rose and grabbed her arm, halting her departure. "I think it's the perfect solution."

He inched closer and his masculine scent heated her blood. He carried a virile scent that disturbed her on a level she didn't want.

"Ever since that night you have haunted my sleep. All I can think about is how good you feel. How wonderful it would be to have you lying beneath me with your legs wrapped around my waist."

Steeling herself against a shudder, she took a deep breath. "That will never happen again." She leaned back against the counter, her breasts rising and falling.

"Yes it will because you want me just as I want you." With his gaze on her lips, Will bent nearer, his fingers giving in to the temptation to touch her delicate skin. He wanted to throw her over his shoulder and carry her to her room, then taste her sweetness all over again.

"This is insane." Her heart stumbled a beat. She stared up at a grin that deepened the dimples on either side of his mouth. "Now move and let me pass. I have work to do."

He wrapped an arm around her waist, halting her hasty departure. "It can wait," he muttered, bending close to Jesse.

He held her so close their hips brushed. His subtle masculine scent enticed her as did the fire she saw burning in the depths of his eyes. She felt powerless.

Raising her hands, she tried unsuccessfully to free herself. "No, it can't."

"What's wrong, Jesse? Afraid of what it would be like lying beside me every night?"

The intensity of his gaze sent a tap dance into full swing at the pit of her stomach. "No, I'm not afraid, just not interested."

"You didn't seem to mind in Philly," he said, lowering his voice to a murmur. "In fact, you couldn't get enough of my lips. I remember kissing every inch of your body." Seizing a chance, he brushed his mouth over hers.

Jesse drew in a breath, yet she didn't push him away. Her emotions were raw. Now was not the time to be kissed but she didn't have the strength to stop him. Standing on her tiptoes, she met his lips halfway. The touch of his mouth sent sparks of sensation radiating downward.

His kisses were slow and skillful. She savored the taste, the honey sweet taste of his mouth. She couldn't hold back the throaty little sounds that escaped her parted lips. Yearning to touch him, she made certain she resisted the urge by slipping her hands behind her rear which was pushed against the counter. The kiss became exploratory as his tongue slipped between her lips and took slow, measured strokes. He ignited a heat so powerful it made her blood pound as it radiated down through her chest, making her weak at the knees.

He was standing so close she felt the evidence of his arousal and knew he wanted her. She felt her control slipping. When his hand slid between the buttons of her blouse, she knew it was time to put things to an end even though her body yearned for a repeat performance. However, she wanted to prove to him that she was in complete control, that his kisses had no effect on her at all. Dragging her lips away, she then ducked beneath his arm.

Will's eyes opened and his arms fell to his sides as his brow lowered in a scowl. He turned around as Jesse headed toward the door. With her hand on the knob, she turned to meet his puzzled expression with a dark, heated expression.

"There is no way I'm marrying you."

Once she was safe in the comfort of her own room, Jesse lay across the bed and allowed the tears to fall freely.

She could already be pregnant with a stranger's child. She touched her belly. She didn't know how to be a mother. She'd never even been a baby sitter until Chanelle's daughter Chante had come along. How could she agree to become a wife to a man she didn't know other than in a physical sense?

She couldn't believe this was happening to her. How was it that her carefully laid out plan had come back to nip her on the butt?

All her life she had dreamed of running Katherine's side by side with her father. However, when that dream was lost to her, she'd thought to continue the family heritage by running the bed and breakfast on her own. Instead, everything was now worse than before. Because of the stipulation in her father's will, the only way she could keep the bed and breakfast was with the help of man. The only way she could restore the house to its original look was with the help of a man. Because she was so heavily in debt, the restoration would become a reality only if she took Will up on his offer.

Rolling over onto her side, she stared at a small bookshelf that held her collection of cherubs. As long as she could remember, she had collected them. They were the one thing her father always made sure she received every Christmas.

Men! She just couldn't understand them. Some days her father had been a tyrant; other days, the most caring gentleman in the world.

And Will?

She fluffed the pillows beneath her head and adjusted herself comfortably. It would be such a relief to throw herself into Will's arms and let him take all her worries away. She was still in awe at his proposal of marriage. She tried not to imagine what it would feel like lying in his arms every night. Her mind relived the velvety softness of his lips. Their kiss had been only a small reminder of what Will was capable of. The quick intensity of her desire had frightened the hell out of her and she resented feeling that way.

Lowering her eyelids, she wished away the memories. The last thing she needed was for erotic thoughts to alter her judgment. No matter how she looked at it, Will was a man and all men thought the same. They used the power that they had over a woman to search for signs of weakness to use against her. Regardless of how tempting the offer was, there was no way she was going to put her future in the hands of William Jones.

By sundown Will had cleared the entire yard. He filled several bags with debris and placed them on the curb for the trash, then headed up to his room to take a shower.

As he moved into his room and quickly shed his sweat-soaked clothes, Will thought about the position Jesse was in. Maybe she didn't think marriage was the answer, but the truth of the matter was that he didn't see any other way. He had heard the emotion in her voice and knew the bed and breakfast was her only connection to her past; therefore, he could understand why she was unwilling to let it go. As he strolled into the adjoining bathroom, he wondered if she'd ever felt that level of conviction for a man. Even though she said she never wanted to get married, he had the impression that if she did, she would give it her all. If his wife had had even a portion of that type of commitment, maybe the two of them would still be together.

Turning on the shower, he adjusted the water temperature and stepped inside, letting the hot spray massage his tired body. He still couldn't believe that he had offered marriage. After being burned once, he'd vowed never to walk that path again. But even before he'd had a chance to give her situation some serious consideration, he had heard those words fall from his tongue. Now, three hours since his proposal, a part of him still felt he had done the right thing.

As Will lathered his washcloth, he thought about the feeling Jesse invoked in him. Never had a woman made him feel the level of desire he felt for her. Listening to her stubborn pride was a joy all its own. He admired her determination in refusing to give up her independence.

Jesse was a sexy little spitball who unknowingly was very passionate. He was certain, though, if he told her so it would earn him a pop right upside his head. Their kiss had stirred his lust to maximum proportions. It had taken everything he had not to lift her off her feet and carry her to the nearest bed.

She weakened him to the point that he wasn't able to think clearly in her presence. His abrupt proposal was a prime example.

Will reached for the shampoo and squeezed a dab in his palm, then lathered his locs. What he should have done was stick to his original plan, find out if she was pregnant or not, and if not, get the hell out of Dodge. Instead, in a matter of hours, he had allowed himself to get emotionally involved with her. Now he again felt some unfamiliar need to protect her.

Rinsing the soap from his hair, he knew he was treading in dangerous territory. He'd made up his mind a long time ago not to get emotionally involved with another woman and had been doing a good job of keeping his head on straight until he ended up in bed with Jesse. Now his plan to remain single and detached was going up in smoke.

Maybe it was for the best that Jesse had rejected his offer. After all, what she did with this house was no one's business but her own.

His wife had taught him a hard lesson and that was, you can't ever force a woman to do what she doesn't want to do. No matter how much love and support he offered, Ebony rebuked it until finally she left him for someone else.

Her rejection had stung, but it had also toughened his skin. And he would not let himself forget how painful it had been. He'd married right after his graduation from Delaware State University. He had thought he had the perfect wife and had loved her with all his heart. Apparently his feeling for her had been a hell of a lot deeper than hers for him. During several brief periods when he had to leave her alone, she had been messing around with a math instructor, he'd discovered. After a bitter divorce he felt thankful they never had any children and vowed to never fall for a woman again.

Despite what had happened between him and Jesse, he wasn't going to allow her close enough to hurt him. He had a suspicion that if he did, her rejection would hurt ten times more than Ebony's.

If Jesse were carrying his child, he planned to stick by her through the entire pregnancy and later become an instrumental part of his child's life. But no matter how involved the two might become, he wasn't going to put his heart on the line for Jesse to step on. His emotions would not be part of their arrangement.

Reaching over and turning off the water, he reminded himself that his emotions really had little to do with it. He was willing to do the honorable thing. No more, no less. His heart wasn't in danger because he wasn't in love with Jesse. Even if she decided to accept his marriage proposal, he'd keep it that way. Besides, even if she agreed, which he doubted, it wouldn't be a real marriage and as soon as the terms of the will were fulfilled, Jesse would practically race him to the nearest divorce attorney.

Of course, if she were pregnant with his child, that would change things quite a bit. Divorce wouldn't be the end of their union. They would always be a part of each other's life. As he dried off, he cursed the fact that there was no easy answer. The next couple of days were going to be difficult.

He strolled back into his room and reached for a bag he had carried up from his SUV and removed a pair of gray sweat pants. He slipped the pants on atop a clean pair of boxers and then took a seat on the edge of the bed and looked around.

To his surprise, he found the room quite impressive. The walls were covered with a wallpaper print with large foliage that gave the illusion you were outside in the middle of a jungle. The newly laid sage carpeting was plush and felt wonderful beneath his feet. There were two double beds with a nightstand between them. There was also a sitting room with a sofa bed and a thirty-two inch television directly across from it. A small table with two chairs was over near a pair of sliding glass doors covered with beige draperies. If the room was any indication of what the rest of the house was going to look like, then he understood her determination.

Although there was a printed comforter folded across the bottom of his bed, the sheets and pillows were missing. After checking the closets and the bathroom and coming up empty, he had no choice but to go ask Jesse.

In search of Jesse, he checked the other five rooms. The room directly across the hall was almost complete while the walls of the other four had been gutted and had yet to be restored. Obviously, none of the rooms belonged to her. He remembered hearing movement earlier at the back of the house and decided that must be where her room was.

He descended the steps and moved through a living room that appeared half finished, then a formal dining room where a large table was draped with cloths and a chandelier was sitting on the floor.

As he reached the back of the house he heard the soothing sounds of soft, classical music.

Hearing light tapping on her bedroom door, Jesse knew it could only be Will. Since his attempt to kiss her in the kitchen, she had done her best to avoid him. With her heart beating twice as fast as it should, she lowered the book in her hand and moved to open the door.

"What do you—" She ran right smack into a hard muscular chest. Despite the cool evening a slow erotic sensation moved down her spine, and she jumped back as if burned.

He was leaning against the doorframe with a smirk on his sexy face. Her hormones went into overdrive and the first thing that came to mind as she watched him standing there was the night she had fallen asleep with her head resting on his bare chest.

Droplets of water hung from his locs that were resting comfortably on his shoulders. A hunger flared to life inside her when her gaze settled on a chocolate nipple surrounded by the fine curly hair that covered his chest and traveled down his stomach and below. Jesse had to clamp her mouth shut to resist rubbing her tongue across her lips. If things had been different, she would have captured one tantalizing nipple between her teeth. As inexperienced as she was, she was shocked at how brazen he made her feel.

Taking another step back from him, she regained control and finally found her voice. "Put some clothes on," she snapped in an irritated tone.

His intense dark eyes held her gaze. "Why? Does my being half dressed bother you?"

You don't know the half of it. She quickly shook her head. "Not at all. It just shows respect. Besides, the last thing I need is for you to get sick."

"It might be worth it just to have you nurse me back to health," he whispered in a low, sexy voice. He was staring at her, his face filled with burning desire. His gaze made intense heat travel through her veins and her heart began beating even harder.

She took another step back. Then her frown deepened. "Don't flatter yourself. What do you want?"

"I need bed linen and a pillow. Unless, of course, you want me to share your bed tonight." His eyes twinkled with renewed amusement.

Even though heat flowed down between her legs, she didn't reveal that his words affected her. She just frowned and narrowed her eyes at him. What Will refused to accept was that she didn't need a man physically or mentally. Ignoring him, she moved past him and padded on bare feet into the kitchen. Will was right behind her.

"Who remodeled your kitchen?" she heard him say.

Slowing her step, she said, "It may be hard to believe but Pace just finished the upgrades."

"Yeah, it is hard to believe."

She stopped and turned back around in time to watch him give the room a slow, appreciative look. She followed the direction of his eyes.

The kitchen featured a large gourmet island. An assortment of pots and pans hung overhead. An abundance of white cabinets that she had accented with decorative strawberry doorknobs lined the walls. Gleaming white tiles covered the floor. The room had been upgraded with stainless steel appliances, including a state of the art double oven.

She shrugged. "Like I said before, Pace isn't all bad. He just has a problem with alcohol."

"And that is a very big problem. One that you can't afford to ignore."

"As broke as I am, I can barely afford to eat."

"Then why won't you let me help you?"

She swallowed, suddenly realizing the tone of his voice had lowered to a seductive whisper. She stood rooted at the center of the room, afraid to look in his direction. She could feel the intensity of his dark gaze burning her right cheek. Pulling herself under control, she murmured, "Let me get those things for you."

He watched her sway past him, then followed her down the hall and up the stairs. The pink robe stopped right below her knees. He couldn't help paying close attention to the way it framed her backside. A hunger flared back to life. The next couple of days were going to be the most difficult days of his life. However, he had to admit her stubborn streak was an added turn-on.

At the end of the hall she opened what appeared to be a linen closet. Rising on her tiptoes, she removed a flannel blanket and two pillows, tossing each into his arms as she lowered them from the shelf. She reached for a set of sheets, then brushed past him and moved into his room.

She began making his bed. He started to say something, then changed his mind. Will knew to argue would be useless. She was stubborn and would use any excuse to start an argument with him.

While spreading the sheets on the bed, she glanced over at him and glared, "Don't just stand there. Put those cases on the pillows."

He bit his lip to keep from grinning. Not only was she stubborn, she was also a bossy little thing.

As they worked alongside each other, his mind was picturing all those soft curves lying in his bed. In that situation, sleep would be the last thing on his mind. He would kiss the frown away from her face, then make love to her until she screamed his name. Something deep stirred within him.

"There are more blankets in the closet if you need them," she said, interrupting his thoughts.

Will saw her swallow and watched her breathing quicken. She had felt it too. That heat, that terrible and tempting desire. Dammit. He was depending on her to be the strong one.

"Would you like to sit and watch a movie with me?" What was he saying? The last thing he needed was to spend the evening watching a movie with her.

Jesse glanced up and met his gaze. "I'm surprised you would even consider such a thing."

He lifted a brow at her tone. She sounded almost appalled at the suggestion. "Why not? We're two mature adults. You might as well start getting to know me because I plan to be around for a couple of days or even longer."

She cleared her throat. "Why don't we wait until I find out if I'm pregnant before you make plans to stay any longer than needed?"

"Alright." For now, he wasn't going to push.

"I think I'll pass on that movie. Do you need anything else?"

Hell, what he needed was her in his arms, in his bed. A lazy smile crept across his lips. "Nope, I've got everything I need."

She glanced at the bed and then quickly averted her eyes. "Well," she said with a weak smile, "it looks like you're all set then."

There was a long, awkward silence.

"Good night, Will." She turned and departed. The clean fragrance of her scent lingered.

He turned and opened a pair of French doors onto a small, newly constructed wooden balcony that faced the rising ocean tide and stepped out. While attempting to cool his hard-pounding desire, he inhaled the salty air. A slight breeze brushed over his bare chest as Jesse's departing words filtered through his mind.

Yeah right, he thought. Good night. Haa! Sleep was not going to come easy tonight. Not as long as they were sleeping in the same house.

CHAPTER EIGHT

The next morning Jesse slipped out of bed and made a quick trip to the bathroom, where she confirmed her suspicion. She wasn't pregnant.

Using her washcloth, she wiped the tears from her eyes. Now what was she going to do? Find another donor? No, she couldn't go through that again. After Will, she couldn't imagine another man touching her, yet she couldn't risk him touching her again either.

Looking in the mirror, she studied her image as the fate of her future weighed heavily on her shoulders. What was she going to do?

With a shake of her head, she released a long trembling breath. There was nothing else for her to do: She was going to have to accept Will's marriage proposal. Instead of feeling a pang of defeat, her traitorous heart lurched with excitement.

Lord! How was she going to bear having him around every day? The scent of him was more than she could bear. Last night had been incredibly difficult. A small part of her had hoped Will would toss her onto the bed. Memories of lying in his arms as he buried himself deep inside of her had haunted her most of the night.

Sunlight streamed into the room. A warm breeze ruffled the curtains and the scent of saltwater tickled her nose. She sighed with defeat. Marriage to Will would be quite entertaining, to say the least.

However, if she did decide to accept his proposal, it would be in name only. There was no way she would ever allow him to make love to her again. It would be a business arrangement, nothing more. And when the year ended, she would send him on his merry way. A slight smile tipped the corners of her lips as she thought about it. She would be the one benefiting, not him. Jesse would finally have her bed and breakfast and the money her father left her. It bothered her slightly to know that Will would be the one getting the short end of the stick. But would he? No man was willing to do anything for free. William Jones would want something, too. The big mystery was what Will would want in return. She tried not to think about one particular possibility, even though her breasts tingled against the fabric of her nightgown. She suddenly realized that what he wanted might be a lot more than she bargained for.

Squaring her shoulders, she reached for a brush and stroked it across her hair to bring some order to her appearance. She then reached for a washcloth again and washed her face, then quickly brushed her teeth. Glancing at herself in the mirror, she didn't miss the hint of lost sleep beneath her eyes. Because she'd dreamed of him all through the night, she had awakened grouchy, irritable and with raccoon eyes. She contemplated applying a little makeup to cover the dark circles. But if she delayed another second, she would find some way to talk herself out of accepting Will's proposal.

Jesse took a deep breath and glanced in the mirror again and decided it was the best she could do, considering the circumstances. She slipped into a robe and padded down to the kitchen. Just as she had hoped, Will was already up, making coffee.

"Alright, I'll marry you," she announced as she strolled into the room. "However, I insist on a prenuptial agreement. This property belongs to me and when this is all said and done, I plan to divorce you and get my life back."

She barely breathed as she waited for his response.

Will leaned against the edge of the counter, crossed his legs at the ankle and raised his mug to his lips. He took several small sips before he bothered to acknowledge her presence.

"Good morning to you, too," he finally said.

Her brow darkened impatiently. "Did you hear what I just said?"

He nodded. "Yes, and I've changed my mind."

Her lips parted. "What do you mean, you've changed your mind?"

Will took another sip, enjoying the way she nervously bit her bottom lip. "I mean I'm not so sure I want to get married. It seems like the only person who would benefit from our union would be you."

She turned away, but not before Will caught the flush moving up her cheeks. He chuckled inwardly. It appeared he wasn't the only one who had been affected by that night.

Jesse sighed deeply, then lowered into a chair at the table. "What do you want?"

He looked her in the eyes. "What are you willing to give me?"

Her face clouded with uneasiness. But Will wasn't ready to let up just yet. Jesse did things to his insides that he wanted to explore, if for no other reason then just to get her out of his system.

A frown deepened the lines between her brows. "How about twenty-five percent of my father's money?"

What she didn't know was that money was no object. His grandfather had left a small fortune to him and his siblings. "I want you to share my bed."

Her eyes snapped to attention. "You're kidding, right?" she asked.

"Nope." Will turned and reached for another mug, hiding the smile on his face. After at first kicking himself last night for even suggesting that they get married, he had come to a different point of view, one that would benefit them both. Jesse would get her inheritance and he would get her back in his bed. He was certain if he fed his hunger for her, he would eventually get her out of his system. "There is no way I can be around you constantly for the next year and not make love to you again." The task would be virtually impossible.

As he moved over to the coffee pot to pour her a cup, he glanced over and saw her staring out the window, obviously stunned into silence.

He refilled his own mug, then carried both mugs over to the kitchen table and straddled the chair across from her.

"So, what do you think about my offer?"

Jesse took the mug from his proffered hand, then reached for the sugar dish on the table. Not once did she look in his direction.

"I don't feel comfortable with that arrangement," she finally said. "I think the money was a much better offer."

"I disagree. And as far as I'm concerned, it's no longer up for discussion. Either you marry me and allow me my right as your husband or you can find some other sucker to satisfy the terms of your father's will." He turned slightly in his chair, pretending that something outside fascinated him as he sipped the hot black liquid.

Jesse's heart raced out of control. She couldn't possibly let him back in her bed. That one night had been more than she could manage. A year of sharing a bed with him would be next to impossible.

She took a sip of her coffee. "There is no way I'm gonna share a bed with you."

"Scared you might fall in love with me?" he asked with a challenging chuckle as he turned to look at her.

The tone of his voice drew her attention. She narrowed her eyes and tilted her chin. "About as scared as you are of falling in love."

His laughter fizzled and she could see the humor leave his expression. His eyes turned icy. Her words had hit a nerve. She didn't know why but as she watched him stare down into his mug, she found herself wondering who or what he was thinking about that brought such pain to his face.

"That will never happen. Not ever again. I loved someone and I got hurt badly once," he admitted. "I don't want to get hurt like that again."

As she listened, she realized there was a bitterness in him that made him distrustful. Someone had obviously cut him deeply. At the same time she realized he'd just opened a part of himself to her. She had a feeling that hadn't been easy for him to do.

"I'm sorry," Jesse replied quietly. "Were the two of you engaged?"

He was silent for so long, Jesse wondered whether he had heard her question. He shook his head finally. "No, married."

She looked directly at him, her eyes wide with curiosity. "What happened?"

"Let's just say she decided I was holding her back. So she found someone who had more to offer," he admitted reluctantly.

She could hear the pain in his voice, see the wounded expression of his eyes, which told her so much more than his words. His wife had left behind scars. Watching the muscle twitch at his jaw she sensed that he still hadn't gotten over being rejected. Even though Jesse wanted to push him into revealing more, the frown on his face stopped her. Instead, she allowed herself to imagine for a moment what it would be like to be married to him. She couldn't speculate on what the days would be like, but she had already experienced a night first hand. She couldn't stop the ripple of pleasure that escalated up her body.

Shaking her head, she came back to reality. Reaching for her mug, she took another sip, then said, "When I was two, my mother walked out on me and my father. I never saw her again." Jesse didn't look at him, couldn't stand the thought of Will feeling sorry for her. She wasn't the first kid to be abandoned and sadly she wouldn't be the last.

"My dad never got over her. He tried to act like he didn't care but he did. He was bitter until the end." She paused long enough to take another sip. She wasn't sure why she was even sharing her past with him. She usually wasn't comfortable sharing her life. The fact that she found herself wanting to pour her soul out to him both worried and surprised her. "He met my mother at a bar. She was his waitress. She had just turned twenty-one, and I guess when she saw this wealthy fifty year-old-man she saw dollar signs. Unfortunately, all that changed after I was born."

Will reached out and touched her cheek. "I want to make a promise to you. If we marry, I will never use or misuse you in any way. Our relationship will be non-emotional. No strings attached. I promise to be your husband in every way from now until the date stipulated in the will. I don't walk away from things that belong to me. I hope you believe that."

She released the breath, unaware she'd been holding until she answered. "I do."

"However, if I am going to be your husband you are going to be my wife and with that comes the duty of a wife—the love, honor, and obey bit."

Her temper flared. "I'll never let a man tell me what to do."

"I don't expect you to. However, I do expect you let me love you in a physical way." He curved his finger around her chin and turned her until their eyes met. "I want you to know that when we are married you will become my wife and your body will belong only to me. I won't share you with anyone."

She swallowed, not knowing what to do, let alone what to say. His nearness immediately made her start thinking about things she shouldn't be thinking. If she granted him what he wanted, it would be hard, maybe even impossible to stay focused just when she needed to stay in control. She leaned back in her chair and put some space between them. In doing so her head felt clearer. She took several deep breaths.

"Well?" he pressed, not giving her any further time to make up her mind.

She folded her arms across her chest. She was in so far over her head that she didn't see any other way out of this mess. She would just have to find a way to stay in control of the relationship. Her decision brought a small smile to her lips. She glanced across at him and noticed he was waiting patiently for an answer to his demands.

She released a deep sigh, then said, "Alright."

Will looked as if he didn't believe her. "I mean it, Jesse. You will belong to me."

The fire burning in his eyes told her he meant every word. Will had every intention of possessing her body. After their one night of passion, she had an excellent idea of what she was in for. Jesse's hand began to shake and she set the mug on the table and rose in one fluid motion.

She was getting married.

Realization suddenly came crashing down. What in the world was she thinking? The last thing in the world she wanted was a husband. Okay, maybe she didn't really have much of a choice but that still didn't change the fact she didn't want to be tied down.

Good Lord! She had just agreed to share a bed with him for the next three hundred and sixty five days. How in the world could she bear such a thing?

Although the memories of him making love to her caused a shiver to course through her body, it did not change the fact that their marriage would be a loveless partnership. Before she got lost in her thoughts, she turned to face him, bracing herself against the counter.

"Would you like some breakfast?" she asked.

His lips quirked in an animated smile. "You cook?" She shrugged a shoulder. "I'm no Martha Stewart but I do okay."

Will emptied his mug, then rose. "How about French toast? I'll even help."

Now it was her turn to look amused. "You cook?"

"They call me George Foreman."

She gave a small chuckle as they both began preparing breakfast.

Jesse pulled out a carton of eggs while he reached for the loaf of bread and looked through her spice rack for nutmeg. Will moved with effortless masculine grace that made her glad she was a woman. But as she started to help him out there was no harmony in their movements. It was obvious they were both unused to having someone else in the kitchen with them.

She turned quickly and bumped into Will. His arms came around her, steadying her. His chest was hard against her arms that were crushed against him holding a package of bacon. She glanced up at him. Will's face was close and his warm breath whispered across her face like a sensual caress.

"Sorry," he said.

"My fault," she said, trying to pull her thoughts together. Dammit, whenever he touched her, she forgot to think, to breathe. He didn't release her and she made no move to break the contact with him. His touch was sending sensations escalating through her entire body. She wasn't sure how long they both stood there waiting for the other to make the next move before Will maneuvered one hand between their bodies and took the bacon from her, setting it on the countertop. Then he tugged her closer in his embrace and his eyes zeroed in on her lips.

"I've been wanting to do this since last night," he said huskily, his lips only a few inches away.

Desire formed in his eyes before she asked softly, "Why didn't you?"

"I was a fool," he whispered against her lips. He lowered his head and captured her mouth with his and a rush of heated desire took over. She couldn't think. She could barely breathe as his touch glided over her bare back. With a sigh she surrendered and opened her mouth and allowed him to slip his tongue inside her mouth.

His tongue probed, coaxed and forced her to respond with all the longing she felt. The kiss also caused a sudden throbbing between her legs. She opened her eyes to find him watching, making sure that she realized that what was happening was reality. Her pulse increased. She'd never really lived for the moment before Will. When he touched her she felt the tension seep out of her body and drew comfort from the strong arms around her.

His hand slid down her spine, cupping her behind covered by her terry cloth robe and pulling her closer. Sensual heat seeped from his hand and radiated through her body. He continued to caress her as his tongue invaded her again, making her feel like the most desirable woman in the world.

Jesse grasped his shoulders, felt his heart pound heavily through the thin barrier of his T-shirt. Her nipples hardened against the soft cotton of her gown. She wanted to rub her breasts against his chest and relieve the ache. The urge was strong and wonderfully painful.

She leaned forward, and their lower bodies melded together. She moaned, wanting more of Will. She wanted to be enveloped in him, wrapped tightly in his strength.

He groaned deep in his throat, the sound distinctly male. His grip on her backside changed and his fingers clenched against her and he rubbed himself slowly against the part of her that needed him. When he moved his hips, Jesse moved against him.

Tilting her head to the side, she granted him easier access. Will's mouth found her throat. His kisses were long and drugging on her neck, his tongue a hot pleasure to her senses. He found the spot just behind her ear. The contact made her shiver in his arms. Senses were stirring that she had only felt once before. It was different from the first time because no longer a novice, she was aware of how her body responded to his touch.

Will lifted her, setting her on the countertop and stepping between her legs. Impatient fingers helped her shrug out of her robe. She inhaled deeply when he slid down the thin straps of her nightgown, exposing the soft curves of her breasts. She saw desire brewing in his dark eyes. Reaching up, he excited her even more as he ran the tip of one fingertip around her aroused flesh. She trembled in his arms. Then he licked his thick upper lip and leaned forward, taking one of her budding chocolate nipples in his mouth and suckling her.

She gasped his name. Her eyes squeezed closed, her body thrilled with exquisite satisfaction. Her fingers burrowed through his locs, holding his head firmly to her breast. His tongue teased her for endless moments before he transferred his magic touch to her other breast, giving it equal attention. Jesse felt herself sinking in a whirlpool of sensations and she sighed with satisfaction at his pleasuring caress. Suddenly what he was doing wasn't enough. Suddenly she wanted it all.

She first jerked at the intimate contact when she felt him move one hand between their bodies, and brush his fingertips across the crotch of her panties. He then looked up into her eyes before he slipped his fingers beneath the material finding her moist wet fold.

She released a sigh from deep within. "Will," she said.

"Just let it go, baby," he said softly. "You are mine, *this* is mine."

She couldn't begin to find words to express the pleasure that overtook her body. She couldn't fight what she was feeling. His touch was unnerving and totaling tantalizing. The only thing she could do was wrap her legs around his waist and lose herself in what he was doing to her.

He resumed suckling her breast as he slipped two fingers inside her heat. They moved in and out, stroking her repeatedly. The contact sent her over the edge. She moaned his name as she squirmed frantically against him.

Her body clenched and she whimpered her pleasure in his mouth. She met each stroke as she cried out his name. His fingers continued to stroke her until a glorious explosion rocked her body. She collapsed against him, resting her head against his chest. Will held her until the tremors stopped and her heart rate slowed.

Aftershocks of pleasure raked her body. As she leaned against him, Will held her with a strength that scared her. Oh my God. What had happened? She was embarrassed and wasn't sure what to do next. Slowly she removed her legs from the hips of a man who'd just given her an unforgettable orgasm.

She shifted her gaze to the kitchen floor, refusing to look at him. "Can I get down now?"

He was rock hard and it was all he could do not to give in to his basic needs. It had been a long time. Longer than he had been without sex in years. Nevertheless, he prided himself on his control. He wasn't going to push her. Not today. There would be plenty of time for that later.

He did the right thing and stepped back from between her parted thighs and lifted her off the countertop. Then he stuck his hands into his pockets. If he touched her again he knew he wouldn't be able to stop. He knew he should say something to lighten the mood but he couldn't think of anything. Besides, he'd never had to before. The women he'd encountered before believed actions spoke louder than words. Rarely had there been any kind of conversation outside of sex.

Jesse was different. In ways he was just beginning to notice. Ways that made him feel too protective of her. He didn't like that.

Jesse lowered her head, obviously too embarrassed to look him in the face. He released a sigh of frustration. Dammit, man, think of something to say.

"I've suddenly lost my appetite," Jesse murmured, more angry with herself than with him. She fixed her clothes, then slid past him to stare out the window.

Voices and loud activity in the backyard drew her attention away from the man she had agreed to marry. Pace and his crew were standing around listening to loud rap music coming from a boom box. As usual, no one was working. Jesse let out an audible sigh. Will crossed the room and stood behind her. Too close. She could feel his breath on her nape and the heat radiating from his body.

He slammed a fist on the counter and Jesse nearly jumped out of her skin. "Cut his check. I'm going to fire the crew." He turned and headed toward the door.

"But what'll I do for help?" She scrambled after him and stopped him with a hand on his arm. His muscles flexed beneath her fingers and she jerked her hand away. How could she be considering marrying a man who made her insides quiver?

Will leveled his dark eyes on her. "I know plenty of men looking for work. Soon as I put word out, they'll be lining up at the door."

Jesse folded her arms across her chest and tilted her chin. "Just because I agreed to marry you does not mean you are now in charge. When you hire, then *I'll* fire."

Will stared down at her long and hard. She expected him to put up some kind of argument. Instead, he turned and strode out the back door.

Jesse closed her eyes and rubbed her temple. Things were going from bad to worse with the speed of light.

She moved over to the table, reached for her mug, and refilled it. She then strolled into her father's office and sank into his old leather chair. Usually it soothed her to sit there. Being in the room made her feel that he was still a part of her life. Even now, if she closed her eyes, she could hear his gruff voice in the background. A single tear trickled down her cheek. She quickly wiped it away. Now was not the time to get soft or more vulnerable than she already was. She had an even bigger problem on her hand.

Reaching for her mug, she brought it to her lips. Her hands were still shaking from the encounter with Will in the kitchen.

She'd just lost control in his arms and they both knew it; her body still hummed with the need to be closer to him.

In her mind, once more she felt those muscles slide around her. That rough callused hand had cupped her breast so gently, massaged until—

She lowered the mug again, then buried her face in her hands. What had she done?

Tying herself to him terrified her, but there wasn't another option.

Owning a bed and breakfast didn't mean anything if she didn't have any money to manage it. Without the repairs, Katherine's would never reopen and the property would go up for sale. Even if she did manage to rent a room or two, once it was up and running she still would need money for food, utilities, and the day-to-day operations. As of last week, her business account had a zero balance. Nope, she had no other choice. But how could she be sure he wouldn't try to take the place from her? How could she be sure he wouldn't hurt her? Jesse stiffened her spine. Losing Katherine's was not an option.

CHAPTER NINE

Will walked around the house making a list of supplies he needed and the amount of time it would take for each repairs. He had to admit that despite cosmetic problems, the house was sound. Nevertheless, needed repairs were many and costly. The wooden stairs that lowered to a footpath that led down to a brown sandy beach were rotting and had to be replaced. The stairs to the front were in even worse condition. The list was growing longer by the second, almost as long as the list of reasons why he shouldn't marry Jesse.

However, he had offered, and she had accepted, albeit reluctantly. And since he was a man of his word, there was no turning back. Still, for some reason, his offer felt right. For the first time in months he felt that he had made a wise choice.

As he rounded the back of the house, he spotted Pace sitting in his truck sipping from a brown bag while several members of his crew stood around talking. The man was blatantly drinking on the job. He slipped the pad and pencil in his back pocket and strolled over to the truck.

"What are you doing?"

Pace scowled when he noticed Will standing beside him. "None of your business." He quickly screwed the cap back on the bottle, then lowered it on the seat beside him.

Will had to do everything in his power not to pass out when the strong stink of whiskey captured his nose. "Pack your gear. You're fired."

Pace tossed his head back and laughed. "You can't fire me." He climbed out of the truck with his chest stuck out.

Will planted his feet apart and watched the drunk. "Clear out."

Pace advanced toward him. "I work for Jesse, not you."

Will's mouth spread into a thin-lipped smile. "Oh, didn't she tell you? We're getting married. So now you work for me."

As he'd expected, Pace lunged forward. Will caught his fist, twisted his arm behind his back and pushed him down onto his knees in the grass. His crew stood around and watched in a daze. They either had enough sense not to interfere or just didn't care what happened to their drunk boss.

Disgusted, Will shook his head. "Pack your shit and be gone within the hour." He then turned and headed toward the house.

He had only taken a few steps when he heard a noise and turned. Pace caught Will in the stomach, knocking him to the ground.

"Stop it!" Jesse screamed as she rushed down the stairs. By the time she reached them, Pace was laid out on the grass, flat on his back with a bloody nose. "What's going on here?"

Will scowled. "Your foreman decided to bring his breakfast to work."

Even from where she was standing she could smell the stink of whiskey. She frowned then, planted her hands on her hips. There was fire burning in her eyes. "Pace, you get off my property or I'm calling the police."

Will smirked. "That's telling him, baby."

Her eyes darted up to him, stunned by his choice of words. He threw his head back with laughter, then moved over. Draping an arm comfortably around her shoulders, he led her back up to the porch. He wiped his mouth and she saw the blood on his hand.

She gasped, "You're hurt."

"I'll be fine."

She saw the evidence of a bruise on his cheek and his cracked lip. "Oh, no, you're not." Taking him by the hand, she led him into the house. Once in the kitchen she made him sit. She reached for a cloth in the drawer and wrapped it around a piece of ice and handed it to him.

"Thanks. It's nice to know that you care."

She opened her mouth, ready to say something, but the words

wouldn't come out. "Oh, whatever." She turned on her heels and moved back out onto the porch to watch Pace's crew loading up their trucks.

Pace gave her a long hard stare, then shouted from the truck before he pulled off, "You're going to regret messing with me!"

Even though the threat disturbed her, Jesse did her best to appear unaffected and simply waved. Once the last vehicle turned at the end of the road, she swung around and returned to the house.

Moving into the kitchen for something cool to drink, she found Will had changed into a clean shirt and washed the blood from his face.

Frustrated, Jesse tossed her hands into the air. "Thanks to you, I no longer have any help."

He moved over and cupped her chin, tilting her head upward. She looked so distressed and lost that an odd tenderness immediately coursed through him. He wanted to soothe away any uneasiness she might be feeling. More importantly, he wanted Jesse to trust him. "Thanks to me this place is about to be done the right way." He grasped her shoulders and steered her toward the door. "Come on. Let me show you where I want to start."

She twisted away from his heated touch. "Hold up. This is going to be a team effort. Either we are going to discuss things together before decisions are made or this is not going to work."

"Alright, we will work together." He looked clearly amused.

Together. That word scared her. She'd grown used to being independent, to being solely responsible for herself. It was strange to think that Will would have a say in her future. It wasn't all bad but the realization was also scary.

"Would you care to show me what you'd like me to work on first?"

His words were dripping with sarcasm. Okay, so maybe she didn't know as much about renovations as he did. However, she did know what needed to be done in order to get back in business.

She rubbed her temple where she felt the onset of a migraine. She was in for a long day, and bumping heads with a smart-aleck musician wasn't going to make her head feel any better. There was no doubt in her mind that William Jones was going to give her a hard time.

"The most important thing is the house. If I can't rent rooms, I can't generate enough income to do anything else."

"True. But if the grounds look like a jungle and the pool continues to have slime and insects in it, no one is going to want to stay here."

She sighed. He was right. The outside was equally important. The beauty of Katherine's surroundings was what brought guests back year after year. She released another weary sigh. It was too late to turn back now. Two months ago she had placed an ad in one of Rehoboth's tourist magazines using an old photograph of the bed and breakfast, announcing their grand reopening. As a result, Katherine's already had reservations clear into July. There was no way she was going to have to call everyone and cancel. With the string of bad luck she'd been having lately, someone would bring her up on criminal charges for false advertising. Her heart pounded wildly in her chest at the possibility. After pondering the situation a few seconds longer, she brushed the idea away. No, that wasn't going to happen. Everything was going to work out.

"Now that you've fired Pace, I don't know what I'm going to do," she commented.

"Don't worry. I'm going to handle it."

"That's just it. I don't want you to."

His knuckles scraped gently along her jaw. "Everything is going to be fine. Trust me." Jesse caught her breath as awareness arched between them. Will lowered his head.

Jesse leaned back. "Don't."

Will halted. "Don't? I thought we had an agreement."

She shook her head. "I agreed to share your bed *after* we are married, not before."

"But I was simply going to kiss you."

She swallowed. "No kissing either."

Will stepped back, frowning. "Kissing is harmless."

"This is just a business arrangement. Besides, we hardly know each other."

"We were good, Jesse. Better than good."

"I know, but…I need time."

"How much time?" he growled impatiently.

"Until our wedding. How can I make love to a man I don't love?" She'd never expected to enjoy making love with a man she didn't love.

"It wasn't love you wanted that night. Hell, it wasn't even me you wanted. You wanted Chris."

She'd stung his pride. "No, no, I didn't want Chris. I wanted a musician who wouldn't follow me home. He seemed the type. You on the other hand…" She shrugged. No need to state the obvious.

"If we are going to make this commitment work, you…we need to work on being friends."

He was right. They would never survive living in the same house if they spent every waking hour disagreeing on one issue after another. They both liked to be in control. That much was obvious. Unfortunately, once she married him, her control would be limited. Could she really bear letting someone else hold the key to her future? She just wasn't sure. She did know one thing for certain: The better they got along, the better chance she would have. What she wasn't going to tolerate, though, was his need to torment her with kisses. Images of the time they had shared less than an hour ago came to her mind and she shuddered. If their relationship was going to last for the next three hundred plus days, then she needed to set some boundaries.

She tilted her head and met his questioning expression. "You're right, we do need to work on being friends. But until I decide I'm ready to sleep with you, no more stolen kisses, no more caresses. Do you think you can handle that?"

His mouth twitched with amusement. "Only if you think you can handle it."

She swallowed a wave of heat and quickly nodded. "Sure. No problem at all."

"Good," he said, although his expression was unconvincing. She had a sneaking suspicion that Will was not one to give up that easily.

"How about we compromise this evening?"

"What do you have in mind?" she asked with a look of skepticism.

"While I finish the backyard, how about you make dinner and later we sit in the family room and watch a movie together?"

She swallowed and tried to tell herself it wasn't a date. "Sure." She must have not looked too convincing because he said, "You sure you can handle that?"

Jesse frowned. "Why not? I'll simply make spaghetti and a tossed salad."

"Deal."

And they shook on it.

Looking out the window, Jesse watched Will cut down a tree with a power saw. The sight tossed her back into her happy, carefree childhood.

She remembered the swing that her father had hung from a large overhead branch. She had spent hours pumping the seat, determined to swing high enough to touch the sky. Several years ago a storm had swept across the coast and had damaged the tree. Now with it gone, she had a clear view of the sandy beach. Without the tree, the room would receive more sunlight.

She watched as Will lifted his safety glasses to the top of his head, then reached for a large branch, and finished breaking it off with his gloved hand. In a T-shirt and jeans and boots, the carpenter's tool belt slung around his hips, he was handsome. The setting sun behind him framed every powerful line and gleamed on that fabulous, sable face.

Turning away, she moved to the refrigerator and pulled open the freezer door.

While she prepared the meat sauce, she thought about what it would be like to be married to Will. Although theirs wasn't going to be a real marriage, she would be sharing his bed. The thought of having him inside her, being filled with his engorged manhood, brought a surge of liquid warmth to her loins. She would have to somehow stay in control, though. Friends, okay. Lovers was going to be a little tricky. However, she was certain if she kept her emotions under lock and key everything would be fine.

Will smelled the heavenly scent of spaghetti several feet away from the door. He stepped into the house to find Jesse standing at the sink draining a pot of noodles.

When she heard the door shut, she glanced over her shoulder and smiled shyly. "Dinner will be done in about fifteen minutes."

"I can't wait. Everything smells delicious."

The timer went off on the oven and she left the noodles in the sink, grabbed an oven mitt and removed several slices of Texas Toast.

Glancing down at himself, Will noticed the grass and sweat that clung to his clothes. He needed a shower. "I'm gonna run upstairs and clean up."

When he left the room Jesse exhaled and allowed herself a moment to relax. Having dinner tonight was not going to be as easy as she had first imagined. As much as she tried to deny it, the two of them sharing a meal was going to be just like being out on their first date.

Exactly fifteen minutes later, she heard footsteps and then he appeared. She tried not to notice how well the fresh clean T-shirt looked on his chiseled chest. Droplets of water clung to his long locs. She forced her eyes back to the stove.

"Dinner is served. Let's eat out on the sun porch."

He nodded and moved to the room behind the kitchen. The room was unfinished with rough walls stripped of damaged drywall panels. A gentle breeze scented with fresh cut grass and sea air trickled through the room from the three screened windows. Before him, the ocean gleamed in the mist; the tide lapped at the sand. Overhead was a skylight which he imagined gave an excellent view of a moonlit sky.

He took a seat at the table. Jesse brought in a glass bowl of her sauce and a separate bowl of noodles to the table.

"How about a bottle of wine with dinner?" she suggested. Will glanced over in surprise and nodded. "Wine would be great."

She moved back into the kitchen and removed a bottle of red wine from the refrigerator, then took it to him. "Here, you get the honor of removing the cork."

He took the bottle from her hand and went to a kitchen drawer for a corkscrew.

She stood and watched him from behind, admiring how wonderful he looked in his jeans, as good as the first time she'd seen him.

When they were seated, she said grace. Then he waited until she had served herself, then dug in.

"This is really good. I thought you said you couldn't cook."

She shrugged. "I can't. Spaghetti is about the only thing I have ever learned to make. I mean, how hard is it to open a can of Ragu sauce and brown toast?"

"Harder than you think."

"I used to make it every Friday for our guests. It was the day our cook usually took the evening off."

He gave her a puzzled look. "I thought bed and breakfasts only served breakfast?"

She smiled at his observation, then nodded. "Most do, but some serve other meals as well. As long as we had guests my father aimed to please. We served breakfast, and dinner and lunch per request. Most of our guests spent the day at the shore shopping and on the beach and never made it back to the house until well after sunset."

As he chewed, Will gazed out the window. "It's very beautiful here."

"Yes, it is."

Will and Jesse enjoyed the rest of dinner, discussing different topics and finding common ground: They both liked Jill Scott, their favorite color was green and they both loved animals, especially dogs.

After she cleaned her plate, Jesse rose and carried it over to the sink. Will also rose and helped gather the dirty dishes.

"Don't worry about them. I'll take care of everything."

"Nonsense. You cooked. The least I can do is help. My mother would kill me if she found out otherwise."

"I'm glad to hear she didn't baby you."

"No way. Hattie raised all of us to be men but refused to wait on us hand and foot."

She washed and he dried while he told her about his brother and growing up in Baltimore.

"Alright, I guess it's time for that movie," he said as she put away the last plate.

Jesse's heart pounded rapidly as she suddenly realized that the two of them were all alone in her house. They moved into the living room and he picked a DVD.

"*White Chicks*. That's my favorite comedy!" she exclaimed, pleased by his choice.

"Good. I haven't seen this one yet."

She reached for a small blanket and draped it over her legs as she curled onto the couch.

"You cold?" he asked.

She shook her head. "No, I mean, not really. My feet are always cold."

Will reached out and put his arm around her. "I hope you don't mind," he whispered close to her ear.

"No, not at all." Jesse could barely get the words out. The heat pouring from him was just as comfortable as being wrapped in a blanket in front of a cozy fire on a cold winter night. She couldn't concentrate on the movie because her mind was on the man sitting beside her.

"Relax," he whispered as if he could sense her nervousness. He pulled her snuggly against him and she rested her cheek against his chest.

Jesse sighed, deciding to enjoy the moment. They were quiet and nothing was said as they both tried to watch the movie. Soon they found themselves laughing along with each other.

Once the credits came on, she lifted her head, rose and turned off the television. When she turned Will was standing also.

Suddenly everything was quiet except for the sound of their breathing.

Unsure what to do next, she faked a yawn. "Well, I guess I'll go to bed now. Thanks for a wonderful evening."

Will curled an arm around her waist and pulled her against him. And she felt the large bulge in his pants pressed against her. She lifted her head, their eyes locked, and slowly lifting her mouth to his seemed the most natural thing to do.

She moaned and opened to the penetration of his tongue. The kiss deepened and her arms curved around his waist. His hand stroked up and down her back.

He tasted her slowly, skillfully stroking the interior of her mouth, dissolving her ability to think. She sagged deeper into the embrace. Will pulled her even closer. He leaned over and clasped her buttocks, lifting her slightly off her feet. His lips drifted to her throat and a soft moan escaped her lips. She squirmed and the movement of her breasts against him drew a strong surge of desire.

Pulling apart, he studied her flushed face, watching as her eyelids flustered open and she stared up at him, desire burning in the depths of her eyes.

"I want to make love to you." Will grazed her right cheek with his lips, then leaned closer and whispered against her earlobe. "But I'll wait until you're ready. I promise you that when I do I'm going to kiss every inch of your body slowly from head to toe. You'll be begging for more. Goodnight, Jess." He turned and went to his room.

She wrapped her arms around herself and stared at him dumbfoundedly, knowing that her desire must have been as visible to him as his was to her.

With a sigh, she went to her room, where she quickly changed into her gown. What was happening to her? she asked herself as she climbed under the covers.

She truly did not need complications in her life. Yet her heart was increasingly at risk where Will was concerned. Jesse curled into a ball, hugging her knees to her chest.

Tonight, her physical attraction to him had reached its limits. If he had persisted, there was no way she would have been able to tell him no. If she wasn't careful, she would be back in his bed before their wedding night. It was as if her body had a mind of its own.

And that scared her to death.

She had no choice but to hold up her end of the bargain, and she already knew deep in her heart that after three hundred and sixty-five nights of lying beside him, allowing him to make love to her, parting would be most difficult.

Every day she was learning that there were many layers to Will's personality. He was stubborn, funny, sensual and witty and when his mind was made up, he stuck to his decision and nothing or no one could stand in his way.

She didn't want to like him. And she most definitely didn't want to lose her heart to him. Jesse groaned. She was in serious trouble.

CHAPTER TEN

"You're doing what?"

Even after twenty-four hours, it was still hard for her to believe it herself. Glancing across her kitchen table at her best friend, Jesse repeated the announcement. "I'm getting married."

Chanelle looked at her with curious amusement. "How? When did this happen?"

While Jesse sliced them both a piece of carrot cake she had bought at the store that morning, she explained everything that had transpired since the day she and Will first met at the lounge.

Chanelle's brow narrowed with confusion. "But I thought you were going to have a baby instead?"

"My plan didn't work. I'm not pregnant."

"Can't you try again?"

"Yeah, but if it's a girl, I'll still lose this house."

Chanelle shook her head. When her best friend had asked her to drive down to the beach for a day of shopping at the hundred plus out-let stores in the area, she never suspected she was going to ask her to be her maid of honor.

"We're talking about that fine brotha you spent the night with in Philadelphia, right?"

"Yep."

Her best friend's lips curled into a smirk. "Maybe it's not such a bad idea after all. He'll definitely make some beautiful babies."

Jesse glanced up from her plate and rolled her eyes. "This will be strictly a business arrangement. I don't have any intentions of sharing his bed."

"You've got to be kidding, right?"

Last night she had come up with the ridiculous notion of convincing Will after they were married that a sexual relationship would be a big mistake. Jesse sighed. She didn't even know why she was fooling to herself into thinking he would even consider such a thing. Yesterday he had flat out refused. Even as she said lay awake last night, she could see why Will refused. It had taken her half the night to settle down after he'd told her he wanted to share her bed. Her insides quivered at the thought. After yesterday, she had to admit the idea was going to be more difficult than it sounded.

Chanelle arched an expressive raven eyebrow. "And what does your musician fiancée have to say about this?"

She dropped her eyes to her plate before saying, "He refused to even consider it."

Chanelle threw her head back and laughed openly.

Jesse was annoyed at being the butt of her laughter. "What's so funny?"

"Did you really think he was going to agree to a celibate marriage?" she asked, holding her gaze.

A slight frown appeared between her golden eyes. "Yes. No. I don't see why it's such a big deal. It's only a one year business arrangement."

"Girl, ain't no man going to go that long without. Besides, that's too much man to pass up. If you're going to marry him you might as well get some kind of pleasure out of it."

Jesse clamped her jaws in frustration.

Chanelle drew in a deep breath of excitement. "Well, I guess we need to be planning a wedding."

"Nothing fancy. Something simple at the house."

"Have the two of you decided on a date yet?" Chanelle asked around a forkful of cake.

"A date?" Jesse repeated, sounding confused.

"Yes, girl, a date for the wedding."

Jesse rested her chin on her hand, then shook her head. "No, we haven't decided on a date yet." She'd hoped to take as much time as she needed to adjust to the reality of their upcoming nuptials. However, the longer she waited, the longer it would be before she could get her divorce.

Chanelle pointed her fork in her direction. "Come on, Jesse, this is supposed to be the most important day of your life. Let's go all out and plan something fabulous."

Jesse regarded her for several seconds, then frowned. "It would be a big waste of money."

"Then let's plan something nice within a reasonable budget. My treat."

She shook her head. "Oh, I couldn't let you do that."

"Yes, you can and you will. As much as you baby sat for me for free, it's the least I can do."

Suddenly losing her appetite, Jesse pushed her plate away. "As long as it isn't more than five hundred dollars."

"Five hundred! The only way I can do that is if I bake the cake myself and pick flowers from my garden."

"Okay. What's wrong with that?"

Just as she expected, Chanelle flat out refused. "I'm not doing it and neither are you. So you might as well accept the fact that if I'm planning your wedding, then I'm going to do things my way."

Seeing the stubborn tilt of her chin, Jesse released an exasperated sigh. There was no way to budge Chanelle when her mind was set.

Jesse should have felt at ease to know that everything her friend did was classy and tasteful. The lovely yellow pantsuit Chanelle was wearing was proof of that. Jesse glanced down at her faded blue jeans and wondered why she couldn't be more like Chanelle. Instead, her nails were a mess. The last time she had seen a manicure was the day in the salon. Even her hair had begun to grow back in a curly mess.

She half-listened as Chanelle began throwing out all kinds of ideas. She flat out refused the catered three-course lunch but agreed to finger foods. She shook her head at the idea of getting married in a church but agreed to a small ceremony at the bed and breakfast. Jesse didn't budge on her decision not to wear a traditional wedding gown. However, she did like the idea of wearing an ivory suit.

They were debating the guest list when Jesse looked up to find Will strolling into the kitchen. She hadn't seen him since early this morning. When she came down, she discovered he'd already eaten. He had mumbled something about going to the hardware store, then turned and left without another word. Chanelle had arrived while he was gone and they had spent the morning shopping for new curtains for the bed and breakfast. When they returned, Will was still gone. Watching the way he moved made Jesse suddenly hunger for something other than food.

"Will, I hear congratulations are in order," Channel cooed as she sized up the handsome brother in one quick look.

He granted her a radiant smile. "Thank you. Forgive me but I have forgotten your name."

"Chanelle. And I advise you not to forget it since you'll be seeing a lot of me." She laughed, the soft sound floating in the air.

"Well, Chanelle, I was just coming to get Jesse so we could go ring shopping."

"A ring?" Jesse asked, her voice cracking.

"Sure, I can't propose and not buy you a ring. Since I don't know what you like I decided we can shop for it together."

Chanelle clapped her hands with glee. "That's a wonderful idea."

Jesse shook her head. "I don't need a ring."

"Yes you do," Chanelle piped in.

Will smiled at her friend. "Thank you. Can you suggest a few places?"

"The best jeweler at the beach is Sorrell's. I've bought several pieces there myself."

He nodded, looking pleased with himself. "Alright then Sorrell's it is."

Jesse rolled her eyes at Chanelle's mild, too-innocent smile. She was so mad it was a wonder smoke wasn't coming out of her ears, but she said nothing.

"I was just leaving." Chanelle rose from her chair and reached for her purse.

Jesse jumped up from her seat in a panic. "Don't you want to come with us?"

Chanelle waved her hand airily. "Girl, this is your time. I'll drop by later this week to see it and then we can get this wedding planned."

Will reached for her hand. Jesse tried to pull her hand away but he held on tight.

Chanelle gave Will a mischievous grin, then sashayed out of the room.

As soon as she was gone, Jesse pulled her hand away. She had been gone all morning with Chanelle dragging her into one store after the other. After spending half the day shopping, she was tired. She had no intention of going anywhere else today, especially not shopping for an engagement ring.

Will noted her hesitation and said, "What's your problem?"

"My problem is I don't want to go shopping for a stupid ring," she shot back, with her nostrils flaring. "What's the point in wasting money on something so meaningless? That money could be better spent on the bed and breakfast."

Will took a deep breath before exhaling audibly. "When I asked you to marry me, I had every intention of doing this thing right. That's the kind of guy I am." His hand encircled her wrist and brought it to his lips, kissing the sensitive area of her skin, enticing her. "So, you're either going to walk out to my Escalade or I am going to have to pick you up and carry you."

Not about to endure his arousing touch a second longer, Jesse pulled her hand away and left the room to retrieve her purse.

"I just can't see the sense of this," she murmured a few minutes later as they headed down the steps toward the driveway.

"It's the way my parents raised me. If we're going to go through with this marriage, you're just gonna have to learn to accept me for who I am." He opened the passenger side door for her.

Feeling as though she was losing control of her life, Jesse hesitated.

Will released an exasperated sigh. "Look, Jesse. What choice do you have? You want to hold on to your property and I want to help you. It's as simple as that. Now get in."

Jesse glared at him with fire in her eyes. She started to get in, then stopped and turned. "Listen and listen good. You better understand something. Don't take this personally but I have plans to live my life the way I want to live it and those plans do not include a husband. So if we are going to do this, don't expect me to change and be something I'm not because it ain't gonna happen."

He stared down at her. "Are you finished?"

Twirling away from him, she climbed in, slamming the door behind her.

As Will went around the SUV and got in behind the wheel, Jesse made work of buckling her seatbelt. Heat had built up inside the vehicle and the air was stifling, already causing her blouse to stick to her skin. She fanned herself with her hand as he fastened himself in. He started the engine, then switched on the air conditioning. Shifting the vehicle into gear, he pulled away from the house.

That man made her so mad, yet as he sat beside her, the natural scent of his skin lingered under her nose and she felt her anger dissipating. Dang, why couldn't she stay mad at him? She tried hard to think about something other than his scent, tried to keep her attention on the road and not let her eyes stray to the virile man sitting beside her. Only he was there and her body knew it. Her mouth could still taste the kiss he had stolen, feel the parting of her lips, the response she hadn't masked fast enough. His scent had even stayed with her while she tried to sleep last night.

As he focused on the road, Jesse glanced at Will out the corners of her eyes. His worn jeans gloved his legs and the T-shirt left his muscular biceps free to be admired. There was no denying it. Will was a handsome man. Having him sitting so close heightened all her senses, putting her nerves on extreme alert.

Not only had she dreamed about him, but this morning the first thing to come to her mind was Will. She had dreaded facing him again, expecting it to be awkward. At the same time, if she were honest with herself, she'd admit she was also a little bit excited. So it was with a mixture of relief and disappointment that she had come down to the kitchen to discover he had already eaten and was on his way out. After the door had shut, she had stolen to the living room window and watched him get into his SUV and pull out the driveway, her mind and body in turmoil.

She should have never allowed yesterday to happen; the kiss, the dinner, the movie, the orgasm. Heat slid to her core at the memory of her wall contracting tightly around his finger. Just thinking about it last night had necessitated her getting out of bed and turning on the ceiling fan.

Every time she thought about how his lips felt and the expertise in his kisses, she allowed herself for just a brief moment to wonder what it could possibly be like being married to him.

Shaking her head at such nonsense, she brought her thoughts back to the present. Everything was spiraling out of control. She could handle the wedding, but she didn't want a ring to symbolize their union.

This was probably the craziest thing she had ever done. Okay, maybe sleeping with a total stranger was crazier but marriage was serious business. Still, marrying Will would guarantee she would not lose the bed and breakfast. Moreover, once her father's estate was probated and a year had passed, she and Will could go their separate ways.

Goodness, she thought as she closed her eyes, they weren't even married yet and already she was planning their divorce. This whole situation was just so unbelievable. First she had given her virginity to a complete stranger and now she was planning to marry him.

Frustrated, she sighed heavily as she glanced out the window at the storefront windows announcing the Memorial Day festivities. This weekend would mark the beginning of the tourist season and there was still so much work to do. It seemed a shame to waste the day riding to get a ring that she didn't want and had no intention of wearing.

"This is really a waste of time," she finally heard herself say.

Will grimaced, holding himself in check. "I said we're going to get a ring and that's what we're gonna do."

"Because you say so?" she challenged.

He gave her a direct look. "No," he said very carefully, "because we agreed that we're gonna get married."

"But there's no need for you to spend money on a ring," she insisted. "This is a business arrangement."

Will swallowed hard. Jesse was testing his patience, which was wearing very thin at the moment. "Think of the ring as a business investment," he told her, his tone flat and final.

"Look," she argued, sliding around on her seat to face him, "don't you see that a ring is going to just make it seem more official?" Her reasoning was falling on deaf ears. She was quickly learning that William Jones had a mind of his own. Well, he was going to have to learn that she wasn't going to jump at his command. She, too, had a mind of her own.

"That's the reason for getting it. I'm an old-fashioned kind of guy. When I make a commitment I follow through. You are going to be my wife and my wife is going to wear an engagement ring symbolizing our commitment to one another." Silence fell between them and that was just fine with Will. His decision to buy her a ring was not up for debate, though he could understand her hesitation about the ring since she'd just told him in no uncertain terms that she did not expect him to act like a real husband.

Well, he hadn't planned on getting married either but that was before he'd made love to Jesse, before he'd taken her virginity. He stole a glance at her. A part of him wished things were different. She was leaning against the door of the truck, her legs crossed, her lips in a full pout. His eyes dropped to her breasts and he wanted like hell to touch her there. His body responded quickly to his thoughts and he returned his attention back to the road. He was going to have to get his libido under control. He couldn't go around lusting after Jesse. The problem was, it was not going to be easy. Just being with her reminded him of what it had been like to hold her in his arms and kiss her beautiful, tempting lips. He liked having her in his arms, that soft curved body against his.

"Why don't you have a girlfriend or something?"

He chuckled. "Why don't you have a man?"

"Because I don't need one."

"Neither do I." His abrupt answer caused her to raise her eyebrows.

Jesse snorted rudely. "You can't expect me believe there isn't anyone special in your life."

"Believe it."

She was silent for a while as she thought about pushing him further. There was no way someone who looked that good could be single.

"Why hadn't you ever been with a man before?"

Startled by the sudden sound of his voice, she jumped, then looked at him. He glanced briefly at her, then just as quickly looked away.

"What?"

He stopped at a red light. "I'm curious as to why you were still a virgin. You are too beautiful a woman for me to think for a minute you've never had a special man in your life."

She was surprised by his interest and wondered if it was genuine or whether he was just being nosey.

She wrung her hands as she spoke. "I, uh, never have had any luck with men. My father was so determined to marry me off that I fought for my independence and refused to find myself barefoot and pregnant like he wanted."

He gave her a sympathetic smile. "You father was definitely old fashioned."

Jesse crossed her arms over her chest. "Yes," she replied, grimly. "Despite what he thought, I do have a brain."

"I can see that. However, I can understand him wanting someone to take care of his daughter. He knew how hard it is to run a business and I guess he didn't want to see you go through that alone."

Jesse glared at him. "So are you saying you agree with the stipulations of his will?"

Will made a left turn at the corner. "I'm saying that I can understand a father feeling strongly about his daughter's happiness."

"I don't need a man to run Katherine's. I have plans for that place that do not require a man." She described more of her plans for restoring the house to its original state. Her face was animated and full of excitement as she shared her thoughts, her dreams. Will was impressed. He admired her determination. She'd thought it all out, and had the drive to make it happen. The only hole in her plans was money. What she didn't know was that he planned to fund the entire project. Thanks to his inheritance from his grandfather and some smart investments, he had enough money to make all her dreams come true.

Returning his thoughts to the matter at hand, he pulled the truck to a stop. "We're here," he said.

"Will—"

"Don't even start," he warned her, getting out of the truck. He walked around to open her door but she was already climbing out. Jesse slammed the door and came toward him.

"Listen, I'm sorry," Jesse said. "I know you mean well, but I just can't go through with this!" she insisted.

Will took her hand and held it tightly. "You can and you will. Come on."

He slid his arm behind her waist and propelled her forward. The touch of his hand against her zapped her resistance. Grimacing, she told herself she had to work on her self-control. She just couldn't turn to jelly every time he touched her.

Fat chance of that.

Reluctantly, she allowed him to lead her into the store.

CHAPTER ELEVEN

As soon as they entered the plush jewelry store, a well-dressed woman approached. "May I help you?" she asked, a polite, welcoming smile on her lips.

Will nodded. "Yes, Ginger," he said after glancing down at her nametag. "We're looking for an engagement ring." Somehow Jesse managed to disengage herself from him. He grabbed her by the waist and pulled her against him, this time holding her a little closer to keep her next to him. "This is my fiancée," he said.

The woman's smile turned brighter as she shifted her gaze from Will to Jesse. "Oh, how exciting! Do you have any idea of the kind of ring you're interested in?" When Jesse shook her head, she simply nodded. "We have some beautiful diamonds and of course other precious stones if you're looking for something unique." She urged them to follow her, then stepped behind a counter and faced them. Using a key to open it, she withdrew part of the display and placed it on the counter. An array of sparkling diamonds glistened against dark red velvet.

Will looked at Jesse. "Which one do you like?"

Overwhelmed by the wide selection, Jesse shook her head. "I can't pick out one of these," she whispered, not even daring to look at the sales associate.

"Yes, you can," Will replied against her ear. Because he wasn't sure of her taste in diamonds, he didn't know what appealed to her. It would be best if she picked out her own. "Go ahead and choose," he encouraged.

"No." Jesse drew in a deep breath, then with forced courage she looked at him again. "This isn't right," she insisted in a whisper, hoping the woman assisting them hadn't heard her. Blood rushed through her veins and the pounding inside her chest increased, blocking out everything around her. An engagement ring signified love and commitment, a promise of forever. Unlike some women, she'd never dreamed of wearing the ring of a man who truly loved her, so naturally she didn't feel right taking a ring from Will.

He didn't love her and she wasn't in love with him. Not at all, she told herself. Her silent denial of her feelings for him contradicted the pounding of her heart. He took her hand and lifted it to the glass, and Jesse tried to pull it back.

"Will," she pleaded. But she could see in his eyes that his mind was made up.

"It's okay, honey," he told her, drawing her closer. "I'll help. I like this one." He pointed to a two-carat diamond set in platinum gold, graced with baguettes on either side.

Jesse lost her breath. "That's much too big," she replied quickly. And would cost a fortune, money she was sure he didn't have to spend. She stared at the choices, her heart hammering. She didn't want to go through with this but she wasn't about to embarrass them both in front of the sales associate. "I...uh...they all look so expensive," she said in a low voice.

With a frustrated sigh, Will tried again. "Okay, how about this one?" he suggested and picked up another ring, this one cut in the shape of a heart.

"Um, no, I don't think so." It was also much too big and expensive.

"Okay, let's try this from another angle," Will suggested, frowning as he picked up a diamond that reminded her of a football. "Try this on," he ordered. Jesse hesitated and he drew her hand closer. She smacked his hand away, then put it on herself, complaining under her breath.

"There. Are you satisfied? It's too big." She spread her fingers wide so he could see.

"Oh, if you like it, we can have it sized for you," the sales associate quickly assured her.

Jesse immediately took the ring off and put it back in its place.

"No, thank you." With hesitation she picked out a couple of rings with smaller stones that didn't look like they cost more money than the SUV he was driving. She tried two of them on. One was too small, the other too big.

Will picked up a round-shaped diamond with a prong setting in a shiny gold band.

"Although we sell many different shapes, that's the most popular," the sales associate assured him. "Do you prefer gold or platinum?" she asked Jesse.

Jess shrugged, hesitant to reveal her thoughts. "I've never really thought about it."

"Well, you should, dear. You'll be wearing this ring for a long time."

The woman's words hit a nerve, and Jesse grimaced. This engagement ring also signified love, honor and obedience, something she was trying to stay away from.

"Try it on," Will suggested. Before she could stop him, he had her hand in his and was sliding the ring on her finger, slipping it over her knuckle. "It fits," he commented thoughtfully, then looked at Jesse's face. Her expression was hesitant and uncertain, but her eyes widened, indicating that she liked the ring.

"It's beautiful, but—"

"Could you give us a minute?" Will said, speaking to the woman helping them. She nodded, putting the display of rings back inside the counter.

Will took both of Jesse's hands in his and turned her so she was facing him. Uneasiness flashed in her eyes as she looked up at him.

"What do you think of this one?" he asked, his tone dropping to a whisper.

"Oh, Will, it's beautiful." Jesse said, staring at the brilliant diamond with open appreciation.

"Then that's the one I want you to have."

Jesse shook her head. "I can't, even though I love it," she answered honestly. For a moment, they just stared at each other, neither of them speaking. A look of frustration burned in his eyes. "It's just too expensive."

Will took a deep breath and tried a different route. "A year from now if you don't want it I can sell it to an independent jeweler."

She stared at the ring. Jesse had felt a rush of pleasure when he'd slipped it on her finger, and her entire body still tingled. She wavered, trying to fully comprehend what was happening. The ring was beautiful and was everything she would have dreamed of if she had been dreaming. It was ridiculous, she knew, because she didn't want to get married, but at that moment their engagement felt real, and despite her protests about getting a ring, it felt so right on her, as if it belonged there, and that scared her.

Looking back at Will, she realized he was watching her. His touch was doing crazy things to her insides, making her think about things that weren't possible.

She gazed up to find him watching her. Then his mouth swooped down and he kissed her on the lips. When he pulled way, she looked up at him.

"Are you sure?" she asked. Her voice was soft, childlike.

He nodded, then moved over to the salesclerk who was patiently waiting.

"We'll take this one. The tone of his voice said the decision was final. "And the wedding bands to match."

The salesclerk beamed. "An excellent choice."

Jesse was certain she was already calculating the hefty commission off the sale. With a sigh, she removed the ring and gave it to the salesclerk, who removed the tags and reached for the matching his and her bands.

"If you want to follow me to the end of the counter, I can write this up for you."

A few minutes later they were leaving the store.

Though Will walked close beside her as they returned to the SUV, he didn't touch her. Touching her made him want her. Shopping for an engagement ring had felt so real that he had come close to pulling her into his arms and kissing her. The trouble was he hadn't expected to feel anything when he put the ring on her finger. He'd gone through the same ritual with his first wife. But something was different about Jesse wearing his ring. She represented everything that he'd once wanted from life.

Glancing out the corner of his eye, he found Jesse quiet, as if she were having an internal battle. No matter how much she tried to deny it, Jesse had felt it too. The twinkle in her eyes when he had placed the perfect ring on her finger was proof enough. However, he would have to remind himself that this was just an arrangement. Jesse wasn't his to have. She'd made the stipulations of the will and debt of their relationship for the next year clear enough. She hadn't wanted his ring. She didn't want him. The only thing he had to look forward to was having her in his bed for three hundred and sixty-five days. That alone made up for everything else. The thought of her lying beneath him wearing nothing but his ring had him turned on.

However, the ring didn't change anything. He had to remember that as well as remember that he couldn't go around thinking with his body. But as they walked across the parking lot, all he could think about was wanting to do a lot more than kiss her.

"Thank you. This wasn't at all what I had expected," Jesse suddenly said.

"Is that good or bad?"

She didn't answer right away. "It wasn't bad."

He reached out and with his hand on her shoulder, stopped her from getting into the car.

Jesse turned and looked at him with questioning eyes.

Will reached into the bag and removed the box. She watched as he removed the engagement ring.

"May I?"

She hesitated, then raised her hand and allowed him to slip the ring onto her finger.

Their engagement was now official.

Before she realized what was happening, he had lowered his head and she was meeting him halfway. Jesse knew she was operating at gut level instead of the common sense she'd relied on her entire life. But she needed to feel Will's mouth on hers. She needed to physically feel him against her.

He angled his head, tilting her head back, supporting her with his palm at her neck. A wave of desire coursed through her body and she found herself melting against his chest.

She shivered as his tongue brushed hers and he tasted her so deeply that she had a hard time figuring out where she ended and he began. She moaned deep in her throat.

It was crazy because even when her mind screamed that it was wrong, her body argued that it was okay. She didn't know what it was, but somehow Will had a way of making her feel soft and warm like a candle that had been burning too long.

She slid her hands over his shoulders and down his arms, exploring the muscles beneath his shirt and she marveled at his strength. Her breasts flattened against his chest and ached for his touch.

She found herself needing something solid to anchor her. Someone to hold on to. Someone to cling to. Not just someone, she realized as his hands traveled down her back, but only one man, William Jones.

He trembled under her touch and shifted so that he was leaning on the hood of the car, cradled between her legs. She felt the thick, hard length of his erection. Her blood boiled and heat poured through her. Overwhelmed, she finally placed a hand at the middle of his chest and eased him back.

He stared down at her, their bodies still intimately pressed together. A sensual flare fired in his eyes.

Finally she shook her head. "What was that for?" she asked.

He didn't answer, just rubbed the sweep of her eyebrows with his thumb. Tingles spread down her neck and arms and deep down she went hot and wet and needy. Staring up at those beautiful brown eyes she had dreamed about last night, she knew that she would still be dreaming about his eyes even after she turned eighty years old.

"Just because," he answered. She felt the heat pouring from him and the brush of his breath across her cheeks.

She bit her lip. "I really don't know if this is going to work. I mean, what if one of us falls in love with someone else?"

His expression was of faint amusement now. Love was the one thing he wasn't worried about. As long as Jesse was in his life, sharing his bed, he wouldn't need anyone else. "I don't expect that to happen."

Her eyes widened. "Why not?"

"Because I'm not looking for anyone. I'm happy with life as it is."

She folded her arms across her chest. "You don't really believe that, do you?"

She caught and held his attention, waiting for his answer. He didn't like the direction the conversation had taken. "Yes, I do. With you in my life, I don't need anyone else."

Her lips formed an "O".

A slight smile tugged at his mouth. "Don't worry. Between my gigs and the bed and breakfast, I don't think we'll have a problem."

Many things about their future might be uncertain but his decision to help her felt right. "I am in this to the end. I'm making a commitment to you and I plan to stick by it until the year is over." He then took possession of her mouth again.

After a great deal of effort on her part, she managed to ease back again. "We shouldn't be doing this."

"Why?" he crooned near her earlobe.

"Because we made a deal."

There was a prolonged silence before Will nodded and released her.

Jesse slid away from the hood. For a second she missed the heat of his body. But as she stood apart she began to feel normal again. Standing on her own two feet was what she'd learned to do best. "We need to get back to the house." She then turned and climbed into the Escalade.

He closed her door, then got into the driver's side and started the engine. The silence between them was almost palpable. After they were down the road a bit, he chanced a glance at her. Her shoulders were stiff, her posture reserved. Taking a deep breath he broke the silence between them and asked if she'd like to stop and get some lunch on the way back.

Jesse shrugged her shoulder. "Sure, if you want," she replied.

He nodded as he turned the SUV onto the main strip. Both sides of the streets were flooded with restaurants, everything from hamburgers to lobster. They decided on something quick so that they could get back to the bed and breakfast and back to work. Will pulled into the first restaurant. Jesse climbed out and walked beside him to the door. As he held the door open, she stepped inside, careful not to touch him.

Bart's was a popular burger joint on the boardwalk with made-to-order burgers. She gave him her order, then moved to find them a booth.

Five minutes later, Will lowered a tray filled with french fries, double cheeseburgers, and thick vanilla milk shakes and slid into the booth.

He stared across into Jesse's sexy eyes. He swallowed hard and forced a smile that wouldn't betray his thoughts. "Everything smells great."

"Mmmm, I can't wait." She reached for a burger and fries, then reached for a bottle between the ketchup and the barbecue sauce.

He watched her sprinkle it over her fries and the smell reached his nose. "What is that? Vinegar?"

She nodded. "Yep. It tastes delicious."

She picked up a fry with her long, slender fingers and dabbed it in a puddle of vinegar. When she looked up at him with a smile before joyfully devouring the fry, he felt an intense throbbing at his loins. He wanted to kiss her again but he knew better. But that didn't stop him from wanting to.

"Mmmm. It's good," she said as she chewed. "I don't know if I would call it a beach thing but everyone loves the vinegar fries."

He studied her for a long moment, wishing he were the droplet of vinegar resting on her bottom lip. He shifted uncomfortably on the bench, then cleared his throat. "Let me try."

He reached across and devoured three saturated fries at once. He instantly scowled at the sour taste.

The carefree warmth of her laughter washed over him. He realized it was the first he'd heard from her.

Will took a sip of his large shake, trying to wash away the taste. "I think I'll stick to ketchup," he said, grinning.

She grimaced. "Yuck. I haven't liked ketchup since I was six."

"Why?"

"I have an older cousin who was always teasing me. One night my father left me in his care while he went to a bingo game in town. I got out of the shower to find my cousin lying on the floor in the hallway covered in blood. I was so scared I ran out the house and down the road in a towel. Later I found out it was only ketchup."

Will laughed and she joined in the fun.

"Where's your cousin now?"

She took another bite, then shrugged. "Military, some special overseas assignment. I haven't heard from him in years."

"Do you have any family around here?"

Jesse shook her head. "No one on the East Coast. I have a few elsewhere but most of them I have never really known. With my father's attitude, most of his family pretty much wrote him off, which meant me as well."

Seeing her sad expression, Will simply nodded.

Jesse took a deep breath and reached for her shake. "What about you?"

"Oh my, my family is large. I have three brothers and a sister. They all still live in the tri-state area. After forty years my parents are still happily married and living in Baltimore."

"Are you close?"

He frowned and reached for his own shake. "Maybe a little too close."

"There is no such thing when you don't have family. I'd give anything to have just one person in my life."

He heard the pain in her voice and reached over and clasped her hand. "Hey, you can share my family with me. I guarantee they are going to love you."

pushed to the surface. She blinked them away. Mayonnaise dripped from her hamburger and down the front of her shirt.

"Hey," Will said, pointing to the stain. "You got a…"

Jesse glanced down at it, then shrugged and bit into her burger again. "It doesn't matter. As soon as we get back to the house I plan on getting dirty anyway."

He felt something stir inside at her words. He could think of a way they could go back to the house and get dirty, dripping in perspiration. He quickly waved it off. "You're something else. Most women would have a fit to find they spilled food on their clothes. You, you just take it in stride."

"I've heard that all my life. What can I say? I'm not like regular women."

"No, you're not, and that's why I like you."

Jesse glanced at Will's food, then looked back up at him. "Eat your food."

"Yes, ma'am." He picked up his burger and attacked it with enthusiasm.

As he watched, she slipped the straw between her lips and sucked down her shake. He felt his jeans grow snug and he shifted uncomfortably again in his seat.

It was time to change the subject.

"I've been thinking." He took another bite of his burger, chewed and then swallowed. "Tomorrow I'm going to set up a charge account at the home improvement store so that we can pick up all of the supplies we need."

She tipped her chin down slightly and looked up at him with those eyes that could trap a man's soul. "Alright."

Her voice sounded so soft, so accepting. Was she finally coming around to the idea of spending the next year together? The thought of sharing a bed suddenly raised the temperature in the room. While she finished her shake, she glanced at him from beneath thick lashes. He was oblivious to everything happening around him, aware only of the glow in Jesse's eyes and the hammering of his heart.

glow in Jesse's eyes and the hammering of his heart.

While they finished eating they chitchatted about nothing in particular. Mostly college and their chosen professions. When they arrived home, two pickup trucks were parked in her driveway.

Will smiled. "Oh, good. They're here."

Jesse gave him a puzzled look. "Who's here?"

Without looking at her, he put the vehicle in park and turned off the ignition. "The crew I hired to finish the job."

"When did this take place?" she asked. Her question was drowned by the sound of his door slamming shut.

How dare he! She groaned as she climbed out of the truck. She had accepted his proposal only yesterday and already he was trying to take over.

Rounding the truck, she followed Will to the group that emerged from the two vehicles. Jesse counted seven men as she moved to hear the verbal exchange.

"Sweetheart, let me introduce you to Donald. Donald this is my fiancée, Jesse."

The man that greeted her had to have been around her father's age with the friendliest smile she'd ever encountered.

Returning his smile was easy. "Nice to meet you."

He brought her hand to his lips and planted a kiss on it. "The pleasure is all mine. I look forward to working with you. You have a fine house here. They don't make 'em like that anymore. While I was waiting for your return, I began a list of things that need to be done to the outside." He reached into his breasts pocket and removed a tiny notepad. "The roof should be the first thing we take care of. It doesn't look like it can handle another rain."

Jesse nodded. One of the back bedrooms already leaked.

He pointed to the porch. "Some of the clapboard needs to be replaced and after I slap on a couple coats of paint the exterior will look good as new."

Observing the excitement on his face, she took an instant liking to him. "That sounds wonderful! Would you like to see the inside?"

He nodded and she led the way. Jesse quickly forgot her anger as she led him through one room after the other while he took notes along the way. Donald commented on every important aspect of each of the rooms. Jesse found she was impressed with his knowledge and expertise. Either he knew what he was doing or he fooled her completely.

When they came back out, he turned to her and gave her a reassuring smile. "I don't think we'll have a problem at all getting this house ready before the summer holidays. I can have an estimate ready tomorrow morning."

His words were magic to her ears. "That's wonderful. How long before you could start?"

"We can be here bright and early Monday morning." He must have noticed her worried expression because he placed a comforting hand to her forearm. "Don't worry. My crew and I will have this house in mint condition before the Memorial Day weekend rolls around."

She sighed with relief and thanked him.

Tears glistened in her eyes as she watched them drive away. Her dream was about to become a reality and all because of Will. So why was she suddenly angry?

She glanced over at him rocking on the back of his heels, noticing the cocky smirk on his face.

Instinctively she struck out at him. She knew the words stemmed from her insecurities, but she couldn't stop them.

"I'd appreciate it if you wouldn't make any more decisions without my approval first." She knew she was being ungrateful, especially after he had bought her the expensive ring and had found what looked to be the best contractor in the entire state. However, if she allowed Will to get away with controlling things now, he would think it was okay to continue to do so in the future.

Will's face lacked expression. "Whatever you say," he murmured, then turned and walked away from her, his back rigid.

She knew her statement was out of line, that it had come from somewhere deep inside her, to conceal the real depth of her emotions.

Will and apologize, but in the end, she talked herself out of it. With a weary sigh, she headed into the house.

Will went up to his room and shut the door. He took a deep calming breath. Things today had been getting seriously out of hand until good ole Jesse reminded him of the facts.

The trip to buy the ring had turned into something he hadn't planned. Even now he could still taste her on his lips, the sensation heating his blood in a most uncommon way, teasing at his control. The anticipation of having her in his bed again was almost unbearable.

He scowled. That was the way it had happened with Ebony and he refused to feel this way about another woman, including his wife.

It was time to give Jamar a call.

CHAPTER TWELVE

Jesse dipped the roller into the pan of paint, then moved over to the wall and began adding a second coat of terra cotta.

In three days with the help of two of her new workers, both bedroom walls had been completed. All they needed now was a couple of coats of paint and new carpeting. She was amazed at how much the crew had accomplished in such a short time. In fact, they had done more in two days than Pace had ever done in two weeks. She had dug in and helped.

Half the crew was now outside while the rest were downstairs replacing the plumbing fixtures in the first floor bathroom and kitchen.

The last couple of days she had risen at the crack of dawn and worked until she dropped. This morning when the crew arrived, she had already completed painting the front bedroom.

She needed to keep busy. It was the only way to keep her mind off Will. No matter how much she tried, she couldn't erase the feel of his mouth, hungry, and expertly tasting and stroking a need inside her.

Sunday over a cup of coffee, he had nonchalantly announced that he had a previous commitment that he couldn't miss and was leaving after he had a chance to speak with his foreman. She was in her room when he left, and he didn't even bother to say goodbye. She wouldn't have had any idea when to expect his return if she hadn't overheard him telling Donald he would be back in two days.

It infuriated her to discover that when she eavesdropped on a conversation Donald was having on his cell phone he was talking to Will. They were discussing her renovations and making decisions as if she didn't have any say-so about Katherine's and it infuriated her.

How dare he take over!

It was just as she had expected. She took a deep breath to calm her nerves. She was acting like an angry girlfriend. Why did she care? She really didn't have a reason to be mad. It was a business arrangement, nothing more, and as long as she kept their relationship in perspective she shouldn't have a problem.

Realizing she was putting more paint on the floor than the wall, Jesse put down the roller and left the room. The problem was she couldn't get him off her mind. He consumed her every thought. Her breath. Her dreams.

Why'd he have to show up here?

She moved to the bathroom and discovered her face was covered with paint freckles. Lathering her hands with a moisturizing soap, she scrubbed her face and hands, then rinsed with cool water and reached for a dry hand towel.

She glanced down at the diamond sparkling on her left hand and paused. Even though she was painting, she couldn't bring herself to remove the ring. She told herself she hadn't taken it off because she was afraid she might lose it but in all honesty it looked too fabulous on her finger to part with. She was engaged. *Don't get too attached to him or the ring because they are both temporary*, a voice inside said.

She had to keep reminding herself, Will proposed to help her get her inheritance, and not because he felt anything for her.

With a weary sigh, she moved out into the hall and went downstairs. As she strolled past the living room, she glanced over at a grandfather clock in the corner and gasped. It was already one o'clock. Where had the time gone, she wondered as she moved quickly to her bedroom. She had an appointment scheduled for two.

It took her forty-five minutes to shower and find something to wear. Dressed in white shorts and a pink cotton blouse, she climbed into her Buick and headed toward the public beach.

The beach was quiet during the spring. A few off-season guests took advantage of discount prices, and would make their way down to the outlets, enjoy the tax-free shopping, then walk along the shoreline.

Pulling off Route 1 she turned right into a small strip mall. Parking, she stared across at the storefront window of Claire's Bridal

Gowns.

Her stomach did somersaults as she stared at the three elegantly dressed mannequins in the window.

"What am I doing?" she whispered to herself as she spotted Chanelle pulling up in a parking spot two places over. If she could have backed out of the spot and sped away without Chanelle noticing, she would have definitely run home and hid under the covers. Unfortunately, Chanelle was heading her way.

"Girl, you either get out of that car or I'm going to drag you out."

Following a long shaky breath, Jesse shut off the car and climbed out.

"Why the long face? This is going to be a lot of fun."

Jesse looked up and rolled her eyes. "That's easy for you to say. You're not being forced to get married."

"I would give anything to be getting married again."

The look on Chanelle's face told Jesse she was dead serious. And it confirmed her suspicion that Chanelle had never accepted the break-up with her husband.

They stepped into the shop and were immediately greeted by a salesclerk.

"Welcome. Which of you is the lucky bride?"

Chanelle quickly pointed to her friend. "She is."

"Come along. We have a large selection of gowns and accessories. Do you have any idea what you are looking for?"

Jesse glanced around nervously at all the racks and shook her head.

"Why don't I start with a couple of measurements and then I'll pick out a couple of selections that I think will flatter your figure."

Chanelle draped her arm around her best friend's shoulders. "That sounds like a wonderful idea."

For the next hour Jesse felt like Cinderella as she tried on dress after dress, including veil and accessories. When she tried on the last gown, she walked to the mirror and gasped. The woman in the mirror was a stranger to her. She was sexy, sophisticated, not at all as Jesse knew herself to be.

The sleeveless gown was made of ivory duchesse satin with pleated silk bands at the waist. The fitted bodice was covered in Alecon lace with a low scooped backline and an A-line skirt with a long row of gold, hand-embroidered lilies extending to the hem of the chapel train. Reaching forward, she touched the glass. It wasn't real, she reminded herself. It was just pretend. As phony as her engagement.

As crazy as it sounded, she found herself wishing the wedding was real, one that would last until eternity.

The salesclerk took the veil and placed it on her head. The floor length veil was attached to a tier trimmed in mother-of-pearl and complemented the ensemble.

Sitting on a couch not too far away, Chanelle cooed, "You look gorgeous."

The salesclerk agreed.

"What do you think, Jesse?" Chanelle asked.

Tears burned the backs of Jesse's eyes. "I think it's…well…" Her voice drifted off. How could she put her feelings into words? She looked like a princess. If only Will were really her prince. If only he were marrying her for real.

She turned and blindly ran back into the dressing room. Sitting on the bench with her arms wrapped around her waist, she cried.

The door swung open and she felt helpless and embarrassed at the same.

"What's wrong?" Chanelle asked her friend.

She tried to swallow so that she could speak but the words didn't come.

Chanelle reached into her purse and removed a fresh Kleenex and dabbed at her tear-stained cheeks. "Oh, sweetie, everything is going to be okay."

Jesse didn't know what was wrong with her. She had never fantasized about a wedding or a husband. She had never considered falling in love and sharing the rest of her life with one person. Yet suddenly her mind was swimming with such images. *What's wrong with me?*

"I'm sorry," she murmured.

Chanelle gave her a sympathetic smile as she passed her several more tissues. "For what?"

"For ruining your fun."

"Fun? Jess, this is your day, not mine. I'm just glad that you have allowed me to share this moment with you."

"Why wouldn't I? You're my best friend."

"And I appreciate that. Our friendship means the world to me." She squeezed her hand.

Jesse dabbed her eyes and returned her warm smile. "See, I feel better already."

"Are you going to tell me what's bothering you?"

She shrugged. "I was having an emotional moment. I think the dress did it."

"I felt the same way the first time I tried on my dress. It's only natural."

There was a light knock on the door. "Is everything okay in there?"

Chanelle rose and met the salesclerk's concerned expression. "Everything is fine."

"Have you decided about the dress?"

Chanelle glanced over at Jesse and noticed her lips quiver. "We'll take it."

The clerk clasped her hands together. "Excellent choice. Let me grab my pins so that we can take some minor alterations."

A half hour later Jesse and Chanelle were sitting out on the deck of a popular Mexican restaurant sipping margaritas.

"What was going on with you back there?" Chanelle finally asked.

"What do you mean?"

"I mean, I've never seen you that emotional before. It was almost like you are falling for the guy."

Jesse sipped her drink.

"You are falling for him! Oh, my goodness. I can't believe it!"

Jesse glanced nervously around, making sure no one overheard them. "Would you keep your voice down. Someone might hear you."

"Someone like who?"

She simply shrugged, realizing how stupid the moment of panic was.

"I've just been kind of confused lately. I think it has a lot to do with us living together and this upcoming wedding."

"Sounds like you regret telling homeboy he can't sleep with you until after the wedding."

Jesse looked down at her hand graced by the beautiful ring Will had bought her. Maybe Chanelle was right. Maybe she was having regrets.

Two days.

That was how long it had been since Will had last seen Jesse.

He was trying to concentrate on the special piece the bride and groom had requested for their wedding song and couldn't.

It had been barely forty-eight hours, yet he couldn't get Jesse off his mind.

Rising from the piano bench, he strolled across an immaculate lawn, amazed at the preparation that had gone into transforming the backyard of the grand estate into an exhibition that would have made Cinderella proud.

It was a day a bride would never forget.

Would Jesse want something similar? He doubted it. He couldn't help the grin that curved his lips. One thing he could honestly say about his fiancée was that she wasn't like most women.

His fiancée.

What he liked most about her was that she was so completely different from all other women. She was stubborn, opinionated, and didn't mind getting cobwebs in her hair or paint under her nails. She didn't use gloves to protect her hands and could use a jigsaw almost as good as he could.

He hadn't planned on performing at Mayor Philip Stemmons'

daughter's wedding but the way things had been heating up at home, he had been left with no other choice.

Home.

Was that how he thought of Katherine's? He shook that thought away. He needed to get all such crazy notions out of his head. However, he had to admit that in the short time he had been there he had grown fond of the place and was just as excited as Jesse to see it transformed.

Jesse consumed his every thought. He'd joined the band for this joyous occasion for no other reason than to get her off his mind. But it hadn't worked. He hadn't called her for the same reason. Nothing helped.

Never before had a woman affected him this way. His past relationships had been physical with no other motivation than to fulfill a sexual need. But the feelings Jesse evoked went beyond the sexual and threatened his equilibrium.

He tried to tell himself she was just like all the others, no better, no worse. She had used him. Of all the women who had come and gone in his life since Ebony, why had a virgin from southern Delaware made such a distinct impression? There wasn't anything special about her.

He was lying to himself and his heart knew it. Yet he wasn't ready to do anything about it.

What was that?

Jesse's eyelids flew open though she lay perfectly still. She waited to see if she heard it again. After several seconds, she took a deep breath and closed her eyes again. She was just starting to doze off again when she heard another sound.

With a gasp, she instantly sat up on the bed and contemplated possibilities. The wind? An intruder?

She took a deep breath. She wasn't living in the city anymore. She was in southern Delaware out in a wooded location. Hadn't she heard on the news just last night that two prisoners had escaped from a prison less than two hours away?

She suddenly wished that Will were there. She could always yell for him if she needed help. At the sound of movement in the other room, she decided she had to investigate. For all she knew, it was a mouse. She hated the nasty-looking suckers but at least if she knew she had mice she could call an exterminator before she opened for business. Besides, since when did she run to a man for safety? Never! She'd been on her own for too long and hadn't had anyone to depend on but herself. And she wasn't about to change now.

Despite her thundering heart, she tossed aside her covers and rose from the bed. Making sure she barely made a sound, she turned the knob and slowly opened the door and stepped out into the hall. Her breathing was shallow as she tiptoed into the adjoining bathroom and reached for the only thing she could find, a plunger.

She moved across the tiled floor with her heart pounding heavily in her chest. The lights were off, yet she could hear movement in the kitchen. Burning with anger, she wrapped her fingers tightly around the stick and held it high above her head as she stepped around the corner. Focusing as well as she could in the dark, she saw a shadow moving across the dining room.

Think girl, think! You can either scream and hope someone hears you or handle it yourself. Her stubborn pride urged her to step quickly behind the shadow and swing.

"What the hell!"

Before she realized what was happening, the plunger was snatched out of her hand. Then she saw who'd been prowling around her kitchen. And what she saw didn't help her heart slow down one bit.

Will!

Her eyes were round and full of fear. "I thought you weren't going to be back until tomorrow?"

"I wasn't, but I got done early. However, if I had known I was going to be clocked upside my head, I wouldn't have bothered."

Jesse pulled her head back until it touched the kitchen cabinet and struggled to clear her scattered thoughts. Unfortunately, they wouldn't get organized, with him standing so close, so she spoke up anyway. "What were you thinking, Will?" She pushed at his bare chest. "You scared the hell out of me. I thought you were a mouse."

They were standing alone in a dark room, lit only by a small circle of light cast by the fixtures over the sink. She tried to ignore the heat of his breath, the press of his solid body against hers as his muscled, bare chest flexed beneath her hands. For a moment she was captivated by the sight of her own fingers intertwined with the dark curls sprinkled across his powerful chest. She swallowed thickly and forced her gaze back up to his.

One of his brows arched up and a loc fell down over his eyes. "You brought a toilet plunger for a mouse?"

Flustered, she recovered quickly and gave a nervous shrug. "Out here all by myself, a girl can't be too careful these day."

He was quiet and she watched the direction of his eyes as they traveled over her body. The flash of pure hunger in his expression made her suddenly self-conscious. Her nipples hardened as she suddenly remember she was standing in the kitchen in one of those skimpy gowns she had treated herself to from Victoria's Secret.

Without even looking down she already knew the baby blue nightgown clung to her curves, outlining her breasts and showcasing a great deal of thigh.

Ignoring his heated gaze, she took in his appearance. He wore a pair of faded jeans that hung low on his lean hips. Her eyes moved lower to the flat stretch of abdomen above the edge of his jeans and a thin line of dark hair that disappeared into his waistband.

His feet and chest were bare. His stomach displayed hard-earned muscles. As comfortable as he appeared, he had apparently arrived quite some time ago.

She was the first to break the spell. "Well, now that I know my life isn't in any immediate danger, I'm going back to bed."

"Whoa," he said as he halted her hasty departure with an arm curling around her waist. "Don't leave." His voice was calm but his breathing irregular.

"Why not?" She knew she should force her mind away from what her body wanted. She knew she should be angry that he was holding her against the heat of his chest. But anger and arousal were so mixed up inside her, she didn't know how to respond.

Will skimmed her cheek, brushing her skin with the back of his hand, setting off a sweet butterfly sensation. He then leaned in closer, too close, and a lazy grin spread over his features. "Because I want to hold you for a few minutes," he said softly.

Shivers went straight up her spine. His lips were mere inches from hers and her traitorous body was on fire. She instinctively reached out and pushed against his chest. "You can't. You promised to wait until after we're married."

"Then we have a bit of a problem. I can't seem to control myself around you," he said, his voice coming out in a low, tense growl. His hands trembled as he cupped her face and stared at her. At her parted lips, her glowing cheeks, her sparkling brown eyes. "Oh, hell, Jesse you're—"

What he didn't say, couldn't say was that he wanted to kiss her until he quenched her fire, but if he did, what would quench his? For the past two days he hadn't been able to get the image of her out of his mind. Now she looked sexier than ever. The tousled hair, those brown eyes, the slim, silky nightgown displaying every curve and clinging to her nipples. He had returned to the house barely an hour ago and already he wanted her in his bed, his lips tasting her skin.

Jesse went very still as he held her. Her eyes wide, locked with his, her right hand clenched on his shoulder, her left hanging by her side. He felt the heat of her, her breasts pressed against the crisp hair on his chest, her breath on his face as he stared back at her, their mouths so close they were only a hair away from touching.

"What are you doing to me?" she whispered.

"Holding you," he whispered back. If he moved, he might unleash the beast within. Even her breathing threatened to kindle his passion beyond his control.

"Why?" she squeaked in a high-pitched voice.

"Because I'm going to kiss you."

She licked her lips. They glistened. Her eyes held a dreamy expression. Her smile was one of anticipation. "What are you waiting for?" she openly challenged.

He drew a deep, painful breath and let it out all at once. His control shattered and he grabbed a fistful of her hair, tilted her head back and kissed her.

He prodded with the tip of his tongue, wanting to master her, to force her mouth open…and found it parted eagerly. A bolt of molten heat flashed through his body. He plunged deep with his tongue, meaning to plunder. Her eagerness matched his. He cradled her tighter against him, trying to remind himself to be gentle, but her fingers raked at his back, demanding more.

"This is crazy," she said.

"This is right," he said, pulling her more fully into his arms. She wedged her hands between them and pushed away slightly.

"What now?" Will growled.

Her eyes were wide, startled. "We said we'd try to keep this non-sexual."

"God, woman, how many times are you going to bring that up? I think it's obvious we're fighting a losing battle."

"I know," she confessed, lips quivering.

"Then why'd you bring it up?"

She took a deep breath but remained silent. She looked vulnerable and Will had the uncomfortable feeling that the blame was his.

Frustrated and aroused out of this world, he raked a hand across his locs, then growled, "Jess, go to bed now. Or I won't be responsible for my actions."

CHAPTER THIRTEEN

A week later

It was midnight and Will was wide awake. He got out of his bed and wandered down the hall to the kitchen. He tried to pretend it was his band that disturbed his thoughts. Jamar and some of the others wanted to tour the West Coast, opening for Jill Scott. But he knew the true reason was the redhead sleeping in the room down the hall.

Too much had happened lately. The renovations were halfway done and he had actually enjoyed every minute of it. Working with Donald was a true honor. He had taught him a great deal. Drywall and wood had always been his areas of specialty, plumbing was not. But after spending a couple days with Donald he was confident now that he could build a new bathroom if he needed to.

He opened the fridge and stared at the contents. Jesse had bought groceries on her way home. He reached past the milk and grabbed the six-pack of beer that had been pushed to the back of the fridge. He took the six-pack outside and stretched out on one of the lounge chairs.

Tipping his head back, he watched the stars. He remembered when he was in the sixth grade, his teacher had taken him on a field trip to Baltimore to the planetarium. He had found studying constellations quite fascinating.

Damn, that was a long time ago. Sometimes he felt years older than he was.

The moon was full and beaming brightly over the ocean. He looked out at the huge waves. Jesse was exactly the kind of woman who could tear him apart—and Will didn't need a second go-around in that painful arena. He pushed back his hair and tied it away from his face. As much as he tried to deny it, Jesse was nothing like Ebony. Beneath the surface, Jesse was passionate, caring and had a level of determination he had never seen in a woman. She was all woman, soft and fragrant and she knew how to defend herself. No, the two were nothing alike, except they both had tried to deceive him. Only now he didn't feel that what Jesse had done had been so bad. He understood why she had deceived him. If he were in her position, he would probably have done the same.

He heard the scrape of footsteps and turned to see Jesse's silhouette in the kitchen. The blue sleep shirt wasn't meant to be sexy even though it did leave her long legs bare, but he found it so. To distract himself he took a long draw on his beer. Maybe if he stayed quiet, she wouldn't notice him and he could return to his room.

But it didn't work. He ached for her and being with her here in this house made that ache deepen. He knew he wasn't going to sleep well or have anything resembling comfort until they'd spent a few hours in bed together.

"Can I join you?" she asked. Her hair was disheveled from sleep. At first he'd suspected she dyed her hair. But dying her hair wasn't something Jesse would do. Besides, the color matched the patch down below her belly button. The thought of running his fingers through it caused heat to flow through his veins.

"Sure. You want a beer?" he asked, gesturing to the six-pack beside him.

She shook her head and hesitated near his chair. "No thanks. I only like beer after it has spent about thirty minutes in the freezer and is ice cold."

He chuckled. "That's not how you drink beer."

"That's how I drink it. With ice chips or not at all."

Nodding, he lifted his head to the wind and stared at the clouds on the horizon.

"Are you okay?" Jesse asked. She moved and lowered into the lounge chair beside him and raised her legs onto the chair.

Such small feminine feet. His looked big and rough next to hers. He wanted to explore all the ways they were different, to strip them both naked and take his time with the exploration.

"Why wouldn't I be okay?" he asked, to distract himself from the images of her naked body dancing in his head.

"Well, it's after midnight and you're sitting in the dark drinking. Something about that doesn't seem like you at all." She raised her knees to her chest. Her toenails were painted a deep luscious red that confirmed what he already knew. There was more to Jesse than she wanted the world to see. Right now she reminded him of a sweet, vulnerable kitten.

He glanced up and realized she'd been watching him stare at her feet. "I can't sleep."

She tucked her feet under her and tilted her head to the side. "Why not?"

"You don't want to know," he said, draining his bottle of beer. He leaned over to replace it in the carton and get a fresh one. He twisted the cap off and offered it to her.

She reached forward and took the bottle. Her shirt slid lower and he had a glimpse of the inner curves of her breast. His body hardened a little more, and he shifted his legs to find a more comfortable position.

She took a sip of beer, scowled, then handed the bottle back to him with a smile. "I wouldn't have asked if I didn't want to know."

"I'm hard with wanting you," he replied. His brown eyes searched her face and probed for the things she wanted to know.

"Oh" was all she managed to say. Her expression was much too innocent.

"I had a feeling you'd say that." He tore his eyes from her and stared off at the ocean again. "Go back to bed, Jesse, before I forget our agreement and make love to you."

She rose and leaned against the railing. Crossing her arms across her chest, she lifted her face to the cool mist, inhaling it.

Jesse knew coming out of her room had been a mistake. Only she couldn't help herself. She had spent the last hour staring at the ceiling in her room trying to think of reasons why their marriage would be a big mistake. She had also been trying to justify her reason for waiting until they married before they made love. She wanted him and she wanted him bad, but there was no way she was going to let him know that. As long as she fought off her attraction until their wedding, then she could justify their sexual union to herself by saying she was obligated. Even though it was something she wanted so bad her body was screaming at her, she had to find a way to wait until they were married before she gave in to her sexual need.

At the same time, she also considered Will a man who loved a challenge and her decision to remain in a platonic relationship until their wedding night was a challenge she hoped he wouldn't be able to resist. In the back of her mind she wanted him to seduce her into changing her mind. Then she could blame it on him.

She knew she wasn't fooling anyone but herself. She had been trying to play it safe and she was failing miserably.

She went completely still when she registered the heat of his body seeping into hers. She shivered when she felt his moist breath on the nape of her neck. She hadn't heard him get up.

Slowly she turned around and faced him. In his eyes she found heat, passion and pleasure. He raised a hand to frame her cheek, his thumb stroking her skin. Jesse shivered not from the breeze but from contact. Her body felt flushed inside and from the way he looked at her, she knew everything between them was about to change and she didn't have the willpower to stop it.

Before she had a chance to think rationally, Will swooped down and captured her lips. The kiss was too compelling to resist and before long she felt herself melt against him.

Her body was hot and alive, incinerating what little restraints she had left. The warm incense of his skin spiced with the scent of beer filled her with drugging pleasure. Impatiently her hands roved over him, sliding inside the open front of his shirt, her fingers spreading across his shoulder, down his chest, across his nipples, digging into his muscles. Her breath came moist and rapid against his neck as he tore his mouth from hers and leaned his head back, gasping for air before lowering it again, reclaiming her lips.

With impatient hands, Will peeled away her shirt, which fell to rest on the wooden deck. His mouth closed over her breast in a hungry swoop that pulled the thread of desire from within her. He cupped each swell, lifting her to him as he feasted. He drew one hard bead into his mouth.

Her insides were quivering like jello and her pulse left her so weak, a moan escaped from deep within her chest. Jesse thought she would die from pleasure. Her knees weakened, and she barely had the strength to hold herself up.

All she could do was surrender and allow herself to be swept away by a wave of new sensations. He transferred his mouth to her other breast, laving equal attention on it as he tended the abandoned one with the circling strokes of his callused thumb. His mouth was warm and gentle and a wave of heat swept through her.

Weakly, she leaned against the railing and hooked her legs around his and flung her head back.

"Don't stop," she gasped.

Unable to fight her emotions a second longer, she rocked against him, the hardened steel of his thigh between her legs sending tingles rippling through her. Will leaned against the rail, balancing with his left foot. He cupped her buttocks, lifted her to fit as closely against his body as he could. Their legs entwined as he nudged his other thigh more firmly against the core of her, his mouth still bathing delicious moist fire over her breasts. Intensity built within her, an escalating need riding the scream welling within her throat. She closed her eyes as her body vibrated with a fire that threatened to ignite her.

Jesse wilted against him. He cradled her as each wave of completion shook her until she simply shivered with aftershocks.

He kissed her forehead, rested his cheek against hers until her breathing steadied into a normal rhythm. Only then did she realize his chest was rising and falling at a pace double hers. She threaded her fingers through his tousled, damp hair.

Gathering her up in his arms, Will carried her quickly inside the house and down the hall to her room. She buried her face against his neck, her breathing quickening. Once there, he bent slightly and lowered her onto the bed and stretched beside her.

Jesse tore at his clothes, pulling the hem of his shirt from the waist of his jeans to expose the body she'd drooled over since the day they'd met. Soft curls sprinkled his chest. Her curious fingers swept up and over his chest. Then lowering her head, she flicked her tongue over his flat nipple until the hardened tip pebbled.

With a frustrated groan, Will rolled off the bed, reached for his belt and slipped his jeans off, then his briefs. Reaching into his back pocket, he removed his wallet and grabbed a small foil packet and set it on the nightstand beside them. He scooped her into his arms and moved her to the center of the bed before fitting his body over hers. His hair fell over his forehead, hiding his expression from her.

Jesse savored the solid weight of him against her, a pleasure she would have regretted never having had. She could feel her own softness giving way to accept him. The roughness of his locs were an exciting abrasion. His broad hands explored her with tantalizing thoroughness.

No inch of her went untouched or untasted until he settled over her once again. The hottest part of him pressed against her leg insistently. Curiosity compelled her to reach for him. Wrapping her fingers around him, she couldn't staunch the well of surprise and perhaps the first twinges of nerves.

"Uh, Will. Here's where my knowledge isn't the best."

"Jess, just relax."

His hand slid between them, his fingers between her folds where he explored, rekindling her need until she forgot how to think. Will reached for the packet, ripped it open and quickly slipped the condom over his aroused flesh. He then shifted more fully over her, until the thick hardness of him was firmly against her.

She dug her heels into the mattress, tipping her hips toward him. Slowly, he eased inside, nudging and stopping, stretching before edging further. Impatient, she squirmed beneath him with greedy whimpers.

Will nuzzled her neck and whispered against her ear. "Patience, boo. I want this to be good for you."

"It is, Will. Hurry."

"I'm going to try not to hurt you." Then she felt the rest of his hardness ease inside her with only a slight sting. She looked straight into his eyes and felt like she was flying.

He pulled almost completely free and returned. Her tight body closed around his hardened flesh. Tonight, she would have all of him, even if only in the most basic of ways.

Then she lost the ability to think or reason, each thrust urging her closer to another completion, except this one would be better, because she would go alone. She locked her legs around his, grabbing his hips in her hands as their sweat-slicked bodies danced against each other.

"Jesse, I need you." The words seemed ripped from him with a begrudging intensity.

She could not unscramble her mind to answer or fully comprehend what he might be trying to tell her. Her hands tightened on his buttocks and she squeezed, pulling him even deeper, filling her as his pace increased, and his breathing grew heavier. He slid in and out of her body with strong powerful thrusts of his hips.

As her body reaped the benefits of his unrestrained passion, she buried her head between his shoulder and neck and closed her eyes tight. She felt the first ripple, then a second and a third until finally she lost count and exploded with screams of ecstasy. Shortly after, a hoarse growl tore through Will, filling the air. That sound alone would have sent her over the edge, knowing she'd given Will a measure of the pleasure he'd given her.

A smile curved her mouth as he rolled over and held her close. That smile was still there when she drifted off to sleep.

CHAPTER FOURTEEN

Will blinked as sunlight poured into the room. He wasn't ready to get up and start his day. He preferred to spend the morning lying here in bed with his fiancée. Turning to look at Jesse, he saw an empty spot instead. He frowned. However, instead of hopping out of bed, finding her and returning her to bed, he decided to give her a few minutes and see if she returned on her own.

He glanced around Jesse's simply decorated room. Done in peach and cream, the room was quite feminine with cream carpet on the floor, and peach sheers that ruffled in the cool morning breeze. The queen-size bed occupied most of the room, leaving just enough space for a dresser and a nightstand. Framed photos of flowers in soft pastel colors adorned the walls. The room's décor was accentuated with a peach and white bed-spread and pillows. The room was indicative of Jesse's femininity.

Shifting slightly, he inhaled her fragrance on the pillow beside him and closed his eyes with a sigh. Last night his fiancée had proven to be more feminine than he'd imagined. Heat stirred in his groin. He remembered the feeling of sliding inside her, the flesh that had surrounded him so tightly.

He hadn't expected either of them to rise any time soon after last night's activities. One climax had led to another and then another until he lost count. Each time they made love it was better than the last. He held her the rest of the night, hoarded each memory of sounds and touch, how she had stroked him, nervously at first and then a certainty and strength he hadn't expected.

Last night was not supposed to have happened. At least not for another week and even then not with the intensity they had experienced. He cursed under his breath as a wave of emotions took him over. He was falling hard.

With one final curse, he rolled out of the bed. Moving to the window, he looked out at the burst of red and gold as the sun began to rise. He opened the window wider and inhaled Delaware's midmorning May air. It was going to be another beautiful day.

Trying to keep his mind off Jesse, he surveyed the property, watching the morning come to life—seagulls swooped to strut the beach, and waves tipped by foam caressed the sand. The pool had been drained and a pool man was coming out in two days to clean and refill it. A landscaper was scheduled for next week. He smiled in approval. The bed and breakfast was quickly shaping up.

The smell of coffee traveled beneath the door and his smile widened. Jesse was in the kitchen preparing breakfast. The thought made his chest swell and suddenly he was anxious to see her.

Reaching for his boxers, he slipped them on, then opened the bedroom door and headed toward the kitchen. He stepped into the room and his eyes immediately zeroed in on her. Wearing a skimpy white robe, she was standing at a window with her back to him. His eyes traveled down to her bare feet. He could almost feel them smoothing his calves as her legs cradled his body, moving again him. He could almost hear her soft cries, taste her…

Sensing company, Jesse swung around and her heart jolted. Will was leaning against the counter. Their eyes met and she saw that sensual awareness had darkened his eyes almost to black. The quiet air sizzled between them.

She groaned inwardly and averted her eyes from his half-naked body. Even from the distance, Jesse could read the message and knew what he must be thinking. Because she was thinking it, too, and had to fight her overwhelming need to be close to him.

She scolded herself as she swung around and stared out at the open window. For a moment, everything that she loved—the ocean, the wind, and salty air caught and tangled around her. There in the sound of the crashing waves, she tried to ignore the power of Will's presence. But even with the distance between them, she could still feel Will's lips, the delicious urgency of his tongue as it met hers, the whisper of breath on her neck as he seared a path to the pulsing hollow at the base of her neck.

Blocking out the memories, she closed her eyes and inhaled the fresh air. She was heading for trouble.

She was unaware Will had moved across the room until she felt the heat of his body behind her. When he wrapped his arms around her and pulled her back against his solid chest, she was unable to deny her need to be close to him and allowed her body to lean into him.

"The bed was lonely without you," he whispered softly, close to her earlobe.

"I wanted coffee."

He turned her around in his arms. "And I want you."

She was no actress, but she put on her most ingenuous smile, shrugged casually and said, "Last night, I guess we both got caught up in the moment."

He didn't smile. Instead, the fire in his eyes crackled and burned.

"Good morning." He brushed his mouth lightly against hers, then looked into her face. Jesse was certain he could see her uncertainty about how to handle the morning after.

Will lightly caressed her cheek. "Are you having regrets?"

"Not really," she answered truthfully.

"Good, neither am I."

Will leaned forward and captured her mouth. Jesse tasted the edge of his hunger, dark and passionate, taut and hot, beckoning her to step out onto a limb and fly away with him. She was relieved. At least he wasn't having any regrets. She wouldn't have been able to bear that.

He lingered a second longer, then pulled back to look at her. "How about we go out for breakfast this morning?" he suggested.

"I was planning to cook." She glanced over her shoulder at the carton of eggs and the package of sausage links lying on the counter.

He shook his head. "It's Sunday. Let me take you out. How about spending the entire day with me? Donald isn't coming today so you deserve to take some time off for yourself."

Jesse opened her mouth, ready to decline his invitation, but the words wouldn't come out because deep down she knew she wasn't ready yet to end this magical time. Monday things would be business as usual but today she wanted to allow herself the opportunity to feel like a woman in love, even if it was only make-believe.

Her moment of indecisiveness stretched and Will gave her a long, curious look. "You sure know how to leave a brotha hanging."

Then her traitorous eyes traveled down below his waist and her mouth fell open. His hardened flesh was fully engorged. He wanted her again and even though she knew it was a mistake, she wanted him too. "Okay. I'd love to spend the day with you."

"So what do we do now?" he asked, his voice a velvet murmur.

She swallowed the lump in her throat. "I don't know. Do you have any suggestions?"

"Oh, I'm sure we can think of a few things." He gave her an exaggerated wink.

It was settled, he wanted her and her mind was made up that she wanted him also.

Without another word, he swept her into his arms and with his mouth pressed to hers, he effortlessly carried her back to her room.

After another round of lovemaking, they decided to eat a light breakfast at home and have lunch down on the main beach to distance themselves from concern about repairs at the bed and breakfast. At twelve o'clock they set out to start their day.

As they turned onto a long tourist strip close to the boardwalk, Jesse peered over the rim of her sunglasses and saw several charming little shops, two of which she intended to visit before they left.

The streets were crowded, but luckily they were able to find parking that faced the ocean.

"It's very nice around here," Will commented as he shut off the engine.

"Yes, I've always thought so." Even though she had lived here all her life, she was still totally charmed by the area of Rehoboth Beach. Sure, she had been on the sandy beaches in California and Florida during spring breaks, but to her nothing compared to the beaches here. She inhaled the salty scent, feeling a measure of peace.

Getting out, Will came around to her door. He helped her out, then caught her hand in his. They walked hand in hand along the mile long strip that was filled with tourists. There were several shops with artists' seascapes and colorful bouquets and art made from seashells. Humid air swirled around them, Jesse was grateful for the light cooler air found close to the ocean.

At Will's insistence, she bought a new yellow sundress and a pair of white mules with small painted daisies. When they left the store, they were ready for lunch.

They took a seat in the deli and ordered Philly steak and cheese and root beer floats. An hour later, they were lying on the warm sandy beach on a large blue blanket she had just bought and underneath a rented umbrella.

Jesse unfolded her legs, stretched her arms overhead and yawned with the lazy reach of a puppy just waking, curled against his mother. Slipping off her sandals, she savored the feel of the sand between her toes.

"Are you having a good time?"

Her gaze shifted to Will's face and she gave him a dazzling smile. "Yes, thanks for suggesting it. I've lived here all my life but rarely ever get the opportunity to enjoy it."

Leaning back on her elbows, she inhaled the salty air and scanned the beach. Several children were building sand castles. Others were sunbathing. The temperature was seventy-eight, in her opinion not warm enough for swimming, however.

As relaxing as her surroundings were, it was obvious why so many people migrated to the coast on the weekends.

Jesse tipped her face to catch the late afternoon rays, knees clasped to her chest, eyes closed.

Will studied the length of her slender neck, the glistening skin. She was wearing capris and a form-fitting pink spandex top that hugged her perky breasts. There was a tightening in his groin as his focus moved slowly up the length of her legs. The gentle breeze couldn't do anything to cool his fevered body.

Leaning forward, he touched his lips to hers. Jesse sagged against him. His kiss had scrambled her brain. He'd done little more than whisper his lips over hers, but that light caress had made her entire body tingle.

In such a short period of time he had managed to penetrate her determination to keep their relationship on a strictly business level. He had appealed to her weak, vulnerable side and in a short time had taken over her mind. As much as she didn't want to admit it, what she felt went beyond lust. It wasn't hard to figure out. Will had somehow found his way to her heart. Closing her eyes, she blushed.

"How are the wedding plans coming along?"

"Chanelle has taken over; she won't let me do anything."

"She seems like a very nice person. Has she at least allowed you to decide on a wedding day?" he said, tongue-in-cheek.

She couldn't resist a smile. "Yes, I have. A week from Saturday."

She saw him blink, yet his expression showed no other reaction. "Next Saturday?"

"The sooner the better," she pointed out.

Will smiled into her eyes. "Yeah, I guess the clock doesn't start ticking until it is official."

Her smile wavered slightly. That wasn't at all what she had meant. Before she could comment, his arms encircled her, one hand at the small of her back. Will bent and captured her mouth. Jesse opened for him with a sigh that told him she wanted his kiss as much as he wanted hers. Her fingernails bit into his skin as she returned the kiss. He cupped her bottom and brought her more fully against him, the wetly intoxicating musk of his body drugging her. She pushed her hardened nipples into his chest. He swallowed her moan as he deepened their embrace.

Pressed against the length of his hard lean body, Jesse poured her whole soul into that kiss as she drank in the sweetness of his mouth. Words were inadequate to express what she was feeling. His tongue engaged hers in an erotic dance of give and take.

Behind them someone cleared his throat.

Jesse jumped back, feeling like a teenager caught necking by the police. That paled, however, in comparison to being interrupted mid-kiss by an elderly couple. Her reaction caused Will to grin. She nodded at the elderly couple standing behind her.

"Clarence, remember when we were young and in love like that?" said the gray-haired woman as she smiled up into her husband's aging face.

"What you mean were? We're still in love like that even after fifty years." To prove it he leaned forward and kissed his wife's soft, wrinkled cheek.

The woman beamed with pleasure, then said to Jesse and Will, "You only get one shot. I can see from the way the two of you are looking at each other that you are deeply in love. I bet it was love at first sight."

Jesse smiled at the couple. As crazy as it sounded, Jesse found herself wishing fiercely that they were the young couple they thought them to be. However, when Will laughed out loud at the woman's assumption, Jesse blushed. He slid an arm around her waist and gave her a look she interpreted as forced affection.

She tried not to hold his reaction against him. The thought of being in love with someone he barely knew would, of course, seem ludicrous to a man who wasn't interested in love or marriage. What struck her as even more absurd was the fact that in the short time they had been together, she felt that he was an honorable man who she could trust even though she knew almost nothing about his background. If she were in the market for a husband, it would be someone like him.

"We could only hope to be as lucky," she responded with a pained smile.

For the life of him, Will could not understand the hurt expression on Jesse's face. By laughing at the old woman's assumption, he'd intended only a diversion. Instead of Jesse being grateful that he had saved them from an embarrassing explanation, she was looking as if he had slapped her. Even though they were starting to make a connection, Will couldn't imagine Jesse wanting to spend the next fifty years together any more than he did.

"Let's get out of here," he said as he took her by the hand, grabbed the blanket and led her toward the boardwalk.

They moved down the sidewalk in silence to where his SUV was parked. When they reached it, he swung her around to face him.

"Are you mad at me for what I said?"

Jesse gazed up into his kind, concerned eyes and answered truthfully. "Yes. I—" Her cheeks colored and she broke off as if she were carefully choosing her words. "I don't know why, but what you said bothered me."

Will moved in closer, leaning her against the vehicle. "Do you want this to be real? I mean…I thought you wanted a business arrangement?" he asked, his voice husky with need.

Jesse exhaled in frustration. "I'm not sure."

He cupped her face with his hands and stared down into her beautiful eyes. "I don't know what I feel anymore either. All I know is that I enjoy being here with you. I love making love to you." Unable to resist, he traced her cheek with his fingers.

She stared up into the face of the man she was falling love with. Alarm and forbidden excitement raced through her. *Oh, Lord, please, not that.*

"Saturday I would like to take you to Pennsylvania to meet my folks."

Her heart soared at the prospect of meeting his family. Suddenly she wanted to be an important part of his life. "Do they know we're getting married?"

He gave her a grin that made her stomach dance. "I thought we'd tell them together." Leaning forward, he pressed his lips to hers, then opened the car door for her and waited until she got comfortable before he moved around to the other side.

Jesse took a deep calming breath. She had better figure out how she really felt soon because he was slowly reeling her in and part of her was eager to be drawn in further.

CHAPTER FIFTEEN

Will knocked lightly on her bedroom door. "Jesse, you ready?"

The door swung open and she stood there nervously gnawing on her bottom lip. "I don't know. How does this outfit look?" She spun around slowly so he could see her from the back.

His eyes bathed her in admiration. "You look fine."

She swung around, eyes wide with uneasiness. "Just *fine*?" she asked, hurrying back over to the full-length mirror and turning from side to side.

Will stared at her, then burst out in innocent laughter. "Boo, you look fabulous." He leaned against the doorframe, arms crossed. He was fascinated to see the normally unflappable Jesse so unsure of herself. He'd never known her to worry about what she was going to wear.

"Will, I'm meeting your family for the first time. I need to make a great first impression."

Minus the scarf that was tied around her hair, she looked awesome. The mauve two piece pant suit had short sleeves and tapered legs that accented her slender frame.

He left the doorway and entered the room. "Jess, you look amazing. Don't worry."

She sighed and sank down on a bed piled with discarded clothing. "Will, I can't do this. Please don't make me go."

He sat down next to her. Her perfume was faintly floral and sexy. But then everything about Jesse was sexy to him. He reached for her hands, which she had clenched tightly in her lap and held them loosely in his own.

She tipped her head to the side and looked up at him. It was a sad, confused look that made him want to do whatever he could to make her happy. He lifted one eyebrow and waited for her to speak.

Jesse licked her lips and then turned her head toward him again. "I don't think I can face your family."

His brow bunched with concern. "Why?"

"Because they're going to ask a lot of questions and I'm going to be forced to lie."

"Such as?"

"How did we meet? How long have we known each other? Our first date? When did we fall in love?"

"Would you rather we told them the truth?" he returned with a sympathetic smile.

"No!"

"Listen, how about while you get ready, I call my parents and break the news?"

"Okay," she said quietly, the word just about sticking in her throat.

"Don't worry. Everything is going to work out. You'll see. But you have to come. I want everyone to meet my lovely fiancée. How would it look if you're not there?"

She gave him a blank look, then finally nodded.

Will leaned over and planted a warm kiss on her lips. "They're going to love you. I promise."

"I hate this suit," she said in a broken whisper.

Will squeezed her hand, then released it. "Then change. Relax, they're going to love you."

Will's eyes narrowed slightly when he saw Jesse stroll down the hallway. She had made him wait another hour for her to get ready and he'd begun to think he was going to have to tie her up and carry her out to his SUV.

His frustration vanished and his eyes widened with approval as he took in every part of her body he had touched and cataloged to memory.

She had decided to wear the yellow sundress and sandals she had purchased at the beach. The knit material was form fitting, hitting every perfect curve. The low scoop neckline teased, and the hem fell above the knee, exposed shapely peanut butter brown legs that she had left bare. Other than the dress she had worn the night he met her, this was the first time he had seen her in anything other than pants.

Gone was the scarf from her hair, revealing vibrant curls that framed her face. She had even painted her lips the way they had looked the first time he'd laid eyes on her.

"Sorry for keeping you waiting," she murmured.

Will rose and moved to stand in front of her. "No problem. You look fabulous." As good as she looked, he would have waited all day if he'd had to.

An enchanting smile formed on her lips. "Thank you. What did your parents say when you called?"

"They said they can't wait to meet you." He scooped her into his arms and brushed a kiss along the side of her face. "Ready to go?"

She nodded and slid her purse straps over her shoulder. He reached for her hand and escorted her toward the door.

As he locked up, Jesse's eyes swept over the white button-down shirt that stretched over his broad chest, then moved down to a pair of freshly ironed khakis and beige Timberland boots.

On the ride to Pennsylvania they talked about the progress of the house. All four suites were ready to be occupied. She had to admit they were doing a fabulous job of restoring her home.

An hour later, they pulled up to a large stone colonial house that sat majestically on a slightly elevated professionally landscaped lot. A long meandering drive led to a two car garage.

They were several cars parked in the driveway. All of his siblings had come home for a family barbecue.

Threading her arm through his, he escorted her into the house. She stepped into an impressive two story foyer with two chandeliers hanging overhead, then followed Will down the hall to a large kitchen with blue ceramic tile on the floor and matching granite countertops. Hattie and William Jones, Sr. were standing at the island chopping vegetables for a salad.

"Mom, Dad, I'd like you to meet my fiancée, Jesse James."

The Joneses turned, smiling at their son and his future bride.

Hattie clasped her hands together in delight before stepping forward and embracing her future daughter-in-law. She pulled back slightly and smiled at Jesse. "Welcome to the family, Jesse."

"Thank you." She couldn't help returning the friendly warm smile. The elderly woman was her height with short, curly salt and pepper hair.

"I can't believe my son is finally getting married. You are the first girl he has brought home in years. Now maybe you can convince him to cut his hair."

With silent laughter, Jesse glanced over at the scowl on Will's face.

"I'm so pleased," William Jones, Sr. said as he moved forward and embraced her. He was a few inches shorter than his son but had the same sable complexion. When he smiled, small lines crinkled the corners of his eyes and mouth. He planted a kiss to her cheek before releasing her.

"My son definitely has taste. How much longer before we'll have a new addition to the family?"

"Dad," Will warned.

William Sr. waved him off. "I'm not getting any younger. I want to see all of my children settled down before it's time for me to meet my Maker."

Jesse smiled at the pouting look on his father's face.

Hattie gave a dismissive wave. "Don't mind my husband. He's dying for a grandson."

Jesse glanced at Will with a curious expression.

"Everyone has girls," he said by way of explanation.

"That's right and I am depending on Will and Wayne to carry on the family name."

Leaning over, Will kissed his mother's wrinkled cheek. "I think this would be a good time to go and find the rest of the family."

He turned to Jesse and urged her to follow him.

Once in the hallway, he reached for her hand. "Don't let my family embarrass you."

"I'm sure their intentions are good."

"Right."

He led her into the family room where several adults were playing a game of charades while their children ran around in the backyard that was visible through a pair of French doors.

"Let me introduce you to my sister first." He led her over to a beautiful woman holding a small toddler. "Jesse, this is April and my niece Monica." Will dropped her hand and scooped his niece up into his arms. She squealed with laughter.

April reached out and gave her future sister-in-law a big hug. "It is such a pleasure meeting you. Let me see your ring." When Jesse held out her hand, she admired the stone. "My brother definitely has taste."

Jesse smiled and agreed. "Yes, he does."

"When Mama announced he was getting married, I was in shock. Shoot, I'm still in shock." She paused and glanced over at her brother who was playing patty cake with Monica. "You're not pregnant, are you?"

Jesse, paused, stunned by her question, then shook her head. "No, nothing like that."

April released a sigh of relief. "Good. The worse thing a woman can do is try to trap my brother. Will is one of those types who won't do anything that he doesn't want to do. However, you must be special for my bother to want to marry you."

It was all Jesse could do not to correct her, to keep from saying that what she and he shared was a deep dose of lust.

"Your daughter is beautiful. How many children do you have?" she asked, noticing all of the children running around the yard out back.

"Three and they're all girls."

At the sound a deep baritone voice, Jesse turned to a tall mahogany man strolling into the room with a frown. "And I already have my shotgun ready."

Jesse chuckled.

April gazed up proudly at the handsome man. "Jesse, this is my husband, Andre. Andre, this is Will's fiancée."

"Welcome to the family." He leaned forward and kissed her lightly on the cheek. "My brother-in-law has good taste."

Jesse blushed openly. "Thank you."

He lowered onto the loveseat beside his wife. "Hey Will, looks like you're ready to start your own family," he chuckled.

Will frowned, scooped his niece into his arms again and returned her to her mother's lap. "Not yet. I've got plenty of time."

Andre winked. "Don't wait too long. Somebody has to carry on the family name."

Will scowled. "You're beginning to sound like my old man." He shifted his gaze to Jesse. "Why don't we go out onto the deck and meet the rest of the clan?" He reached for Jesse's hand and led her out the side door. "Don't pay any attention to that baby talk. There are more than enough babies in this family."

She nodded in understanding.

Out on the deck, two women and two men were all trying to talk at the same time. However, conversations ceased when Will and Jesse stepped through the door.

"Jesse, these are my older brothers." He introduced her to his brothers Sheon and Clayton and their wives Talise and Dana.

The women both smiled and gave a warm greeting while the men both pulled her into their arms and gave her a warm Jones welcome.

"I can't believe my little brother has finally decided to settle down," Sheon said as he rubbed loving hands across his wife Talise's protruding stomach.

Will smiled. "It takes some of us loners longer to find our soulmates."

Clayton raised an eyebrow. "Even get it wrong a couple of times before we do."

His comment earned him an elbow to the chest. Everyone, including Jesse, knew Clayton was referring to Ebony.

"I have to warn you, you are marrying into one weird family," Sheon commented as he poured a glass of lemonade and handed one to his wife Talise, then offered Jesse a glass. "You better run while you still can."

To her surprise, Will came up behind her and wrapped his arms around her waist. "If she can accept me and all my flaws, I think she can handle this family as well."

"Jesse, it isn't too bad," Dana said. "I've been married to Clayton almost eleven years and I've regretted my decision only once every three or so years."

"Then the two of them kiss and make another baby," Will whispered loud enough for everyone to hear.

The group dissolved into laughter.

"So how did you guys meet?" Clayton asked.

Jesse's heart pounded and she glanced nervously over her shoulder at Will. "Darling, would you like to tell them?"

His eyes sparkled at the endearment. Then his lips slid into a wide smile. "We met at a gig I had in Philly. I was in the middle of a performance when my eyes met hers from across the room. I said to myself, 'Will you've got to get to know that beautiful woman.' We've been inseparable ever since."

At the look in his eyes, Jesse's heart began to beat rapidly. "It happened so fast I've barely had a chance to catch my breath," she said barely above a breathless whisper.

Twisting her in his arms, Will lowered his head and captured her mouth. The kiss had nothing to do with convincing his family. Instead, he tried to communicate with his kiss what he couldn't find the words to express.

"Enough! Go get a room or something," Clayton barked.

When Will pulled away, Clayton punched him playfully on the arm. Jesse dropped her lashes and blushed.

As the women all went in to help bring out the rest of the food, Will led her across the backyard to where a man was playing catch with a girl around eight years of age. He glanced over and smiled when he noticed them coming.

"Well, here he is. My other half." He tossed the ball one last time, then headed their way.

When he turned, Jesse gasped. He looked so much like Will it was uncanny, only he was built like a prizefighter.

"Jess, this is my twin brother Wayne."

Her eyes shifted from one to the other. "You didn't tell me you were a twin."

He shrugged. "It is so second nature to us, it completely slipped my mind."

She took the proffered hand. "Wayne, it's nice to meet you."

"The same here," he said as he raised her hand to his lips. "Is there any way I can persuade you to leave my twin and marry me instead?"

Will snorted rudely. "He's the unfaithful type. In two months he'll be on his way."

Wayne smiled then winked at Jesse. "I don't know. This lady here might be the one to make me change my doggish ways."

His brother had a zest for life that was turning his mother's hair white. "Ha ha!"

"Uncle Wayne, hurry up!" the little girl called.

"Sorry, a bachelor's job is never done." He waved and jogged back over in time to catch the ball tossed in his direction.

"That little princess is Candace, Sheon's oldest daughter. The twins playing with the doll house are Clayton's. On the slide are Kyla and Carmen, April's kids. As you can see, everyone has kids but me and Wayne."

"He seems to be enjoying his niece."

Will nodded. "He's excellent with kids as long as they're not his own. Wayne is a true bachelor. Sports car, flashy clothes, a different woman every day of the week."

Jesse nodded her head knowingly. Watching him, though, she sensed there was something more beneath the surface. A warm and caring person, just like his twin brother.

Will encircled her waist. "Let's go eat. I'm starving."

Two hours later, Jesse leaned back in the chair, feeling stuffed. She had had her fair share of barbecue, potato salad and homemade baked beans. After her second slice of chocolate cake there was no way she could swallow another bite.

"Have you decided on a date yet?" Dana asked from across the patio table.

Jesse glanced at Will for help. With the entire family sitting around the table, she knew the announcement was going to go off like fireworks on the Fourth of July.

"Yes, next weekend."

"Next weekend?" His mother's face fell. "Why the rush?"

Clayton chuckled. "Don't tell me you have a bun in the oven."

Will gave a playful scowl. "Not at all. Jesse is an old fashioned kind of girl and believes in saving certain things for after she is married."

Jesse's head snapped to his smug expression. She couldn't believe he had just lied and told his family she was a virgin.

Talise reached across the table and patted her hand. "Ain't nothing wrong with that."

Jesse gave a weak smile. "Well, uh, we've decided to do something small and intimate."

"How small?" his mother asked.

Will clasped her hand under the table. "Family and just a few friends."

"How about having it here?" his father suggested.

"Jesse owns a bed and breakfast and has always dreamed of having her wedding there."

She glanced at him again with surprise. How did he know that she had dreamed that when she was a little girl, before she decided she didn't ever want to be married?

"How enchanting!" Talise squealed. "If there is anything I can do, please let me know."

"That goes for all of us," Mrs. Jones commented with a tearful smile. "We're just glad to have you be part of this family."

Jesse smiled on the ride home. The Joneses had welcomed her into their family with equal warmth. She felt so bad deceiving them into believing their wedding would be a union of love.

"You have a nice family."

"Thanks. Sometimes they drive me crazy but I couldn't imagine life without them."

"I know what you mean." Ole Man was all she had ever had, and when he passed she had felt all alone in the world. Even with his faults, he had been her father, and she had loved him very much.

The rest of the drive was accomplished in complete silence, except for the tunes of Will Downing coming from the speakers. Jesse stared out the side window while Will concentrated on the road.

Jesse was relieved when they pulled into the circular drive. She wanted to get away from him as quickly as she could so she could have some time alone to make sense of her emotions.

She wanted Will, not as a temporary husband but as a permanent fixture in her life. Not just in her bed but also sharing her heart. But she was frightened because her heart was now on the line and she was almost certain that he would never share her feelings. Today had been an act for her and his family's sake. The performance was so extraordinary that not only had he fooled his family, but he'd had her wishing that things were the way he represented them. The touching, the looks he gave her, the gentleness. She wanted all of those things to be real.

She wanted him to love her.

When the car came to a complete stop, she climbed out and made it up the stairs before she heard his door shut. She unlocked the door and stepped into the entryway just as he came up behind her. Soft light from a new chandelier illuminated the newly finished foyer.

She turned and stared up at him and said, "Thank you for a lovely afternoon."

"You're welcome," he replied with an irresistible grin.

"Well, I think I'm going to spend the rest of the evening in my office."

Just as she turned to leave, Will's arm snaked out around her waist and pulled her gently into his arms. With a gasp she found herself flush against his solid body. He looked so deeply into her eyes that it rocked her to her core. Then he lowered his head, pressed his mouth against the space below her ear. Jesse curved her arms around his neck, unable to stop her hands from shaking.

"Will," she moaned in a hoarse whisper.

She felt him hard and throbbing against her stomach as she raised her hips to meet the pressure of his body. When he shifted his lips in search of her mouth, she met the sweetness of his kiss. He devoured her mouth and she welcomed his tongue stroking deep into her mouth while he rocked against her. Will moved one hand up her rib cage with agonizing slowness to the underside of her breast. Her nipple pebbled against the lace bra and she shifted restlessly.

"What do you want?" he asked, his voice smooth with sexual taunting. "This?" he closed his hand over her breast and she couldn't hold back a groan of pleasure.

He had never needed anyone. Not even his ex-wife. But Jesse had managed to touch places in his heart that Ebony had never reached. Her power over his emotions was frightening and exciting.

He felt around behind her, found the zipper of her dress, lowered it in one slow movement, then pushed the fabric from her shoulders. The dress fell to the floor, and without pausing a beat, he reached for the clasp in front and released her bra, baring her breasts. She shrugged it off onto the floor and shivered at his sensual approval. Her small breasts invited him. He lifted his thumbs to her nipples, and she arched into them and moaned as he teased her nipples into tight buds.

"You are so very beautiful."

She lowered her lashes and blushed. "You don't have to say that."

"I know I don't. I'm saying it because it's true. You are a beautiful, intelligent woman and you're mine," he murmured possessively.

She just smiled as if she still didn't believe him. Linking her arms around his neck, she gazed at him with steady eyes. Her breasts filled his hands and surged at the intimacy.

Lifting her from her feet, he carried her to the bed, laid her down and kneeled beside her.

He slid his hand down between her thighs. He found the elastic band of her thong and rubbed his thumb on the soft sensitive skin underneath. She held her breath as a rush of pleasure soared through her.

Jesse pulled him down on top of her. He was still fully clothed, and she lay beautifully naked beneath him.

He took her slowly.

Will brushed his lips across hers, kissed her throat, delicately touched his tongue to her breasts. When Jesse moaned softly, he drew a swollen nipple into his mouth. She arched against him and moaned. The sound vibrated through him and sent him into a frenzy. He moved to her other breast, teased, suckled with a hunger that left her panting.

Her hands were moving down between them. Further down. She unfastened his slacks and eased the zipper down over the bulge of his masculinity. He drew a sharp breath as her cool palm slid into his briefs, found him and wrapped her fingers around his erection. She moved her hand as he'd taught her, improvising now with little squeezes, heightening the intensity of his pleasure.

Will closed his eyes and tried to restrain himself. Intense pressure heated his groin. Burying his face at her throat, he tasted her sweetly moist skin, gritted his teeth on another wave of near release, then stilled her hand with his.

"Enough!" he growled before he rose from the bed, shed his clothes.

He lowered beside her on the bed, then gently moved her legs apart. He kissed her to keep her busy while he located the delicate nub he'd found before and teased it until she tightened and shivered with her first climax.

She was ready.

He moved in between her parted thighs. Jesse locked her legs around his hips, opening herself to him. Their eyes met, held, acknowledging a fusion of bodies, of souls.

He was about to ask if she was all right when she shocked him by taking control of the situation. Locking her ankles behind his butt, she yanked him hard against her. Suddenly, he was in all the way.

Jesse grinned up at him as if pleased with her participation.

There was nothing left for him to do but close his eyes and savor her hot, silken flesh folding around him. He dared not move for several seconds for fear of immediately coming.

Then he dedicated every ounce of his energy to pleasuring both of them. He lifted his hips, drawing nearly out of her, then smoothly glided inside again. He repeated the delicious motion several times.

He didn't stop when she cried out his name. He didn't stop after she'd had what he estimated to be her third wave of ecstasy. Only when her beautiful eyes glazed over and her fingers combed through his hair, fisting among the locs, and she whimpered with exhaustion did he plunge one final time and allow his own release.

When his seed spilled into her, he silently rejoiced. Overcome with emotion, he had neglected to use protection tonight. The possibility of her carrying his child filled him with a sense of wonder and joy. Spent emotionally and physically, and wrapped in each other's arms, the two of them fell into a deep sleep.

On Monday they shopped for new furniture for the living room. After spending an entire morning going from one outlet furniture store to the next, Jesse finally decided on a contemporary burgundy leather couch, loveseat and chair, and coordinating large oak tables. Will insisted that she buy a home stereo system for the room, which included DVD player and surround sound. After they were both completely satisfied with her purchases, they returned to Katherine's to find that the landscapers had come while they were gone.

"Oh my goodness, Will, look!" Jesse stared in awe at the beautifully done lawn. Bare spots had been filled with sod. Bushes were trimmed. Flowers had been planted. Trees had been pruned. It reminded her of the way things had been when she was a little girl.

"I must say this place is shaping up quite nicely."

She climbed out of the car and stood back and took it all in.

They had added a second coat of winter white paint to the picket fence. The porch had been replaced with a composite material that was

guaranteed to last forever. The house had been scraped and was scheduled to be repainted the next day. She was so happy that she didn't even
bother to wipe away the tears that pushed to the surface.

Will stepped behind her and wrapped his arms tightly around her
waist. "You okay?"

She took a deep breath and nodded. "I couldn't be better and I owe
it all to you."

"No you don't. We're a team, remember?"

She simply nodded at the reminder that they were business part-
ners. For once she wished she could just forget about the agreement.
Releasing a sigh, she stepped away from his embrace and ignored the
puzzled expression on his face.

She carefully moved around an area that had been sectioned off,
where fresh cement would be poured to replace the spaces in her sidewalk. Hearing a car, Jesse turned to find an old Oldsmobile moving
around the circular driveway. When the couple stepped out, she practically jumped out of her shoes.

"Agnes! George!" She dashed over to them. "Oh my goodness, it is
so good to see you!"

They returned her warm embrace.

"Where have you been? I asked my dad last year and he said the two
of you had moved to Florida to retire."

George scowled. "Yep, and that place was so hot I couldn't take it a
minute longer."

Agnes nodded in agreement. "All he did was complain. But I have
to admit the beaches were nothing like ours. Young folks were everywhere, not to mention the traffic was always horrible."

"As soon as my son got a job transfer and moved out of our house,
Agnes and I decided it was time to come home."

"Oh, I'm so glad to have you both back." Suddenly remembering
Will was standing there watching, Jesse turned and did the introductions. "Oh, I'm sorry. Agnes, George, this is my fiancé, William Jones."

"It's a pleasure meeting both of you."

"Enough with the formalities. We're all family here." Agnes pulled him into a warm embrace. When she stepped away, she smiled over at Jesse and shook her head. "Someone has finally snatched my girl. When she was growing up I didn't think she would ever stop playing with trucks and climbing trees. I tried buying her a doll and that thing sat in the box."

Jesse couldn't resist laughing as she remembered growing up with Agnes and George. They had been her family.

"Agnes ran this house for years," Jesse said by way of an explanation.

"So this is the fabulous cook you were talking about."

"Humph! I was the cook, the maid, George was the groundskeeper, the maintenance man, the tour guide. You name it, Jesse Sr. had us doing it," she said without malice. In fact, Jesse caught the proud tilt of her chin.

"It looks like the two of you are getting this house back together. It was a shame how your dad let it go to pot. That last year he just didn't seem to care anymore. Getting him to spend money was like pulling teeth."

George placed a comforting hand to Jesse's shoulder. "I'm so sorry we weren't at his funeral. By the time we heard about it he was already buried and gone."

Jesse's eyes glistened at the kind words. "Thank you."

Will moved and laced his fingers with hers. "How about we show them the rest of the house."

They Butlers followed them inside and marveled at the shiny wood floor. The vaulted ceilings of the living room featured textured wood beams that gleamed in the natural sunlight that filled the room. In the dining room the old nineteenth century table had been restored by an Amish woodworker. He had removed the old finish and replaced it with a lovely mahogany finish. He had then tightened the legs on all eight chairs and replaced the torn cane seats. The second floor color schemes received oohs and aahs from the couple. They found the details of each room warm and richly welcoming. It was the kitchen, however, that caused Agnes to cry. The upgrades were something she had wanted for years.

"I can't believe how lovely this house is. Your guests are going to love it."

"I sure hope so." Jesse glanced up at Will, then reached for both George's and Agnes's hands. "I would really love it if the two of you would come back and work for me."

Agnes looked to her husband. She was grinning happily at the possibility of getting her old job back. "Well, George what you think of our girl's offer?"

He scratched his chin. "Well, I don't know. We're supposed to be retired."

Will noticed something in the man's expression and realized that Jesse needed to take another approach.

"We could really use the help of both of you. I travel a lot with my band and I hate the idea of leaving my wife here all alone. Besides, there is no way we can manage things by ourselves."

George gave a proud tilt of his chin, then smiled. "Since you put it that way, I might see a reason to come back. After all, I can't have our girl here all alone. Besides, you need someone who's familiar with this place to keep it in top shape. I know how temperamental this old house can be."

"So does that mean you'll come back?" Jesse asked.

Agnes looked at her husband, the excitement of working again quite apparent.

"Alright, we'd be glad to come back," George finally said.

Jesse jumped up and down like a little kid as she hugged them both again.

"Oh wait a minute! I need one more favor from you."

Agnes squeezed her hand. "Sure, anything for our girl."

Jesse turned to George. "Would you be so kind as to give me away at my wedding this weekend?"

When his eyes came to rest on her, tears blinded him and choked his throat. "You just made an old man very happy."

CHAPTER SIXTEEN

Jesse's wedding day found her sitting on her bed, sipping a cup of coffee and watching the rain through the window. Fat droplets tapped against the glass and the trees trembled in the wind. Chanelle had prepared the bride-to-be a breakfast fit for a queen, but Jesse had no appetite.

Her mood was as dreary as the day. The big day had finally come and she couldn't help worrying that she was making a big mistake. She loved her soon-to-be husband. She wished the wedding today was the real thing, that Will was marrying her because he loved her. Unfortunately, Will was only honoring his end of the bargain, nothing more. She would just have to learn to accept their relationship for what it was: a one year commitment in order to save her bed and breakfast.

The giggles she heard coming from the kitchen brought a smile to her lips. Chanelle had insisted that she and her daughter spend the night at the bed and breakfast so Jesse wouldn't be alone. After all, they were both going to be in the wedding anyway, she argued.

Jesse brought the cup to her lips. As she sipped, she reminisced on the past several days. During the day, she and Will had worked side-by-side with the awesome new crew as they put the finishing touches on Katherine's. Each night they'd spent wrapped in each other's arms until they fell asleep in blissful exhaustion. Thursday evening Will had left for an engagement on the Eastern Shore after assuring her he would be back in time for their wedding on Saturday. The last two nights had been the loneliest in her life.

Jesse jumped when she heard a knock at the door. She turned on the bed to find Chanelle, in a bathrobe and hair rollers, moving into the room carrying a large garment bag.

"Time to start getting ready," she announced in a merry voice as she dropped the bag on the bed.

"What's that?" Jesse asked curiously.

Chanelle looked at her as if she had lost her mind. "Your wedding dress."

Jesse stared at the bag for a long moment, feeling again that she was about to make a big mistake. She uncurled her legs from beneath her and rose. "I think I should just wear that cream pants suit you convinced me to buy for that disastrous New Year's Eve party last year." A local singles club had hosted a party during the holiday. Jesse had found herself surrounded by the most desperate-looking men in the city. She had spent the evening fighting off advances. Before the clock struck midnight, she'd had to deck a cocky short dude.

Chanelle gave her a chastising look. "I am not going over this with you again. Whether you want to admit it or not, today is the most important day or your life." She reached down and unzipped the garment bag and removed the dress. "So, whatcha think?" she asked, holding the dress out for Jesse's perusal.

Jesse gasped. Small soft pink roses had been embroidered along the skirt of the dress. Reaching out, she touched the stitching. It was silk. The dress was gorgeous.

"It's beautiful. Thank you so much," she said, lifting her lips in a small smile. "I want you to know how much I appreciate everything you've done for me. I couldn't have put this together without you."

Chanelle laid the dress across the bed, then gave her a dismissive wave. "Girl, puhleeze, what are friends for? Besides, it wasn't my idea, it was Will's."

She shot her a curious look. "Will's?"

"Yep, he asked me to meet him at the bridal shop a week ago."

Jesse was stunned as she tried to picture Will spending an afternoon at a bridal shop, sipping cappuccino and nibbling on imported shortbread cookies.

"He's something special," Chanelle added.

Jesse looked at her with a puzzled look. "Do you think I'm doing the right thing?"

Chanelle stared at her friend. She had observed Jesse and Will together and after spending an afternoon with Will, there was no doubt in her mind that the two were perfect for one another. She had seen the twinkle when he mentioned her name.

"There is no doubt in my mind that Will is gonna be a wonderful husband," she soothed.

If only I knew that for sure, Jesse thought. It was on the tip of her tongue to remind Chanelle that Will wasn't going to be a *real* husband and their marriage wasn't going to be a *real* marriage, but Chanelle looked so excited she hated to spoil her fun.

Chanelle glanced down at her watch. "We're getting close to the magic hour. So come on. Let's get you dressed so that I can fix your hair and makeup."

"How do you know when you meet your soulmate?"

Chanelle shot her a curious look and Jesse looked away, afraid if her friend looked too deeply she would be able to read the extent of her doubts. Chanelle drew closer and took her hand in hers. "You'll know." She rubbed Jesse's cold hand between hers.

"Just like that?" Jesse asked quizzically. When her friend nodded, she furrowed her forehead in concentration and paused for a moment. "Will it be like a shock of electricity?"

"Something like that. Why? You think you might be in love with Will?"

She looked away but not before Chanelle caught a strange flash of light in her eyes. "Girl, don't leave me hanging like that."

Jesse closed her eyes, aware that her friend was watching her, aware that she cared too much about Will.

"Yes, I'm in love with him."

Chanelle rushed around the bed and threw her arms around her. "Oh, that is so wonderful! I had a feeling this was going to work out."

Jesse answered with a weary smile, "I just wish he felt the same."

"Have you told him how you feel?" Chanelle asked as she took a seat beside her on the bed.

Jesse sadly shook her head.

"How you expect him to know if you don't tell him?"

"I don't think he'd want to know."

"And I think you're wrong."

She wished she had Chanelle's confidence. Would Will ever love her? Her heart ached at the question because love wasn't supposed to be part of the arrangement. Their marriage was supposed to be a business arrangement made for the sake of fulfilling her father's will. They'd never discussed the possibility of one of them falling in love with the other. But there was no turning back now. Everything was going to be alright, she told herself. It had to be.

With a deep breath, she stood. "Alright, I've got a wedding to get ready for."

An hour later she stepped out of her room in a white terry cloth robe. She stepped into the multipurpose room at the back of the house to find that it had been transformed with the Butlers' special touch. Fresh flowers were beautifully arranged around the room. An archway had been rented and stood in the middle of the floor, vined with an assortment of silk flowers. They had even gone so far as to strategically arrange several chairs on both side of an ecru colored runner. In the back of the room were two long tables filled with punch, champagne, a three-tier cake and finger foods.

"Oh, Jess, you don't even have on your wedding dress and you still look so beautiful," she heard Agnes say.

She turned around to find the older woman smiling with approval. Chanelle had curled her hair, then decorated it with pieces of baby breath.

Jesse moved and took the woman's hand. "Thanks, and I want to thank you for everything. You've done a fabulous job of decorating." They had made it simple, small and intimate, just as she had wanted.

"It was the least I could do. I just wish your father was here to see you," Agnes said, dabbing at her eyes.

"I wish he were here too," Jesse whispered. Especially since he was the reason she was going through with the farce of a marriage, she thought. If it hadn't been for her father, she might not have even met

Will. And she might have never fallen in love. Would she have wanted that? No. Yes. She didn't know.

Tears burned the back of her eyes. Quickly she wiped them away, taking care not to smear her mascara. Chanelle would have her head if she did.

Agnes gave her a motherly scold. "There'll be none of that today. Now, hold out your hand. I have something for you." She reached into her pocket and dropped a pair of diamond teardrop earrings into the palm of Jesse's hand.

"Oh, these are beautiful!"

"I want you to wear them. My George gave them to me for our first anniversary."

Jesse shook her head. "Oh, I can't wear these."

A frown wrinkled Agnes's forehead. "Don't insult an old woman. We have to stick with tradition and you need something borrowed. Besides, I couldn't think of anyone I would rather have wear them than you. You were always like a daughter to me."

Tears threatened again as she gazed lovingly at the person who was the closest thing she had ever had as a mother. "Thank you." She wrapped her arms around the old lady. When she pulled away, she found that her eyes weren't the only ones that were misty.

Agnes dabbed at her eyes again. "Now go back into your room until we send for you."

"But—"

"No buts. Don't you know it's bad luck to see the groom before the wedding?"

Knowing there wasn't any point in arguing, Jesse turned on her heels and reached her bedroom just as the doorbell rang. She glanced out the side window. Outside, the clouds had given way to sunshine. Climbing out of their cars were Will's parents and his sister April, as well as two of his brothers. Her stomach did a nervous quiver. In an hour they would also become her family. She gave a sad smile as she thought of how welcome they had made her feel. For someone without a family of her own, their warmth and kindness meant the world.

Jesse checked her watch and frowned. What was keeping Will? Panic put a lump in her throat. What if he were having second thoughts? she asked herself. They would have to call off the wedding. No, it was too late to do that. Besides, if he were going to cancel, he would have done so long before his family arrived. She told herself the Will she knew wouldn't do something like that to her. After all, the wedding had been his idea.

Hearing a light knock on the door, she turned to find Chanelle entering the room. She had changed into a pink-colored Chanel sheath. Somehow, she always made the simplest outfit look exceptional. Her daughter Chante came in right behind her in an adorable pink and white sundress accessorized with pink ribbons in her hair and pink ruffled socks and white patent leather shoes.

Jesse's lips curled at the sight of her goddaughter. Her round chocolate eyes were shining brightly. "Don't you look adorable?"

"Thank you, Aunt Jesse."

She leaned down and kissed her goddaughter on the cheek, then looked up at Chanelle with a worried expression.

"Have you heard anything from Will?" Chanelle asked.

Jesse shook her head, trying to mask her disappointment. "Not yet."

She squeezed Jesse's hand. "Don't worry. He'll be here."

"I hope so."

"Alright, take off that robe and let me help you slip into your gown."

Jesse removed her robe to reveal a satin slip. Picking up the dress from the bed, she stepped into it and slid her arms through. Chanelle then zipped it up and stood back to take a look.

"Aunt Jesse, you look pretty!"

Jesse turned and faced a full-length mirror in the corner of the room. The dress had been made for her. It was satin without all the lace and frilly things she hated in a dress and was so simple, just the way she liked it. The material was light and flowed along every curve without being tight or itchy.

Agnes entered the room just as Chanelle was handing her a beautiful bouquet. "Your sweetie has arrived," she said.

Jesse couldn't have resisted the smile that curled the corners of her lips even if she had wanted to.

"You look so beautiful." Agnes leaned forward and planted a motherly kiss on her cheek. "I'll let everyone know you're ready." She then turned and left the room.

Jesse felt butterflies in her stomach.

"You're gonna be just fine," Chanelle said encouragingly as she hugged her best friend.

"I love you," Jesse whispered close to her ear.

"I love you too." She moved away. "I'm gonna go and get ready. I'll see you in a few minutes."

After she left, Jesse slipped her feet into a pair of satin pumps, then sat on the end of the bed and waited until George knocked at the door.

"Is my girl ready?"

She rose and smiled. "Ready as I'll ever be." With a deep, calming breath, she moved over and took the arm he offered her.

To the sounds of Jagged Edge's "Walk Out of Heaven," she slowly moved along the runner to the archway where Chanelle, Chante, and her husband-to-be were standing. Her nerves knotted tighter with each step. Right away she noticed a difference in his appearance.

His locs were gone! He was even more attractive with the short, even cut. She wondered why he would do such a thing after it had obviously taken him years to grow the locs. She would be sure to ask him later.

His face lit up when he saw her coming, causing her insides to stir. She could almost believe he genuinely cared for her, that he wanted this too. Her pulse raced and she took a deep breath.

Chanelle had been right. This *was* the most important day of her life because in the next few minutes she would be marrying the man she loved. Maybe their relationship had started out as a charade, but for her it was now the real thing. No matter how brief their marriage might be, she was going to cherish every minute, and do her darndest to be the kind of wife he would find impossible to walk away from.

Taking her place by his side, she glanced up at Will and smiled. "You were late," she whispered.

As he gazed deep into her eyes, Will took her hand and squeezed. "Sorry, boo. I'll make it up to you later."

She didn't miss the mischief twinkling in the depths of his eyes. He smelled fabulous and his black suit emphasized his broad shoulders and dark complexion. Even if she had been a real bride, she would have considered herself lucky to have won the heart of such a handsome man.

The moment they both turned to face the minister, everything seemed to slip into fantasy. She felt strange, as if it was someone else's world, someone else's wedding. It wasn't until the minister greeted them that she returned to reality.

Will looked nervous. She wondered what was going through his mind as he recited their vows in front of all of their loved ones. His vows were the ones young girls dreamed of hearing and she hung onto his every word. She turned and stared at him as she repeated her vows after Reverend Willis. His lips curled upward and she found herself smiling back at him. In her heart, she meant every word as she pledged her life to him.

"Do you have the rings?" the minister asked.

Will nodded and dug into his pocket and withdrew two wide platinum bands. His steady gaze locked with hers.

"Jesse, will you have this man as your lawful wedded husband…"

Will studied the beautiful stranger who was about to become his wife. Her silken voice wrapped around the words. "I will," she said, then looked up at him with those soft eyes rimmed with dark, thick lashes.

The minister turned to Will. "Please join hands and repeat after me…"

Will took Jesse's left hand in his, held the delicate ring suspended over the sculptured fingernail of her fourth finger.

"I, William Jones, take you, Jesse James, as my wedded wife, to have and to hold from this day forward…," the minister intoned.

Will listened and responded dutifully, but after a moment he began to feel something strange happening in his chest, as if someone were doing a tap dance in the center of it.

He slid the band onto her finger and felt her hand tremble in his. When it came his turn, her hand shook so much she nearly dropped the ring before she could push it over his knuckle. He squeezed her fingers to reassure her, and when she squeezed back, he felt something inside him stretch painfully tight.

It didn't seem possible, he thought with wonder, but in spite of the circumstances, in spite of the lies, in spite of the fact that they were virtual strangers, and in spite of the fact that he'd decided long ago never to marry again, this wedding was making him sweat more than the wedding he and Ebony had had all those years before.

"By the power vested in me by the State of Delaware," the minister said, "I pronounce this couple to be husband and wife.

Jesse's chin quivered, her eyes burned. She blinked hard and looked at the man who stood beside her.

Her husband.

As she met Will's gaze, Jesse lost all sense of time and place. The flash of heat in his eyes was unmistakable. Jesse opened her mouth to say something but found she'd completely lost track of her thoughts. Will took her in his arms, brushed her mouth with his own, then deepened the kiss, pulling her body tightly against his. She forgot about all the barriers erected between them. All she could think about was that this man was her husband and he had every right to kiss her this way in front of their friends, family and in the sight of God. She returned the kiss with all the love she felt in her heart. His scent and taste invaded her bloodstream like a narcotic while his lips sent shockwaves through her entire body.

"Jeez, Will, save it for tonight." Clayton's teasing words fizzled the moment.

Will pulled back slightly and Jesse's hand fluttered from Will's chest to her own.

Reverend Willis nodded his approval and faced the group. "Ladies and gentlemen, allow me to introduce you to Mr. and Mrs. William Jones."

Jesse was vaguely aware of the applause, of Chanelle hugging her tightly and Mrs. Jones, tears in her eyes, kissing her cheek. "My son couldn't have made a better choice," she heard her say.

Mr. Jones kissed her and shook his son's hand as he congratulated them both.

Wayne kissed her cheek and winked. "I'm telling you, you should have held out for me."

She tried to laugh, but couldn't.

Luckily, her attention was drawn away in that moment by an audible sigh. She looked over and saw Agnes beaming as proudly as if this were the love match of the century.

"I have a special wedding surprise for you two," Chanelle said with a quick glance.

"That's really not necessary," Jesse said. She stepped away from Will, then glanced around to make sure no one was listening. "You know this marriage isn't real," she added in a whisper.

"Of course it's necessary." She looked at Will, back to Jesse and then said in a low conspiratorial whisper, "I've got you a sexy nightie, including some personal effects." She wiggled her eyebrows suggestively.

Jesse's face relaxed with laughter. "You are too much."

While the rest of their guests moved into the dining room for the reception, the preacher led them into Jesse's office and passed her a pen. *Jesse James Jones* she signed on the marriage license. Her stomach felt like the middle of a beehive and her pulse pounded with the enormity of what she'd done. She'd never wanted to marry, never wanted to give a man that kind of power over her and yet the sunlight bouncing off the bands on their hands told her she had. Will had not only saved her bed and breakfast, he had given her the kind of wedding she would remember long after it was over.

She walked over, curved her arms around his neck and kissed him on the cheek. "Thank you."

He shot her a curious look. "For what?"

"The dress, this day. It seems…real."

He cupped her elbows, drawing her full attention. "This is a real marriage, Jesse. Don't doubt it. Now we're going on a real honeymoon."

Jesse's eyes blinked in surprise. "Honeymoon?"

Will simply nodded. "Somewhere away from sawdust and the annoying sound of power tools. So grab your purse. Your chariot awaits."

"B-but I haven't even packed."

"No need," he said, pulling her closer. "I have everything we'll need in the SUV."

She shook her head. "Will, I can't—"

Before she could get another word out, he lowered his mouth to hers and kissed her hard and passionately. When he pulled away she stared up at him, stunned at what she saw. Had she seen love in his eyes? Or was that her imagination?

"I missed you," he confessed with a smile.

"I missed you, too," she whispered, loving the way he made her feel.

Afraid that he would see the love illuminating her eyes, she released him and walked back to the reception.

They spent the next few hours surrounded by their loved ones until Will announced that it was time for them to leave.

Jesse bid everyone goodbye, then allowed her husband to escort her out to his SUV.

CHAPTER SEVENTEEN

Chanelle watched them pull out of the circle drive, then went back into the house to help Agnes clean up.

"Chanelle, chile, go home. I don't need your help."

"Not on your life. George looks anxious to get you home alone. Besides, I don't have anything else to do tonight except drop by Blockbuster's and pick up a chick flick." Chante had latched onto April's kids and they had taken her home for a sleepover.

Chanelle reached for a dishtowel, then headed for the dining room to clear the table. She was so busy rushing out of the room before Agnes could further protest that she didn't see the man heading in her direction until they collided.

"Oh, I'm so sorry. I—" The words died on her lips when she realized it was Wayne.

There was no mistaking he was as handsome as his twin. He was tall with shoulders that were a mile wide and after feeling his hard chest against her cheek, Chanelle knew he was at the peak of fitness. He wore slacks which could not hide legs as firm as tree trunks and a black suit jacket that outlined his powerful masculine physique. With short dark curls and a humorous, kindly mouth, his face was definitely handsome but rugged enough not to be called pretty.

Even though Wayne looked like his brother there was something different about him. She could feel it from where she stood and rather unexpectedly it had set her pulse in a tailspin. It was a kind of magnetism which radiated across the distance separating them and caressed her.

"Forgive me," he said.

"You're forgiven." She instantly found herself staring into piercing light brown eyes.

They were the sort of eyes which probed to one's soul, and when they locked with Chanelle's, that was exactly what they did. In a matter of seconds something elemental connected between them and her heart turned over in response. The air seemed to crackle and dance around them as if positively charged. It was pure chemistry and a glance was all it had taken to set off an attraction that was instant and mutual.

At a bump in the road, Jesse opened her eyes.

Will glanced away from the road long enough to say, "Wake up sleepy head."

She saw him smile across at her. Rubbing her eyes, she sat up in her seat and returned the smile.

"Where are you taking me?" she said around a yawn.

Will took his eyes off the road long enough to give her a boyish grin. "You'll see. We're almost there."

With a love for surprises, Jesse decided to wait patiently. Glancing over at the digital clock on the dashboard, she gasped, "I can't believe I've been sleep for almost two hours."

Will nodded his head knowingly. "I'm sure you had a long, restless night. I know I had."

"Oh, let me guess, the dreaded bachelor party," she drawled with a humorous roll of the eyes.

"Hey, a brotha can only take so much," he laughed.

"I'm sure," she murmured. She playfully punched him in the arm and they shared laughter. She then turned to stare out the window in time to read a highway sign.

"Are you taking me to the Poconos?" she asked, her eyes dancing with excitement.

"Yep."

A huge smile curved her lips. "I haven't been there since I was a kid. Ole Man used to take me to the Jack Frost Resort during my spring break. That is, if there weren't any guests."

He couldn't help returning the excitement. "Does that mean you are an experienced skier?"

She shook her head. "Not hardly. I try but I've never been any good at it. However, I can ice skate and I love the snowmobiles."

"Too bad it's not winter. You could show me the ropes."

"That would have been fun."

"Can I let you in on a little secret?"

She turned at the sound of the serious tone. "Sure, what is it?"

"Where we're staying children aren't allowed."

She raised her brows in question.

Will grinned like a boy with a big secret. "I think I've found the perfect setting for our honeymoon."

She met the desire in his eyes and as a warm feeling flowed through her, she lowered her eyelashes so Will couldn't read what she was feeling.

Other than occasional small talk, they were quiet for the rest of the drive. To insure the limited need for conversing, Jesse slipped a Beyoncé disk into the CD player.

With her eyes shut, she thought about the vows they had taken earlier. In her heart she had meant every word. The wedding had been a real wedding as far as she was concerned. And the honeymoon he had planned was even better. She felt a throb of pain beneath her breast as she wished that Will felt the same. She said a silent prayer. From this day forward, no matter how much it might hurt in the end, she was going to do everything in her power to win her husband's heart.

"We're here."

She opened her eyes as he brought the SUV to a stop in front of a fabulous resort.

Will hopped out of the vehicle and walked around to open her door.

Jesse stared up into the eyes of the man she loved and had to catch her breath.

"Ready?" he asked.

Jesse read so much meaning into that one single word. When she nodded her head yes, she was affirming her decision to win the heart of the handsome man standing before her.

They moved into the hotel lobby and the name said it all. Caesar's Palace was both elegant and classy.

Fifteen minutes later, with keys in each of their hands, she followed him into the spacious suite complete with a relaxing heart-shaped whirlpool bath for two. Her heels sank into the thick red carpeting. Jesse quickly moved from room to room of the suite, completely infatuated by the erotic and luxurious details. She stopped right in her tracks when she discovered a round king-size bed with mirrored headboard.

Since theirs was a marriage of convenience, she hadn't expected a honeymoon, let alone anything of this magnitude. Dropping her eyelids, she took a moment to calm her racing heart.

"You okay?" Will asked as he carried their bags into the room.

She stared up at the concern in his eyes. *God, I love this man.* "This suite is fabulous."

Will shared in her excitement. "I'm glad you like it."

Jesse wrapped her arms around his waist. "Thank you."

He returned her smile and pulled her closer to him. "You're welcome," he whispered against her lips before he kissed her.

"Why don't we go eat before I feast on something that isn't on the menu."

She felt her stomach clench. For someone who had just discovered the joy of lovemaking, she was anxious to share the thought—provoking bed with him.

Will cupped her chin, tilting her face to make certain he had her attention. "When I make love to you tonight, I don't want any hunger pains standing in our way. Besides, you're gonna need carbs. I plan to take my time properly reintroducing myself to every inch of your body."

Jesse took a deep breath. When he reached out for her, she knew he could feel the trembling his words had caused. Will leaned forward and dipped his mouth over hers for a kiss that lingered. She immediately wrapped her arms around his neck and molded their bodies. The private area between her legs began to ache with the overwhelming need to have him buried inside her again. Will deepened the kiss and she met each stroke of his tongue. The kiss was different from before. This time it was demanding, greedy, igniting heat within her. When Will finally broke off the kiss, he held her in his arms until their breathing returned to normal.

They arrived at the dining room and ordered the special: lobster tails, baked potato, and steamed vegetables. Will didn't think he had ever waited so long for a restaurant to serve his food. Any other time, he would have enjoyed the meaty texture of lobster. Tonight, however, nothing seemed to have any flavor at all. Was it the food, or was it his desire to make love to his wife?

Wife.

Why did the word have such a magical ring to it?

When they finally arrived back at the suite, Jesse found the flowers, candy and champagne Will had ordered delivered to their room. She squealed, then grabbed her suitcase and quickly disappeared into the bathroom. While she was gone, Will tried to pull his thoughts together.

What are you doing? he asked himself. This was just supposed to be an arranged marriage and nothing more. But last week he had heard an ad on the radio about romantic weekend getaways at the Poconos and before he knew it, he had been sitting in front of a travel agent booking a honeymoon package.

Reaching into his duffle bag, he still couldn't figure out why he had done it. But there was no question that the radiant smile on Jesse's face made it worthwhile. Deep in the back of his mind, he knew he wanted to do everything in his power to bring happiness to his wife's life, even if their marriage was just a temporary arrangement. She deserved to be wined and dined and pampered and he planned to do just that. He pushed aside the feelings that tugged at him. He was going to think about today, right now, and he would worry about the rest when they got back home. Hearing a throat being cleared, he looked over his shoulder.

Jesse was posed dramatically in the archway dressed in a very skimpy white teddy with matching g-string.

He released a long whistle.

"Does that mean you approve?" she asked as she slowly turned in a circle, insuring he got a tempting view of her backside.

"Damn right. You look good."

She sashayed toward him with a little extra swing. He knew it was for his benefit and he appreciated every agonizing movement.

"Come here," Will commanded.

He didn't have to ask her twice, which was good, considering he had been waiting all night for this moment. Tonight they would take it slow. Tonight they would do it right. Tonight when they made love it was going to be as husband and wife.

Stopping in front of him, their eyes locked and Jesse saw a combination of curiosity and sexual intent. Will leaned down to kiss her and she closed her eyes and sighed.

His tongue went deep, stroking every crevice of her mouth. His hands slipped up her arms, bringing her closer. Jesse also slid her hands over him, feeling his hard, lean and muscled body. Anticipation traveled to every nerve in her body.

As he trailed kisses along her throat, his hands peeled away her teddy. While she reached down for his belt buckle and unfastened his pants, he cupped her breasts and stared down into her eyes. His intense expression was setting her aflame.

"You're beautiful," he whispered hoarsely, and her body ached for more of his touch.

This time she didn't question his words because he made her feel like the most desirable woman on earth.

He balanced on one foot and tugged off one shoe and then the other one, tossing them aside, his eyes never leaving her. Clothing fell swiftly and invisible barriers seemed to be tumbling as well. When he straightened, she pulled off his briefs to free him, drinking in the sight of his strong male body that left no question about his desire and readiness.

His large hands cupped her breasts again and squeezed them gently. She trembled under his touch and closed her eyes as her body vibrated with fire. She sighed, letting him caress her, wanting his hands all over her. She bit her lips and wiggled with pleasure.

She slid her hand to his chest, trailing her fingers down over his flat muscled stomach, touching his manhood.

"Jesse." He ground out her name when her hand closed around his thick arousal. Her fingers were eager and bold. Just when he thought he couldn't bear one more stroke, he swung her into his arms to carry her to the round bed that drew his attention like a magnet.

He laid her gently at the center of the bed. Her lips were swollen, her eyes hazy with passion. Will leaned down to kiss her breasts, his tongue stroking her nipple as he sucked and teased. Exquisite sensations stormed her senses and she gave herself to him. Her eyelids fluttered weakly and a groan escaped her parted lips.

Her surroundings were dreamlike, unreal. What was real was that she was about to be loved by her husband. What was real was warm flesh against warm flesh, kisses that sent her temperature soaring, looks that made her tremble. Why did she feel she belonged in his arms forever?

"Jesse, I want you so damn badly," he whispered silkily. He rained kisses from her forehead to her ankles. He gently caressed the bare flesh between her thighs.

Restless, Jesse came up to kiss him hungrily, knowing no matter how much he desired her, she wanted him more.

"Let me love you, Will," she whispered, certain that he would never realize the true depth of her request.

She did want him with all her being, even though she was honest enough to know that he would never love her as deeply in return. Tonight she wanted to give and take and have it all. Tonight, she was willing to risk a broken heart. Even though the marriage was a farce, tonight was real.

Strong shoulders, smooth back, narrow waist, his manhood: She wanted to explore and touch and kiss all of him. As she did, she heard his groan and was surprised that he shook. She was amazed what she could do to him, expecting him to be accustomed to women as expert at loving as he was. But that wasn't the case. He was coming apart in her arms until he grasped her and shifted her roughly. "Jesse—"

He cradled her in his arms, kissing her as passionately as she kissed him. His hand caressed her thighs, sliding in her inner thighs. She opened her legs to him. While she caressed him, his fingers trailed high, reaching the juncture of her thighs and then touching her intimately. He stroked her, taking her to a new height. He laid her down and moved down to trail his tongue where his hand had been. He was between her legs, watching her as he kissed her.

She closed her eyes, arching and gasping, lost in scalding sensations, yet fully aware this was Will who was loving her and who wanted her.

Thoughts spun away while lights flashed behind her closed eyes and she dug her fingers into his shoulders, arching and wanting more of him, wanting him deep inside her.

"Will!"

Her breathless pleas only made him take even more time to please her. With a great deal of effort, she moved, turning to take his manhood in her hand, to kiss and caress him until he groaned and moved between her legs.

Will's breathing was harsh when he moved in place over her body, and she inhaled, feeling breathless as she looked at him. Virile, handsome, so incredibly sexy, he knelt, poised and ready to love her. His eyes were dark with need, a look on his face that heated her blood to boiling. Then she closed her eyes as he lowered himself, the tip of his shaft teasing, moving against her.

With a cry, she wrapped her legs around him and arched beneath him, pulling him closer. His mouth covered hers, and she clung to him, writhing and wild with her need.

Will tried to hold back in order to drive her to the highest point of need. Sweat covered his body and his pulse drowned out all other sounds. She was silk and softness and a marvel to him. She was more passionate than he could have imagined.

The fire in her red hair only hinted at the fire in her body. He kissed her deeply, wanted to plunge himself into her softness, to feel her moving beneath him. Her soft moans against his ear were his undoing. He slid into her and closed his eyes and expelled a sigh. She was wet and tight, fitting him like a velvet glove. She arched her hips, meeting his every stroke. He began moving his body, easing in and out of her satin heat. The flame of passion burning hotter than it ever had. He picked up the pace, pumping faster in and out of her body.

Closing his eyes, he held back until he felt her body climaxing around his flesh. Then seconds later, he abandoned his restraint and allowed his warm liquid to flow inside of her.

Hours later Will opened his eyes to find rays of the sun peeking through the sides of the curtain. With a deep sigh, he slid Jesse's head from his chest and onto the pillow beside him. Slowly, he rolled out of bed and moved to draw the curtains tighter to block the sunlight from the room. He didn't want anything to disturb Jesse's much needed sleep.

Turning away from the window, he stared down at the woman lying on her stomach beneath the satin sheets. His body still hummed from the aftershocks of their lovemaking. He had made love to her most of the night and she deserved her rest. He, on the other hand, hadn't slept much. There was just too much on his mind.

Will slipped on his boxers, then strolled out of the room into the living room. Finding the room chilly, he switched on the gas fireplace and took a seat in the chair nearest the fire. It wasn't long before he felt warm again, except it was nothing like the warmth he had felt lying beside Jesse.

He closed his eyes and tried to understand what he was feeling. Never had he felt so consumed by a woman. All he could do was think about the woman who was now his wife. Last night pleasure had washed over him repeatedly until he felt on the brink of insanity. After they had climaxed together for the umpteenth time, Jesse had lain in his arms with the fragrance of their lovemaking surrounding them. It wasn't long before Jesse had stirred slightly in her sleep and her hand had somehow ended between his thighs. The next thing he knew, her fingers were wrapped tightly around his hardened flesh. He almost lost it when she asked if she was hurting him as she stroked him up and down. Her lack of experience with men, the fact that he was her first, her only, made the tug to his heart that much stronger.

Will opened his eyes and stared into the dancing fire. What was really going on? he asked himself, even though the answer was becoming quite apparent.

Jesse was destroying his perfectly devised plan not to get emotionally involved. She was toying with his mind and tearing away at the wall he had put around his emotions. She had somehow shifted his thoughts away from their business arrangement and found a way to his heart. Yet he wasn't mad because Jesse had no idea of the effect she had on him.

Will tried to dismiss the connection he felt. *Man, you don't need this. Remember, this was how it all started with Ebony. She manipulated her way into your soul, then reached inside and crushed your heart. Bro, you don't need another woman messing with your head. One year is all you committed to. A business arrangement and a sexual partner, nothing more. Stick to the plan! Go back to school, obtain your master's then get the hell out of Dodge.*

But even as the voice in his head continued to remind him of his original intentions, a part of him wanted much more.

His heart fluttered, then began to beat rapidly. The last thing he wanted was to become a victim of love again.

He couldn't bear the thought of putting his heart on the line only for Jesse to turn her back on him after the terms of her father's will had been fulfilled. He couldn't help thinking about how good she made him feel or the hope that even now she might now be carrying his baby.

Though reluctant to admit it, he knew that he had once again intentionally refrained from using protection. Visions of his baby growing inside of her womb aroused him in ways he couldn't begin to explain.

After Ebony he had sworn he would never love deeply, never be caught in the trap of loving a woman and becoming vulnerable. But now nothing seemed the same. If loving Jesse made him susceptible to pain, then so be it. If he was falling in love, then he would just have to accept it. Because nothing else had ever felt so right.

"What are you doing?"

Will saw Jesse standing in the doorway wearing nothing but the red satin bedroom sheet wrapped around her waist. At the sight of her firm small breasts, he suddenly grew hard.

"Trying not to disturb my boo."

With her eyes crinkled in a smile, she shuffled forward while trying to stifle a yawn. "The bed was lonely without you."

As she moved towards him, breath whooshed from his lungs. Desire was still blazing from her eyes. He tried once again to fight the control she had over his body, but as his loins throbbed and his manhood grew hard and erect, he once again gave up the fight, deciding that now was not the time to try to resist something that was being handed to him on a silver platter.

Jesse stopped in front of the fireplace, then dropped the sheet. With a wicked smile, she tore her eyes away from his and spread the sheet out onto carpet, then lowered her body to it. Will balled his fist tightly, trying once again to resist what she was about to offer. Finally, he pushed aside his determination to come to some kind of understanding. At that moment nothing else seemed to matter except the sensation of burying himself inside her again.

Watching, she licked her lips provocatively, then crooked her index finger, signaling him to join her.

Will slipped off his boxers and lowered himself on top of her welcoming body.

"I always wondered what it would be like to make love in front of a fireplace," Jesse cooed.

"Your wish is my command." He then slid eagerly into her wet female heat.

CHAPTER EIGHTEEN

Will pulled away from Katherine's. It had been a week since their honeymoon. They had returned to find that the foreman and his crew had completed the entire upstairs level of the house. When he kissed his wife goodbye, a few minutes earlier, Jesse was lining the shelves in the kitchen.

He wanted to turn around and go back to be with Jesse. The intensity of the need he felt to be with her surprised him, tied him in knots.

He was in love.

He hadn't wanted to fall in love. Yet being with Jesse was the best thing that had ever happened to him. He couldn't wait to get back to the bed and breakfast and see her, hold her and kiss her.

She was a beautiful, sexy woman who was intelligent, fun to be with, kindhearted and exciting. He wanted to be with her all the time, and the thought of her walking out of life a year from now made his breath catch.

Through the busy day Will had struggled to concentrate on what Donald was saying, yet found himself trying to catch a glimpse of his beautiful wife. Jesse was constantly on his mind. It amazed him to feel this way, as if Jesse were the most important person on earth. Earlier that day he had almost walked in front of Donald's moving truck. Thank goodness one of his men pushed him out of the way in time.

Love was making him do some crazy things.

Will turned his SUV at the next corner, and as he stopped at a traffic light, thoughts continued to flood his mind. He raked his hand across his short hair. The new look was going to take some getting used to. He'd had a long standing bet with his band that if he ever thought about getting married again, he would cut his hair. He had made the bet because he'd never thought he would marry again. But, losing his hair had been a small price to pay for the happiness he'd had found with Jesse.

As he pulled away from the corner, he scowled. Even with everything he was feeling, he was unable to tell Jesse he loved her because he didn't want to become vulnerable again. Given his current behavior, he was almost certain that this time if his feelings were trampled over, if she rejected him, he would definitely go over the deep end and lose his mind.

The band was scheduled to perform next week in Virginia Beach. He had agreed to go, although the thought of spending one night away from his new wife was mentally unbearable.

Stopping at a main intersection, Will spotted a small florist on his right. As soon as the light changed, he pulled in front of the building and climbed out. Fifteen minutes later, he came out carrying a large vase of red roses and humming a silly tune. As soon as he climbed into the car, he reached for his phone and called the house.

Jesse's voice was soft, making him remember last night too clearly.

"Jesse, hey, what are you doing?"

"Helping Agnes decorate. She has a wonderful knack for home décor."

"Sounds like fun." There was a brief pause before he blurted, "I miss you."

She giggled, then said in a soft tone, "I miss you too."

"How about if I make dinner reservations for seven o'clock?"

"Dinner would be wonderful. Where at?"

"It will be a surprise."

"Sounds wonderful."

"See you in a bit," he said, wanting to say so much more, shocked again by his intense reaction to her. As soon as she hung up, he dialed for information and made reservations for dinner.

In a daze Jesse replaced the receiver and walked to the bedroom they shared, staring at the bed while her thoughts spun with vivid memories. She was so in love with her husband that her stomach pained her every time she thought about loving him.

In spite of what might happen, she loved Will. Even though she knew that she needed to keep some distance between them if she was going to survive the next year, she couldn't. She loved him too much and no matter how hard she tried to pretend otherwise, nothing was going to change.

At half past four, Jesse was dusting the living room when she heard his SUV. She hadn't expected him for at least another two hours. She glanced down at her shorts and tattered shirt. A scarf was tied around her hair.

The car door slammed shut and as she watched him stride toward the house, her pulse jumped. In jeans and a white shirt, he looked incredibly sexy and appealing. In his hand was a crystal vase filled with deep red roses.

He opened the screen door and his hot gaze met hers.

"Hi." A smile fanned the corners of his eyes. "I brought you flowers."

"They're beautiful," she said without taking her eyes from his. He set the roses on the coffee table as he crossed the room to her.

Her already racing pulse accelerated and she flung herself at him. The moment she wound her arms around his neck, Will walked her backwards toward the bedroom.

While they kissed, her hands were all over him as much as his were all over her. She hadn't known it was possible to desire someone the way she did him. Still kissing him, she unbuttoned his shirt and tugged it out of his jeans frantically, barely aware when he pulled her T-shirt over her head and tossed it away. In their slow walk to the bedroom, clothing was strewn everywhere.

"I want you, Jesse," he whispered hoarsely. "I haven't been able to think about anything else all day."

"The workers are in the house," she reminded.

His response was a throaty sensual sigh. "So…"

She nibbled on her bottom lip. "They might hear us."

He smirked, his expression hot and intense. "All they will hear is a man making love to his wife."

He seized the opportunity to kiss her as he filled his hands with her bare breasts, slowly caressing each nipple. She closed her eyes and moaned with pleasure. Urgency tore at both of them.

Her hungry need for him overwhelmed her. She caressed him as he lifted her onto the bed and gently lowered her into the center. He then locked his gaze with hers before he moved between her legs and entered her swiftly.

Jesse arched beneath him, clinging to him and moving with him, giving herself completely to him. She ran her hands over his smooth, muscled back down to his thighs, memorizing each inch of him. A low-strangled groan caught in her throat. How she wanted it to last forever. When they crashed with release, ecstasy filled her as she held him, knowing they were one.

"I couldn't wait to see you," he said when their breathing slowed to normal. He held her close in his arms, his fingers caressing the lower half of her back. "I'm torn between wanting to take you out and wanting to stay right here in bed and love you the rest of the day and night."

Jesse couldn't get enough of him either. She wanted him in her arms, loving her, more than she wanted anything else. She really didn't care whether they went to dinner or not.

The following morning was long. It was mid-May and the temperature was hot, the sky bright and clear. Will helped pour a new concrete slab just below the wooden deck in back for picnic equipment. It was only a few feet away from the swimming pool, which had been drained, then cleaned and filled. The clear water sparkled beneath the sun. Will's eyes traveled to a younger crew member named Ernest, who was installing a new fence around the pool to keep small kids and animals from wandering over and possibly falling in and drowning.

Eager for a hot shower, Will went into the house but stopped in his tracks to watch Jesse. She was finishing the walls of the main floor hallway with an elegant burgundy and taupe border she had found at Home Depot two days ago.

Watching her, Will realized he was becoming quite familiar with all Jesse's moods—the way she became animated and excited when something pleased her, the way she pressed her lips into a tight line when she was concentrating, the far-off look in her eyes when something was bothering her.

Like now.

Jesse had said very little to him all morning. Last night they had mutually decided not to go out and instead had ordered pizzas and had spent the evening in bed discovering several different positions they hadn't tried yet. Afterwards he had held her in his arms as they slept. But this morning at breakfast, she had said very little and now it was after two o'clock and he was starting to get the impression he had unconsciously done something to upset her.

"Is something wrong?" he asked, watching her.

She glanced to her right, shrugged, then resumed working. She smoothed the wallpaper, insuring that it would stick.

Will moved to where she was standing and lightly touched her arm. To his irritation, she shrugged away as if she didn't want his hands on her. Reaching for her again, he turned her around so that she was forced to look at him, then pinned her against the wall with his hands on either side of her.

"Baby, I want to know what's bothering you," he said, concerned by her distant demeanor. He didn't like seeing her this way. He craved her smiles, her laughter.

"I'm just tired," she answered with a sigh. Jesse knew it sounded more like an excuse than an answer. She just wasn't up for the discussion. Last night while in the heat of the moment, she had allowed the words

"I love you" to slip from her lips. They had sounded so natural that she hadn't regretted expressing her feelings. When he hadn't responded, she had accepted the fact he didn't share the same feelings. What bothered her was that she had allowed herself to fall hopelessly in love with her husband and was powerless to do anything about it.

"It's more than that," Will said as he reached up and cupped her chin.

Jesse stared into his eyes. "It's been a busy week, that's all," she insisted, finding it hard to breathe with him so near. When she realized he wasn't going to give up, she felt heat rise to her cheeks. "We've been keeping some long hours. I barely had four hours of sleep last night."

Will shook his head. "I guess you're right." Images of their bodies entwined caused an instant erection. He wondered if she had any idea of what she did to him.

Agnes stepped around the corner and Will turned toward her, his movement bringing his body into contact with Jesse's. When she started to move away, he snaked an arm around her waist, keeping her next to him.

Grinning, Agnes winked at them and disappeared into the linen closet. She came out shortly after with fresh towels. "You two aren't gonna get any work done like that," she told them, a big grin on her face.

"We were just talking," Jesse retorted, aware that her body felt short-circuited. She wanted to put distance between them but her feet wouldn't obey. Unconsciously, she lifted her hand and pressed it against his chest. The muscles in his abdomen tightened in response. As she aroused his passion her own grew stronger.

"Yeah, right. George and I used to talk just like that when we were y'all's age," Agnes quipped, clearly amused at catching the lovebirds in an intimate embrace. She strolled out of the room whistling.

Still holding Jesse next to him, Will looked at her with fire burning in the depths of his eyes. He felt his control slipping. Her mouth was so damn tempting. Raising his hand, he cupped Jesse's face and lifted it. Before she had a chance to protest, he swooped down and claimed her lips. On impact the kiss sent the pit of his stomach into a wild dive. Heat stabbed at his chest, then slowly flowed through his veins. When she did-n't pull away, he brought her closer to him. She felt delicate and soft and all woman.

He groaned his satisfaction as she moved her hand over his ribs, aligning her body was his. Her breasts grazed his chest, increasing his desire. He darted his tongue into her mouth, and groaned with satisfaction when his tongue found hers. His hand slid from her back to her waist, then languidly up to her rib cage and hovered near her breast. As if hungering for his touch, she arched toward him, pressing closer, moving against him, encouraging him.

His hips pinned her against the door, and she lifted her leg. Will gathered her closer, his hands going to her bottom and lifting her firmly against him, the barrier of their clothing adding friction to their passion.

He groaned again as her palms caressed his back, then moved lower to his hips, then lower still as she pulled his hardened flesh against her.

Lord, he couldn't get enough of this woman. Just touching her made his blood race in his veins. He wanted her right here, right now.

Knowing he needed to stop himself before things got any more out of control, he gave her one final kiss and pulled his mouth away.

Jesse opened her eyes and her haze cleared almost instantly. Her breathing was ragged.

"Damn," he whispered. "I have no control when I'm near you."

"Neither do I," she sadly admitted. It was useless to fight her heart. He started to touch her again, but she stepped away. "I better get back to work."

"Let's go out to dinner tonight," he suggested.

She smiled. "Sounds wonderful."

He kissed her one final time, then headed toward the stairs. Before he made the climb he turned around and said, "Make sure you wear something nice. Tonight I'm taking you somewhere fancy."

CHAPTER NINETEEN

Will left the house to find Donald and two others putting the last of the maintenance free siding on the house. Originally Jesse had been against the idea. He knew her hesitation had been a question of money. Finally they had agreed that everything would be paid for out of the check Will would receive from the lawyer next week. Two hundred and fifty thousand dollars could go a long way if she was tight with spending. As soon as the siding was finished, the newly painted red shutters would be put back on the house. Everything was coming together way ahead of schedule. The city inspector was scheduled to come out next week for the final approval.

Will got in his SUV and pulled away from the house, planning to make a quick trip to a men's clothing store he had spotted yesterday. He wanted a new suit for tonight. Thinking about Jesse, he missed his turn and found himself on a dead end street. With a light chuckle he swung the vehicle around. In the process, a sign caught his attention.

For Sale.

He pulled the car over and got out.

A magnificent stone manor crested a hilltop overlooking the ocean. It looked to be set on well over three verdant acres. Mature deciduous trees surrounded the home and created a park-like setting. The house had vintage charm and grace and was calling his name.

At that moment he made a decision. Reaching into his back pocket, he removed his cell phone and dialed the phone number on the sign.

Jesse stared at herself in the mirror. Could she pull this off? Could she actually wear this gown in public?

The white fabric clung to her body like a second skin. But that wasn't the problem. The halter dress left her back completely bare. Which meant that she'd forgone a bra, something she had never done before.

She checked the clock and her heart did a somersault. Will would be banging on the door at any minute. Wanting her dress to be a surprise, she had literally locked Will out of the room.

She scrambled around the room for her shoes and evening bag and was slipping into her shoes when she heard Will tap on the door. She nearly tripped as she ran to the mirror for a final inspection.

"Are you ready?" she heard him call from outside her bedroom door.

"No, I mean, sort of. Not quite." She needed a moment to breathe, to gain the confidence to face him. "I'll be right out."

She slipped on a wrap that complemented her dress and opened the door, nearly bumping into Will. Cool and collected, he wore a classic black suit, a crisp white shirt and a slim black tie. She detected Burberry cologne.

She closed the door behind him. "You were supposed to wait for me in the living room."

He flashed a rebellious grin. "Since when do I listen to what you tell me to do?"

She couldn't resist a grin at his comment. What he didn't know was that she wouldn't have it any other way. She loved this man and everything about him.

"So, how do I look?" She spun around slowly, making sure he viewed her dress from all angles. "Wow" was all he could say and for Jesse that was more than enough.

"This is nice," Jesse said as she and Will were escorted to a secluded table at the Seafood Cove. Jesse was pleased to find that he had made reservation at a cozy restaurant and piano bar with a magnificent view of the ocean.

Once they were comfortably seated, she stared out the window at the captivating view. "I've lived here all my life and I didn't even know this place existed. How'd you find it?" she asked.

"While I was at the florist the salesclerk suggested the place to me."

"Excellent choice," she replied.

"I need to run to the men's room. Order me the special." He rose, planted a kiss on her cheek, then strolled away.

The waitress arrived and departed. Jesse began to wonder what was taking so long. She glanced down at her watch. It was almost nine o'clock.

The lights dimmed and she turned slightly in her seat to face the stage as an older, elegantly dressed woman strolled onto the stage.

Then she saw him. Will moved over to a baby grand piano on the stage and began to play. Fascinated, she watched the way his fingers glided gracefully across the keys while the woman sang Alicia Keys's "Fallen." Her heart flooded with love.

At the end of the song, the crowd applauded, and he rose from behind the piano, then bowed. When the lovely singer beckoned him to the microphone, tears sprang to Jesse's eyes as she saw how nervous he looked.

"Thank you for allowing me to celebrate with you. I'd like to dedicate that song to my beautiful wife, Jesse. Sweetheart, please stand so everyone can see how fine you are."

Star struck, she rose and waved at the applauding crowd before quickly sitting again.

"Before I join my lovely wife for dinner, I would like to take a moment to say something. Jesse, baby, I love you and I want to spend the rest of my life showing you just how much."

Heart pounding, tears running down her cheeks, Jesse sprang from her seat and ran up onto the stage and into his arms, where they shared a passionate kiss. The crowd roared when they finally pulled away. He took her hand and led her to the middle of the dance floor.

"Did you mean what you said?" she asked as they began dancing.

He kissed her nose. "Every word. I've just been afraid to tell you how

I feel."

"What about with your first wife?"

"I never felt this way with her."

Her heart sang as he held her tightly in his arms. Life couldn't possibly get any better than this.

Sitting back on the bed he watched as she shrugged out of her gown. When it dropped to her feet, she reached down for it and playfully tossed it at his head. Will inhaled the floral scent that was so much Jesse, then watched in fascination as she finally stood in front of him in nothing but a lacy white bra and matching thong and red pumps. She was the most stunning woman he'd ever seen. His eyes traveled from the soft curves of her breasts to the smooth flatness of her belly. If he looked at her for a hundred years it still wouldn't be enough time to absorb the full depth of her beauty.

Her lips lifted in a seductive half-smile. "Are you going to just sit and stare or are you going to show me just how much you really love me?"

He smiled. "How badly do you want me to make love to you?"

"Badly."

He slid off the bed and stood before her, then leaned down and covered her mouth in a hungry kiss. Within seconds they'd shrugged out of the rest of their clothes. She wrapped her arms around his neck and he carried her over to the bed and covered her aching body with his. She cried out as his bare chest met her bare breasts. Safe and secure, she opened herself to him fully. He tasted her as if she were honey. Her body begged for him. Tears rushed to her eyes as her mind flooded with emotions. As she gasped and writhed beneath him, Will filled his hands with her swollen breasts, then took one nipple, then the other into his mouth. When her impatience grew to explosive proportions, Will thrust inside her and Jesse found her release almost instantly. It wasn't long before the two drifted off to sleep wrapped in a cocoon of love.

CHAPTER TWENTY

"You're pregnant," Agnes said.

Jesse rose from the toilet and moved to the sink, where she splashed cold water onto her face. It wasn't until she patted her face dry with a towel that she allowed her eyes to rest on Agnes's sympathetic face.

"I can't be pregnant."

"Don't tell me Ole Man never talked to you about the birds and the bees."

"He talked to me alright." She clearly remembered the brief discussion. "Keep your legs closed until you're married." Luckily, she'd had friends like Chanelle to help educate her.

"Come on into the kitchen so I can make you some tea."

Feeling slightly dizzy, Jesse moved down the hall and flopped into the first seat at the table.

"How long have you felt this way?"

"Almost a week."

"Are you late?"

Jesse's eyes traveled over to the calendar on the wall and her pupils grew wide as she realized it was the middle of May. Where had the time gone? Her period was a week late and she hadn't even noticed.

It had been well over a month since Will had first appeared on her doorstep. So much had happened in the past weeks. Katherine's had been completely renovated and they were expecting their first guests in two weeks. Moreover, she had fallen in love with the most wonderful man in the world and had gotten married. And now she was carrying his child. She placed her hand over her still flat stomach as excitement filled her.

"I can't say that I'm not excited. It will be nice to have a little person running around the place again," Agnes said, setting a cup of tea in front of Jesse. "I bet Will will be thrilled."

Jesse glanced up and they shared a knowing smile. She had a feeling he'd be happy but at the same time she wondered. He hadn't been happy when he thought she had tricked him. Brushing it off, she told herself things were different now. They were married. Their child would be surrounded by love.

Her thoughts turned to the Thursday appointment she had with Mr. Dawson, her father's attorney. She stared out the window, realizing she was nervous about the appointment. About what she wasn't quite sure, considering she already knew the contents of her father's will. Maybe it was knowing that after Thursday, everything would change. Next week Katherine's would belong to Will.

As she sipped her tea, her thoughts returned to her pregnancy.

"Agnes, don't say anything yet. I'm going to surprise Will this weekend."

"My lips are sealed. However, I plan to pull my knitting needles out and started making a pair of booties."

As soon as Will stepped into the house, the mango scent of the potpourri Jesse had placed around the house filled his nostrils. His heart swelled as he anticipated holding her in his arms. He hadn't seen his wife in two nights. That was much too long to not feel her warm body against his. In fact, he had been so anxious to get home to his new wife that as soon as their performance in Virginia Beach concluded, he hopped in his car and made the three hour trip home. His watch indicated it was well after three o'clock. Will was tired and hungry, yet all that mattered was holding Jesse in his arms.

Quickly he shut the door and locked it behind him. With his overnight bag on his shoulder, he moved down the hall to the last room on the right. Before entering he took a deep breath, then turned the knob. Finding her lying in the center of the bed fast asleep, he felt a familiar tightening in his chest. If anyone had told him a month ago he was going to fall in love, he would not have believed it.

Watching her lying there looking so sweet, so small and innocent, his heart began to pound uncontrollably. He needed to hold her. Now that he had admitted to her how he felt, he wanted to hold her in his arms and show her how he felt.

Dropping the bag, he quickly removed his clothes, making as little noise as possible. He didn't want to wake her. Not yet. He was looking forward to the look on her face when he joined her in bed. After slipping off his boxers, he moved over to the bed and joined her under the covers. The scent of a floral bath splash filled his nose as he leaned forward and kissed her.

"Will," she mumbled sleepily against his lips.

"Yes, baby," he whispered as he gently pulled her into his arms.

"You're home," she said softly with a smile.

"Yes, baby, I'm home." He kissed one eyelid, then the other, until they fluttered open. When she smiled up at him, he captured her mouth in a deep, searing kiss.

When he pulled away, her heart was pounding as hard as his.

"I missed you," she confessed. "Did you miss me?"

"You better believe it." He rolled on top of her. "However, just in case you've forgotten, let me show you how much."

Will and Jesse settled in two stiff leather chairs positioned directly in front of Mr. Dawson's desk. The lawyer peered at them through his thick bifocal glasses after confirming all the legal documentation had been signed and notarized.

"Your father was a strange man," he began.

"You can say that again," Jesse mumbled.

He gave her a comforting smile, then leaned forward across the desk. "As I told you before, at first I thought this was some kind of joke.

But when your father threatened to find another lawyer, I realized he was serious. I tried to talk him out of such a ridiculous provision but talking to Jesse Sr. was a big waste of time."

Jesse cut Will a knowing look out the corner of her eyes.

The lawyer cleared his throat. "Well, I'm glad to see that things worked out after all. I hated to see all this money go to the Hare Krishnas."

Will gave her a puzzled look. "Why would he leave his money to them?"

She shrugged. "My father's way of being funny. He knew there was no way I was going to let them get his money."

"Anyway, now that we have everything in order, all I need is for you to sign here and the money's yours."

Jesse reached for the documents and Mr. Dawson cleared his throat.

"I'm sorry. I was referring to your husband."

There was a tense silence as Jesse nibbled nervously on her lip and tried to hide her disappointment, even though she had already known the check for two hundred and fifty thousand dollars was to be made payable to Will, not her.

Her husband reached over and squeezed her knee to reassure her that everything was going to be okay. She hoped so. However, she couldn't avoid being apprehensive despite the fact that she knew he loved her. Pushing her fears aside, she pretended to stare out the window.

Before Will signed the documents, the lawyer once again went over the terms of the agreement. She listened, though she pretended not to. The lawyer explained that although the money was Will's to do with, whatever he wanted, he would be forced to return the full amount or be sued if the marriage ended in less than a year.

After Will agreed to all the terms, he signed the next twelve months of his life away.

Jesse was unusually quiet on the way home. Will glanced at her as she sat with her eyes closed. He was almost tempted to tell her that as soon as the check cleared he was writing another one to her for the full amount. That is, after he bought her a decent car to drive. The Buick was on its last leg.

He had everything carefully laid out for the weekend before Katherine's Bed and Breakfast officially reopened. He was going to take her out on the town in Philadelphia and confess his financial wealth to her. He wanted to reassure her that he didn't need her money. He had his own. What he did need was Jesse permanently in his life.

They had stopped on the way home and picked up a bucket of chicken and a movie. Jesse was already turning the key in the lock by the time he'd grabbed the items and headed up the walkway.

"Boo, is something wrong?" he asked.

Avoiding his eyes, she shook her head. "No, I'm just tried."

He noticed the lines of worry around her eyes. "Want me to give you a massage?"

"No, I'm just gonna take a hot bath, then a nap."

Will tried to hide his disappointment. "Alright. I'll be in to check on you in a few minutes."

Jesse nodded, then headed to their suite. He watched her leave, then pulled out his cell phone and made an urgent call to his broker.

Jesse went into their suite and didn't stop until she reached the bathroom. She lowered the toilet, took a seat then reached inside her purse.

While Will was in the video store, she had run into the drugstore next door. Now she removed the home pregnancy test. Her stomach fluttered with anticipation. Regardless of what had occurred at the lawyer's office this afternoon, she was excited about the possible pregnancy.

She carefully read the back of the box, then followed the instructions. After a few minutes she checked the strip. It was positive. A smile tipped her lips and her hand automatically dropped to her stomach, which she stroked with wonder.

She suddenly forgot about her earlier anguish. Eager to share her exciting news, she went in search of Will. As she stepped back into the bedroom, she spotted a small card on the floor beside the bed. She stopped and picked it up. It was a realtor's business card. Why was Will looking at houses? Determined to find out what he had been up to, she moved from the room and down the hall. Jesse found him in the living room, his back to her as he talked on the phone.

"Jamar, man, everything is going according to plan. I'm supposed to meet with the realtor tomorrow and give her the deposit. I know, I know…now that I have the money, I can stop pretending and tell Jesse the truth."

Stunned by what she heard, Jesse felt anger and hurt wash over her. He had used her.

Tears rushed to the surface and she had to hold a hand over her mouth to muffle a sob. Turning, she raced out of the room and back to her bedroom.

She had been wrong about him. Will wasn't different. Men were all the same.

Now that I've got the money I can stop pretending.

She suddenly felt a knife twist in her heart. She had allowed Will inside her heart and he had used her. Unable to contain herself, she returned to the living room. There was no way a man was going to make a fool of her and get away with it.

Will glanced up when he heard her heavy footsteps. The smile on his face suddenly disappeared when he noticed her eyes blazing with anger. "Boo, what is it?"

"I would have never believed it if I hadn't heard it for myself."

His eyes lit with realization when he noticed the card in her hand. "Baby, let me explain."

"There's no way you can explain this. I knew you were going to try and take over. I knew you would use me."

"What are you—"

"I don't want to hear anything you have to say. All I want you to do is be out of my house by the time I get back."

Tears flooded her eyes and a sob clogged her throat. Shaking her head, she turned and left the room, before he could say a word.

Not wanting to be in the same house with him a minute longer, she grabbed her purse and headed out to her car. As soon as she pulled out of the driveway, she called Chanelle's house. There was no answer, so she left a message that she was on her way over.

Tossing her phone on the seat beside her, she sighed. This couldn't possibly be happening to her. She felt a sharp pain in her center when she thought about what he had done with her trust, her love.

Stunned, Will stood on the porch. Where was she going? He had intended to give her a few minutes to calm down before explaining about the house. But before that could happen, he had heard the car door slam and her peel out the driveway. What was going on? he wondered.

CHAPTER TWENTY-ONE

Chanelle had just returned from dropping her daughter off at a classmate's house for a sleepover when she heard Jesse's car coming around the corner. The noisy car could be heard a mile away. She had offered on more than one occasion to buy her best friend another car, but Jesse had refused.

She understood why Jesse refused. She was too stubborn to accept help. But what Chanelle could never get her friend to understand was that she wanted to do it because she loved Jesse like the sister she'd never had. Their friendship meant more to her than all the money she'd earned from her best selling novels.

She strolled up the walkway, putting her key in the door just as Jesse pulled her Buick in behind her Mercedes. The instant Jesse jumped out of the car and stormed up the walk, she knew something was wrong.

"What's the matter?"

"My husband is a phony. That's what."

Chanelle opened the door and stepped inside, signaling Jesse to follow her into the kitchen. Setting her purse on the counter, she took a seat at the kitchen table and waited for Jesse to do the same before asking, "Why do you think Will's a phony?"

"Because he is. I heard it directly from the horse's mouth. He married me for my money."

Not one to quickly take sides, Chanelle leaned across, resting her elbows on the table. "Why don't you start from the beginning and tell me exactly what you heard."

She listened as Jesse poured out her pain, stopping her only long enough to get a box of Kleenex. When she was done, Chanelle sat there quietly shaking her head.

"Well, aren't you going to say something?" Jesse demanded. It angered her that her friend hadn't quickly jumped to her defense.

Chanelle's eyes widened. "I'm just having a hard time believing he would do something like that. I really thought he loved you."

"I thought he did, too. Now I know it was all just one big lie."

"How dare he treat my best friend this way! I have a good mind to go track the dog down and give him a piece of my mind."

Jesse shook her head. "No, that wouldn't do either of us any good. I knew the risks involved when I first agreed to marry him. I just hoped that he was different, that everything was gonna be alright."

"Is there anything I can do?"

Fresh tears appeared and Jesse blinked several times, trying to hold them back. "I'd appreciate it if I could stay here until I have a chance to decide what my next move will be."

"You know you're welcome to stay here as long as you like. Chante will be happy to have her auntie around."

"I could really use one of her smiles right about now."

"She's staying with Katie, but I'm picking her up around ten tomorrow morning."

"That's fine. I wouldn't be very good company anyway."

"How does a bottle of white zinfandel, a sausage and mushroom pizza and a Julia Roberts' movie sound?"

Tears streamed down Jesse's face at her friend's kindness. "I think that will be just what the doctor ordered."

Will was flabbergasted.

While he was out putting a final coat of paint on the white picket fence, Jesse had called and left a message that she wouldn't be home tonight. He couldn't believe it. Before he realized what he was doing, he'd jumped into his car and headed for his brother's apartment. He rang the bell and waited for Wayne to appear.

When Wayne opened his apartment door, he seemed surprised to see Will standing on the other side. He stepped aside and Will walked in and headed straight for the kitchen.

"Well hello to you too."

"She left me."

Wayne lifted a dark brow. "Who left you?"

"Jesse. She left me."

When Wayne chuckled at his brother's forlorn expression, Will's jaw clenched with stretched patience. "Don't worry. She'll be back," Wayne said.

"How the hell do you know that?"

"Because Chanelle told me."

He stiffened. "Chanelle?" Then he recalled introducing the two at his wedding and the long, lingering look his brother had given the tall beauty. "Is Jesse with Chanelle?"

"Yeah. She and I had a date tonight until your wife showed up upset over your behind."

Will shook his head, relieved to know that Jesse was safe. He had been so worried that something might happen to her. In all his frustration he hadn't even thought about the possibility that maybe she had gone to visit her best friend.

Wayne moved over to the refrigerator door and opened it. "Here, have a beer."

Will shook his head. "I've got to get over there and talk to her. She is upset with me and I need to know why."

"I think you need to hold your horses and give her a little time to think first. You also need to do the same." Wayne gave him a can then moved into the living room and signaled for his brother to follow. "Here, take a load off your feet and stay awhile." He flopped down in a big chair and popped the cap on the can. "I never thought I'd see the day when my brother was strung out again over a woman."

"Neither did I," Will admitted, calling himself a fool. He sank down on the couch.

"So what did you do this time?"

He popped his beer and shrugged his shoulders as he took a drink. "I have no idea. I was on the phone with Jamar talking about the house I had just bought for Jesse and me when she walked into the room, waving my realtor's business card, and yelling that I used her."

Wayne took a long swallow, then shook his head. "I never could understand women."

"Neither could I but this is one woman I am willing to try to understand."

"You really love her, don't you?"

Will rolled his eyes in his twin's direction. "What kind of question is that? Of course I love her. I would give my life for her."

"Have you shown her?"

"Shown her what?"

Wayne pursed his lips, running out of patience with his brother. "How much she means to you."

He shrugged. "I thought I had. I don't know what else I could have done."

"Well, obviously there is something else you could have done. Otherwise, she wouldn't have left."

Will scowled at his brother's words, then gave him a puzzled look. "Since when did you become the expert?"

"I'm no expert. I just know what I know."

Wayne had obviously forgotten who he was talking to. No one knew him like Will. Wayne ran away from relationships at the first sign of commitment. So for him to be trying to give advice was a sign that his brother was either slipping or had changed.

"What's up with you and Ms. Chanelle?"

Wayne reached for the remote control and clicked on the television before he answered. "Nothing much, just been talking on the phone."

The phone. Will could not believe his ears. One thing his twin hated doing was talking on the phone. It was obvious Wayne was quite intrigued with Chanelle. He chuckled.

"What's so funny?"

Will shook his head. "You. Me."

"What's that supposed to mean?"

"It means…I never thought I could feel this way about a woman again and I do. Having Jesse is the difference between living and just existing. She completes me and without her I'm nothing." He tilted his can but before he took a drink he added, "When you're able to understand what I mean then you'll understand why I was laughing. Love sneaks up on you when you least expect it and makes you do things you would have never imagined doing."

Wayne looked totally unconvinced. Will already knew it was just a matter of time before Wayne would know exactly what he meant.

The next morning Jesse rose early and went out onto a large deck out back and sat down. She'd had trouble falling asleep last night. She'd told herself it was because of the strange bed, not Will. After all, she'd slept alone for years. There was no way she could have gotten used to sleeping in his arms that quickly.

She lifted her feet and tucked them beneath her. The morning was chilly, but the heavy terry cloth robe she had found on the back of Chanelle's guest room door was doing a fabulous job of keeping her warm.

No, she wasn't going to allow herself to admit that she had done the one thing she swore she would never do—lose control.

She heard the patio door slide open. When she glanced over her shoulder, she found Will stepping out onto the deck. The sight of him took her breath.

"Good morning, Jess."

She tried to pull her eyes away from the man who had stolen her heart. "Good morning. What are you doing here?"

"I was hoping I could convince my wife to come back home. The bed is lonely without her."

He looked tired. Despite herself, she was glad to see him.

"How did you know how to find me?"

He shrugged as he took a step forward. "It wasn't that hard."

She gave him a weary look. More than likely Chanelle had called and had told him her whereabouts. As she watched him, she wondered why he had come looking for her. It was obvious what he had been up to, so why was he here trying to apologize?

As if he could read her mind, Will said, "For one thing, I would like a chance to tell you something I should have told you sooner."

Finding a fly on her leg, she swatted at it, grateful for the distraction.

Will sat at the bottom of her lounge chair and lifted her onto his lap. Her heart stalled and she bit her lip. He put a hand under her chin and tilted her head back so she was facing him.

"Jesse, I want to know why you left."

She shook her head because she couldn't tell him the truth. She couldn't let him know how hurt she was to find out he had deceived her. "I just needed some time to think."

"I don't understand. I buy a house, us a house, and you get mad and storm out. I thought maybe you might want a place of your own and maybe let the Butlers live at Katherine's."

"But you didn't ask. Then you used the money that we were supposed to put back into the company."

Realization flared in his eyes. "You thought I was spending your money?"

She nodded.

"Silly rabbit. I spent my own money."

"Your own money?"

He closed his eyes and shook his head with an animated laugh. "I guess I really messed up."

"Yes you did. Now, please explain."

"I have my own money. I just had my broker wire half a million into my checking account."

He explained to her that his grandfather had left him and his brothers and sister a fortune. "The minute I saw TWIN WILLOWS I just knew—"

Jesse gasped. "Did you say TWIN WILLOWS?" He nodded. "You're telling me that you own TWIN WILLOWS?"

"*We* own the TWIN WILLOWS."

She shook her head in disbelief. "I've admired that house for years. It used to belong to Samantha Harris. She had blonde hair and blue eyes and always had the prettiest clothes. I couldn't stand her or her snooty friends. Anyway, whenever the school bus would pull up in front of her house I would stare at her home and I tell myself that someday I would have a house just like that."

"Well, now you've gotten something better. You've got the real thing."

"I wonder what happened that put it on the market?"

"The notice on the window said foreclosed, so I think rich girl wasn't quite so rich anymore."

Jesse felt guilty for the pleasure she felt at the thought of the Harrises going broke.

Will's face sobered. "Listen, Jess, I've been a fool," he said quietly with eyes so honest and intense.

He buried his face in her hair and inhaled. "I was lying in bed last night and all I could think about was my life with you. I don't care about the band or anything else. Only my life with you. Can you please forgive me?"

Her heart swelled in her chest. "Why didn't you tell me about this from the beginning? Maybe then I wouldn't have thought you were out to control my money."

He lifted his hand to her cheek. "Because I guess I wanted to wait until I knew for certain what I was feeling was real. Now I know no amount of money can replace what we have. I want to share everything with you and be everything with you. I can't let you go." He slid his fingers over her bare skin as if to reassure himself she was really there.

A knot formed in her throat and Jesse's eyes burned with the threat of tears. She struggled.

"I love you, boo. We're in this together. I want you to be the mother of my children."

Tears spilled over and she began to tremble. She had yet to tell him about her pregnancy. Even though this was probably as good a time as any, she had hoped to spring the news on him in a more romantic setting, like in the bed. She bit her lip and blinked back another round of tears.

"Woman, you're killing me. Are those tears of joy or sorrow? Can I get my wife back or what?"

"You are so silly." She locked her arms around him and laid her head on his chest. "I love you, Will," she said, her heart so full she thought it might burst.

"I love you too."

She lifted her head and looked at him. His eyes were filled with such a powerful combination of passion and love it stopped her breath. He dipped his head and she met his lips as he kissed her. Suddenly everything was the way it was supposed to be.

Jesse returned home to find Donald and his crew had cleared everything out and moved on to the next job. It was almost as if they had never been there. Katherine's had been restored to perfection. The view up the driveway was so breathtakingly beautiful tears filled her eyes again.

"Oh no, not again," Will mumbled with a playful groan.

She socked him in the arm for laughing at her frequent waterworks. Then it hit her. Pregnant woman were known to be increasingly emotional, which could explain her recent bouts of tears. "For laughing you can fix your own dinner tonight."

Will laughed again. "How about I pick up Chinese and we spend the evening curled up on the couch with a good action flick."

"Make it a suspense movie and you're on."

"You drive a hard bargain." He climbed out of the Escalade and came around to her side. After she got out he took her hand and led her up the walkway.

"I can't believe how beautiful this place is," she said in a soft, far-off voice.

"It's all because of you. You made me see something that I didn't see because deep in your heart you knew. I have a lot of respect for you, Mrs. Jones."

Jesse was completely flattered by his compliment. "Well, thank you very much, Mr. Jones."

Glancing around, she said, "Now that all the work is done, there isn't anything left for me to do."

"Oh, I can think of a few things."

"Really? Like what?" she asked innocently.

Will scooped her into his arms and ran up the stairs. "I can show you better than I can tell you."

While he went into town for takeout Chinese, Jesse remembered the small bassinet that had once been hers. She'd found in the back of the shed the last time she was out there.

The building was actually a large barn that instead of housing livestock, had been used to store equipment and years of junk. She gave a sigh as she left the house and went to it. It desperately needed to be cleaned out. Maybe now that the house was ready for guests, she would be able to set aside sometime to tackle that chore. That is, if Will allowed her too. She had a strong feeling that once she revealed she was carrying his child, she wasn't going to be allowed to do very much. The thought of his child growing inside her brought a smile to her face as she moved out back to the shed. She would love for her own child to have the opportunity to sleep in the same bed she had.

She reached for the door and before she could turn the knob, the door swung open and an arm snaked out, grabbed her wrist, and yanked her inside.

The smell of stale beer hit her like a splash of cold water. She quickly shook her arm free and backed up.

She swallowed her surprise. "Pace, what are you doing here?"

"I came to get what's mine." With each word he advanced forward, forcing her to take several steps back. When she felt hands at her waist, she flinched and swung around to find Darrius, one of Pace's men, standing there.

"I don't have anything here that belongs to you," she said, trying to sound calm.

Pace shook his head. "See, that's where you're wrong. This property was supposed to be mine."

"Why would my father leave the bed and breakfast to you?" she asked as she edged to the side. Darrius lunged for her, but Jesse spun out of his reach, ducked and scooted around a riding lawnmower, but stumbled on a brick before she could escape. By the time she found her balance, Pace had grabbed her and jerked her to him.

Pace gave a wicked laugh. "The plan was for you to come home and marry me."

He was trying to scare her and he was, but she refused to let him know just how scared she really was. She jerked her elbow back into his gut, taking satisfaction in his surprised grunt of pain. She scrambled toward the door again, but Darrius blocked her way. "Going somewhere?" he asked.

Before she could dash in another direction, Pace came up on her right and wrapped his arm around her neck, squeezing tightly as she squirmed to be set free.

"Everything would have gone according to plan if it wasn't for that punk," he slurred near her ear.

"Take your hands off me," she demanded.

"Not until you make it up to me."

"And me," Darrius said as he lumbered closer. "I'm gonna show you what you could have had."

"You're gonna regret this," she warned as she struggled to get free.

They both laughed at her warning.

"That husband of yours can't save you now." Pace said.

Will parked the truck in the circle drive, grabbed the bags and headed into the house. Finding the trash full, he remove the bag, but before he could make it across the tile floor, the bottom burst and its contents spilled onto the floor.

He swore under his breath as he moved to the cabinet beneath the sink and retrieved another bag. He stooped down and was picking up a banana peel when something caught his eye.

A pregnancy test.

He reached for it and glanced down at the stick. The results were no longer readable. Did this mean she was pregnant? The thought of her carrying his child flooded his heart with love.

He carried the bag to the dumpster on the side of the house and noticed Pace's truck parked beside a tree.

Tossing the bag and closing the lid, he then went in search of his wife.

"Lay one hand on my wife and you're a dead man."

The words rushed through the barn like a gust of high wind. Pace stopped dead in his tracks. Darrius froze like a deer in front of headlights.

When Jesse looked at him with eyes filled with fear, a wave of fierce protectiveness welled inside him

Pace gave a distorted laugh. "Back away," he said, dragging Jesse.

Will fought the impulse to go to her because he didn't want to risk her life. "I protect what's mine," he warned, promising himself he would wipe the smirk off the man's face at the first opportunity.

The warning was uttered in such a deadly tone, Jesse ceased squirming to stare into her husband's eyes. What she saw answered so many unanswered questions. She saw a mixture of love and fear. At that moment she felt something hard and cold against her back.

Pace had a knife, and was planning to kill her. Everything inside of her went still.

"Put the knife down, Pace."

He laughed, then pulled her tighter against his smelly body. "Sorry, but I can't do that. This little lady is going with me." He backed her toward the rear, placing the blade against her throat.

Jesse's heart was beating a mile a minute. She didn't want to die. Not before she had a chance to tell Will about the baby.

Darrius now had a pocket knife in his hand, and he stood there with his eyes fierce and challenging, waiting for Will to make his move.

As they continued to move toward the back, Will continued to move forward. He had to come up with a way to save his wife.

Watching Jesse's eyes, he noticed that she was looking down at the shovel as they passed it. Her eyes traveled over to him and she gave him a slight smile and nodded her head. She was getting ready to make a move and wanted him to grab the shovel. He hoped he was right. If not, there was no telling what would happen. Sure enough, as soon as he came abreast of the shovel, Jesse screamed "Now!" and sank her elbow hard into Pace's groin. Will grabbed the shovel and swung it at Darrius's head, knocking him cold. Then he made a dash for Pace before he could recover and landed a solid fist to his nose.

Standing over Pace's body, he tore his eyes away from him long enough to look at his wife. "Boo, are you alright?"

She looked into the eyes of the man she loved. "Yes, Will. I'm fine."

"Good. Then go call the police before I'm no longer responsible for my actions."

By the time she returned, he had both Pace and Darrius tied up.

"I called 911. The sheriff should be here shortly." Although she looked calm and collected, there was a slight tremor in her voice that let him know she was still terrified.

He reached for her hand. "Are you okay? He didn't hurt you or the baby?" He pulled her into his arms, needing to shelter her.

She drew a deep breath. "How did you know?"

"I found the test. So it's true?"

"Yes," she confessed in a soft voice.

He returned her smile, feeling some of the tension of the last few minutes easing. He then swept her into his arms. Only minutes ago, he could have lost both of them forever.

Their lips met in a deep kiss and Jesse suddenly realized that this moment marked the true start of their marriage. No matter what the years might bring, she would make a real home with Will and would always cherish their life together.

EPILOGUE

A year later...

Jesse sat near a window facing the ocean, her son in her arms suckling greedily at her breast. Staring down at his little face, she felt a smile of pride tipping her lips.

The last year of her life had been the kind of year any new bride and expectant mother would dream of.

Katherine's had been filled nonstop since reopening. After they moved into TWIN WILLOWS, the Butlers moved into the bed and breakfast, and the newlyweds focused on renovating their new home and preparing for their new addition. Just as she had expected, Will had barely let her raise a finger. Instead, he spent her entire pregnancy spoiling her often with gifts and unlimited love and devotion.

As she stroked his soft red curls, her darling little boy opened his eyes and met her loving smile. William Jesse Jones had inherited his mother's hair and his father's brown eyes and complexion. Hearing a car, she swiveled her chair to find that Will had arrived home. A smile rose to her lips.

Six months ago Will had given up touring with the band, although he occasionally performed at the piano bar where he had first confessed his love. Instead, he had enrolled in graduate school, and on the weekends gave private piano lessons out of their home.

William Jr. closed his eyes and was only seconds from falling asleep. Jesse rose from the chair, moved over to his baby bed and laid him inside. As soon as he was lying peacefully, she planted a kiss to his cheek and went downstairs in search of her husband.

"Thanks Ole Man," she said as she moved toward the stairs. Because of a will, she had found love.

ABOUT THE AUTHOR

Angie Daniels is a chronic daydreamer who loves a page-turner. Already an avid reader by age seven, she knew early on that someday she wanted to create stories of love and adventure. During the fifth grade she began her journey writing comical short stories. As her talent evolved she found herself writing full-length novels that offered her readers a full dose of romantic suspense. "I enjoy writing whodunits because they allow me to use my imagination to the fullest extent. When I combine it with a love story it's like spreading icing on a cake."

Angie was born in Chicago but after spending the last fifteen years in Missouri, she considers it her home. She holds a bachelor's degree in business, and a master's in human resource management. She enjoys the option of occasionally working on contract or just staying at home to write full-time. You can contact her via email at **angie@angiedaniels.com** or visit her website at www.angiedaniels.com.

Excerpt from

TAKEN BY YOU

BY

DOROTHY ELIZABETH LOVE

Release Date: October 2005

CHAPTER ONE

It had to be nervousness.

How else could she explain the anxiety she felt as she waited to meet the man who tiptoed around her dreams and didn't know she existed?

Not only was Reese McCoy a stranger to her, but he the famed football player, model and successful businessman. So much rolled into one man. That was probably why her heart was racing.

At Atlanta International airport, Leila stood in the shadows fifty feet away from the gate, scanning the crowd for the face she had seen many times in newspapers and on TV. She hadn't discovered any of the details about his personal life until the previous night when she had discussed him while viewing his pictures in the photo album of her friend Chi. The album was followed by an exciting look through a male pinup calendar. The barely clothed pinups hinted at a story about Reese McCoy that completely enticed and motivated her to reexamine the photo album.

This time around she had noticed that the less publicly known pictures in the album revealed expressions of happiness that seemed to lessen more and more as time passed by. Leila found that somewhat unsettling.

When Reese McCoy finally deplaned the aircraft from Scottsdale, Arizona, he flashed that wonderful smile—one Leila had come to like—at the airline attendant greeting passengers. His black pants and matching shirt nicely emphasized what she knew was an incredibly fit body underneath.

Lord, she thought, tingling, he's too fine in person.

Reese suddenly turned that alluring smile toward her. It masked the troubles she had heard he was having. Yet, still, it caused her breath to catch, pant a little. Too bad she had never met him in person before now.

Leila was about to wave to get his attention, but he turned and looked about, searching for someone. Leila knew he was looking for his friend, but wished it could have been her. She also knew that would never be the case. It seemed Reese McCoy had very little time for things outside of business, especially something as bothersome as a serious relationship.

Suddenly, his gaze returned to hers. This time their eyes locked for several moments. A slow, meaningful smile danced across his face. Leila couldn't stop her own mouth from reacting to his contagious smile. When he winked, she realized she was again staring. Did he think that she was just another pretty face on the long list of many that his tempting smile could entice? Embarrassed, she glanced away to refocus on her reason for being there.

Amazingly, in the short time she looked away he closed the distance between them.

Standing a few feet away he said, "Hello, pretty lady."

Probably a practiced line, she thought. He had no idea who she was or why she was there.

"I'm here to pick you up," Leila somehow found the confidence to say without breaking her stare.

He chuckled. "I haven't been to Atlanta in awhile, but come-on lines have certainly gotten bolder. I guess my next question should be, Your place or mine?"

"My place." Leila enjoyed his surprised look. She'd caught him off guard. Maybe he wasn't as practiced as she thought.

"Ohhh... yes," he growled softly, slowly, as his eyes roamed over her body. "I do miss Atlanta."

I think I'm flirting! That boosted her ego as she extended a hand for a shake. "I'm Leila Chamberlain. A friend of both Parker and Chi. Parker will call you about the change in plans, but he asked that I pick you up. He's stuck out of town on business and won't be back until very late. And Chi can't get away from the hospital. So I'm to babysit you until he returns." Leila was well aware that Reese had come to town to serve as Parker's best man.

"Babysit?" Reese chuckled, looking away.

Leila wasn't sure, but it looked as if there were a hint of something akin to regret behind that sienna stare. He recovered quickly. "I should start over," he said, accepting her hand to shake. "Nice to meet you, Leila. It's a pleasure."

Leila laughed then. "Parker thought you would be upset because all your plans for tonight changed at the last minute. He said something about you being a stickler for preplanning. I can't wait to tell him you used the word pleasure."

"Mention it's because of his choice of babysitters." Reese adjusted his carryon luggage over his shoulder. "I'll follow your lead."

His sinfully charming grin had returned and that caught her off guard. "I guess we should get your luggage."

"That's one option."

That certainly has a double meaning! She, however, stuck to the agenda. "We have a stop to make. I'm to remind you to get fitted for your tux today. We can go there next if you like."

"Although Chi and Parker's wedding is one of the reasons I'm in town, I have a few business errands to run. I'll get the tux later. I guess I need a rental car now."

"No, you don't." She dodged a traveler hurrying toward them. "Parker's Jeep and a key to his home are at my place. I'll take you there."

"You were serious about going to your place?" Reese smiled at her.

"I never kid around about inviting a man to my home." Leila stepped onto the down escalator that led to the underground rail system, which carried passengers to terminals. "It's also my place of business." She casually tossed that comment out.

The smirk on Reese's face showed he was possibly considering less than appropriate 'business' options. Or maybe he just found her seriousness to be funny. "Oh, really."

They rode down the escalator in silence, then joined a horde of people waiting for the train. When it arrived, everyone dashed aboard and attempted to find a spot to stand in the already crowded car. Leila moved to hold one of the stationary bars as Reese stood sardined between her and the people behind them. He managed to grasp the bar just above her hand. She could feel the heat of his body touching her back.

"Thanks for coming to pick me up," he said, leaning forward.

"No problem." Leila looked back over her shoulder at him. The mere inches between them sent heated awareness through her. She took in his wide, firm chest and strong, muscular arm, as his spicy cologne enchanted her. The train jarred to a stop at each terminal as it made its way to baggage claim, and each jerk brought Reese closer to Leila. Of course she could have taken a step forward to stop that from happening, but bumping into the tall, lanky man in front of her was not as appealing as bumping into Reese.

"What is Mr. Chamberlain going to say about your entertaining me while my friend's away?" His breath was on her ear.

"My father gave up on advising me years before he died," Leila said. She knew he was attempting to find out more about her personal life. Although single and available, she wasn't quite sure if she wanted to admit that yet.

It tickled her pride knowing she'd done very little to capture his interest, yet clearly she had. Well, if not counting the blatant stares, the flippant invitation to her home, and the unnecessary closeness they were now sharing.

Her senses seemed sharper. She was aware of his heat, aware of his attraction, and aware they would soon be alone together. Intrigued at how his mere presence had fully consumed her thoughts in a rather short period of time, she reflected on the little she knew of Reese. Her reaction to him was purely physical, the worst kind, and she needed to contain it. He was quite stunning in those calendar layout pictures. His barely clothed body posed next to August made that month definitely hotter.

What gave her pause was that he was an ex-football player, therefore probably a playboy. He had lost custody of his son during a bitter divorce, and his ex-wife lived in town. He had buried his only family, an aunt, several years ago and had taken her death hard. The recent downturn of his shipping business had relegated him to a struggling firm.

The train doors opened and they headed to baggage claim. As Reese watched for his suitcases to appear on the luggage conveyor, Leila stole a glance at him. He looked just as rugged and daring as he had in the younger photos, but now the fine lines of wisdom that cradled those eyes suggested experience she wanted to know more about.

His skin coloring reminded her of warm pecan pie, her favorite. She unconsciously licked her lips as she recalled the pictures showing more of that skin. Both he and Parker had posed as calendar models. Parker had done it as a dare. Reese, however, had needed the money and exposure.

In all the pictures she had seen, a smile completely brightened his handsome face. Unlike now. The smile was genuine but the cheerfulness seemed to have faded somewhat. She liked his faint beard that surrounded lips that promised heaven in a mouthful. Instantaneously, her mind drifted to a scene where she was experiencing that mouth, those fine hairs against sensitive parts of her body.

"I would pay big money to know your thoughts," Reese said,

watching her. He looked as though he already knew them.

"I didn't think I would recognize you from the pictures Parker showed me." Leila was proud of how well she came up with a valid reason, even veiled excuse, for blatantly, probably heatedly, staring at him again. "You haven't changed much in the past few years."

His smile disappeared as if memories from the past plagued his thoughts. "Pictures can lie. I'm nothing like that guy anymore."

He was frowning and she blamed herself. From lust to accusation. I should shut up and just get the man to his vehicle, Leila scolded herself.

"I just meant…" Leila was about to say, 'You look the same physically,' but it was too late because he had turned to retrieve his bag from the spinning conveyor.

She was sure his statement had nothing to do with physical changes, but more with the circumstances that surrounded his life. She didn't know the details, but Parker had labeled them as "difficult times." Since Parker had also labeled his first fiancée's death, his sister being shot and the accident that almost killed the love of his life, Chi, as "difficult times," Leila figured Reese's life must have been just as trying.

He collected the last of his luggage and followed Leila outside into the warm June afternoon. They went to Leila's car in short-term parking. She easily maneuvered the car out of the airport only to encounter caterpillar slow highway traffic.

"Is this typical for this time of day?" Reese asked a few minutes later, looking at the time.

"Not on I-75. There must be an accident ahead."

"How far away is your place?"

"Without traffic it's about twenty-five minutes."

"This can go on for awhile." Reese reached into his overnight bag to retrieve his cell phone and dialed. "Bill? It's Reese McCoy," he announced when the person answered. "I'm in town, but stuck in traffic. First, the plane was delayed. Now this. Can we delay our meeting until this evening?" Reese listened. "No, no. That's okay. I'll get there as soon as I can. I really need you to see my plan and consider supporting it... Yeah... Bill, it's a solid plan. Don't shoot it down until you have a chance to review it." The longer Reese talked, the flatter his tone got. He hung up and stared at the phone for a few seconds, visibly shaking off a difficult mood.

"I can take you directly to your meeting," Leila offered. "Pick you up and take you to get the Jeep afterwards."

"I'm not sure how long I'll be or where we're headed afterwards." Reese watched the traffic come to a halt. "The sooner I get to Parker's, the sooner I can shower, change and get to the meeting." His look suggested appreciation. "But thanks for offering."

Leila liked the sincerity she saw. "I have a better idea. You can change at my place, it's closer and we need to stop there anyway. I'll get off the highway as soon as I can. Maybe get around this." She turned and leaned back to get a map from her briefcase on the backseat. "I keep a city map with me for moments like this." When Leila looked up, she found Reese had turned toward her, looking down the V of her white blouse.

"Take your time."

"Are you sure? That call sounded important."

"It was. But I'm in no rush to listen to them shoot down my plan. This...," his eyes roamed provocatively up her chest to her eyes, "...delay is taking my mind off it."

His somber look from moments ago had disappeared, replaced with a warm, much more pleasing smile. Visions of teenager years "necking" in the car danced in Leila's head. The inches between them would only take seconds to remove.

She wasn't sure which one of them moved first, but somehow his mouth seemed much closer to hers. Her heart jiggled a little and she found herself breathing heavier. Then something in his eyes called to her.

Sampling him was a fantasy that had crossed her mind several times while looking at pictures of his fantastic body. Now she was sure she was the one to move closer this time.

The honking from the car behind startled her.

"Oh!" She jumped and let out a nervous little laugh. Looking quickly about, she then moved back under the wheel. It took her a few seconds to realize the car was already in gear and all she needed to do was remove her foot from the brake pedal. She felt like a clumsy teenager instead of the professional, sometimes sassy, business owner that she was.

That was a stupid gesture I just made, she said to herself, then turned to Reese. "Traffic is moving."

"Uh huh," he grunted, his smile widening.

Luckily, since she couldn't think of anything else to say, jazz from the car radio filled the air. It bothered her that she'd neither resisted nor gone through with the kiss. A kiss she'd been wanting to experience since the moment she'd dreamt of him. This kind of indecision was another example of why she would always be the lonely maid of honor and never the bride. She could dream about having a man but couldn't pull off impressing one as an experienced flirt.

Remembering the map, she busied herself with searching for a convenient route as she followed the slow-moving traffic.

"How long have you lived here?" Reese asked.

"I moved back about four years ago. It's changed a lot since I was a kid." She studied the map, then looked up at the road ahead. "I think I can get around this by getting off at the next exit."

"I'll leave my comforts in your competent hands."

Leila looked at him. His comforts. Was he picking at her for failing to resist him and failing to kiss him? Certainly kissing was a bit much for someone she had just met. She played it safe and pretended to take a greater interest in getting around the heavy traffic. The ride through the busy districts was the perfect distraction.

They arrived at her home, or partial home, as Leila called it, about thirty minutes later. They had talked very little en route because Reese spent most of the time on his cell phone discussing shipping matters. The gist of what Leila picked up on was that his cinching an important business deal was imperative to the expansion of his company. Based on

Reese's solemn tone, she figured things weren't going well.

Reese noticed the day care sign. "You have a kid we need to pick up from day care?" he asked as she parked the car.

"I live on the floor above it," Leila said, getting out of the car.

"Interesting place to call home." He went to get his luggage out of the trunk. "How come?"

"I own the building. The day care center is my business."

"Very clever." He glanced around at the upscale business location.

The day care was the size of a two-story warehouse with a large playground and expanse of land behind it. Several cars were in the parking lot. A few parents were picking up children. On the playground, several kids played on slides, swings and monkey bars, while others played a game of putt-putt golf. Several kids cheered when another whacked the small ball between the legs of a gigantic sized parrot.

Upstairs, Leila's apartment door opened into an extremely spacious room. She had a flair for the dramatic and had reconfigured the room into sections with cream Roman columns separating the foyer and hallway from the living room. The floors were bleached hardwood with matching paneled walls. Large plants were aplenty. A deep purple, leather sofa sat against the back wall, on the other side of the glass top table, matching chairs faced the sofa.

The unusually high windows on the back wall spanned up to vaulted ceilings and allowed a view of blue skies and green tops of leafy trees. A view she considered her peak at heaven. No one could have imagined that a busy playground, a major road and several businesses were just beyond those walls. It was just like she wanted it to be.

Reese's cellular phone ran again. "Hey, Suzette," he said casually.

The female name got Leila's attention. But she shouldn't be eavesdropping. Or at least, not look as if she were eavesdropping. Leila went to her desk at the far side of the room and opened the top drawer, pretending to be busy as she tuned in to Reese's side of the conversation.

"I'll rearrange my schedule," he was saying. "I don't want to change the plans for this weekend. Okay. Bye."

Leila sensed he was studying her downcast head. She put down the mail she held and reached back inside the top drawer to get a stuffed envelope, which she handed it to him. "These are for you. Jeep keys, Parker's house key, and directions to the tuxedo shop."

"Parker is finally getting married." Reese shook his head. "I still can't believe it."

She angled her head, confused. Leila wasn't sure if she appreciated the comment. "For a best man, you don't sound too supportive."

He looked at her, his expression tame. "Parker deserves to finally find happiness."

For some reason she wanted to be annoyed at Reese. Possibly as a means to dampen her fascination with him, but his sincere look wouldn't allow her to use his comment as a reason. Well, the man did live several states away and, according to Chi, was on the rebound from a terrible divorce. If that wasn't reason enough to sway her interest, then obviously his looking forward to seeing this Suzette person should have been. It wasn't. Leila fought down the urge to flirt, to compete.

She walked around him. "You wanted to shower and change. Let me show you to the bathroom."

Reese stepped inside a bathroom that only an interior designer could have imagined. The high ceiling was painted with clouds and the borders with leafy red and purple roses. It had a Jacuzzi tub, a freestanding glassed-in shower stall, and more Roman columns. The center wall featured a vanity area on one side and a loveseat with bookcase on the other.

"Very nice. I like your taste." Reese set down his luggage.

"Thanks. I live too close to my job. So home had to be an escape for me." Leila opened the closet door and handed him a towel and washcloth. She pointed and said, "Everything else you'll need should be under the sink."

She turned and noticed him unbuttoning his shirt. When he started to casually pull the shirttails from out of his pants, she froze. Not out of panic but out of pleasure. She'd dreamt about seeing that body up close and personal.

Then Reese placed his hands on his hips and the shirt opened even more. "Anything else you want to tell me?" Reese asked.

Again she was staring. His chest was more enticing than the one she'd conjured up in her dream last night. She dragged her eyes up to his. His cocky grin didn't help matters. It was one thing to secretly drool and pant like a cat in heat. Being caught, however, was rather embarrassing.

"I need to go downstairs to check on the day care." Leila found herself struggling to find something other than him to gawk at. Failing, she walked toward the safety of the door.

Unfortunately for her, he stopped her by catching her by the arm as she passed. Leila stepped away from him but he refused to release her.

"What is it?" she whispered.

"There is something else," Reese said, pulling her closer to his inviting body.

She sidestepped. "I've delayed you long enough from your meeting," Leila said to his hand since she wasn't brave enough to look him in the face. He might see just how in need of his touch she was.

The telephone rang. Again she jumped and inwardly cursed because of it. She really needed to gain control of herself. "Let me get that." She looked at the telephone that hung on the bathroom wall by the loveseat behind him. Though parts of the too-large bathroom looked and felt like a den, it was still too intimate a setting for her with Reese there. She decided to take the call elsewhere.

At her desk, Leila found herself breathing heavily when she answered. "Chi! Hi! Your timing couldn't be better... We just got here. Reese was about to jump in the shower..."

"Stop him!" Chi said. "I need to talk to him."

"Oh, okay, hold on." Leila hurried to the bathroom door and called out. "Reese, it's for you!" When he picked up the bathroom telephone, she went to hang up the one on the desk.

As she did, Reese stepped out of the bathroom, the cordless telephone resting on his bare shoulder. He had taken off his shirt and shoes, and his pants were partly unzipped. "I think that's a fantastic idea. I'm sure of it," he said to Chi. "I assume you've already talked to Leila?"

Leila came to stand in the hallway, watching him watch her. His stare was disconcerting. So sexy, so disarming, so distracting. Thankfully, the man would be leaving her home forever once he showered and changed. Moments earlier when he touched her, she'd had the impression he was going to do something quite thrilling. That would have been a mistake for her, in light of the Suzette call, but for some reason she felt disappointed that it hadn't happened.

Luckily, he was leaving and her life would soon return to normal. She could sit back and think about her crazy reactions to him later. Whatever he had just said to Chi, Leila hadn't heard; she was too busy enjoying his near nakedness.

In less than an hour he will be gone, she reminded herself. She exhaled slowly to calm her racing heart.

"Leila," Reese said, "Chi was wondering if you could help with something tonight."

"Sure," she said. "Of course."

"More wedding guests are flying to town."

"Does she need me to pick them up from the airport?" she asked.

"It seems Parker has run out of room for everyone. So Chi was wondering if you wouldn't mind entertaining me tonight…," Reese paused to smile, "by letting me use your bedroom."

Although he was perfectly clear, Leila asked, slightly flustered, "What?"

He removed the distance between them and said again, very slowly, very provocatively, "I want to stay the night with you."

A WILL TO LOVE

2005 Publication Schedule

January

A Heart's Awakening
Veronica Parker
$9.95
1-58571-143-8

Falling
Natalie Dunbar
$9.95
1-58571-121-7

February

Echoes of Yesterday
Beverly Clark
$9.95
1-58571-131-4

A Love of Her Own
Cheris F. Hodges
$9.95
1-58571-136-5

Higher Ground
Leah Latimer
$19.95
1-58571-157-8

March

Misconceptions
Pamela Leigh Starr
$9.95
1-58571-117-9

I'll Paint a Sun
A.J. Garrotto
$9.95
1-58571-165-9

Peace Be Still
Colette Haywood
$12.95
1-58571-129-2

April

Intentional Mistakes
Michele Sudler
$9.95
1-58571-152-7

Conquering Dr. Wexler's Heart
Kimberley White
$9.95
1-58571-126-8

Song in the Park
Martin Brant
$15.95
1-58571-125-X

May

The Color Line
Lizzette Grayson Carter
$9.95
1-58571-163-2

Unconditional
A.C. Arthur
$9.95
1-58571-142-X

Last Train to Memphis
Elsa Cook
$12.95
1-58571-146-2

June

Angel's Paradise
Janice Angelique
$9.95
1-58571-107-1

Suddenly You
Crystal Hubbard
$9.95
1-58571-158-6

Matters of Life and
    Death
Lesego Malepe, Ph.D.
$15.95
1-58571-124-1

2005 Publication Schedule (continued)

July

Class Reunion
Irma Jenkins/John
    Brown
$12.95
1-58571-123-3

Wild Ravens
Altonya Washington
$9.95
1-58571-164-0

August

Path of Thorns
Annetta P. Lee
$9.95
1-58571-145-4

Timeless Devotion
Bella McFarland
$9.95
1-58571-148-9

Life Is Never As It Seems
J.J. Michael
$12.95
1-58571-153-5

September

Beyond Rapture
Beverly Clark
$9.95
1-58571-131-4

Blood Lust
J. M. Jeffries
$9.95
1-58571-138-1

Rough on Rats and
    Tough on Cats
Chris Parker
$12.95
1-58571-154-3

October

A Will to Love
Angie Daniels
$9.95
1-58571-141-1

Taken by You
Dorothy Elizabeth Love
$9.95
1-58571-162-4

Soul Eyes
Wayne L. Wilson
$12.95
1-58571-147-0

November

A Drummer's Beat to
    Mend
Kei Swanson
$9.95
1-58571-171-3

Sweet Reprecussions
Kimberley White
$9.95
1-58571-159-4

Red Polka Dot in a
    World of Plaid
Varian Johnson
$12.95
1-58571-140-3

December

Hand in Glove
Andrea Jackson
$9.95
1-58571-166-7

Blaze
Barbara Keaton
$9.95
1-58571-172-1

Across
Carol Payne
$12.95
1-58571-149-7

Other Genesis Press, Inc. Titles

Erotic Anthology	Assorted	$8.95
Eve's Prescription	Edwina Martin Arnold	$8.95
Everlastin' Love	Gay G. Gunn	$8.95
Fate	Pamela Leigh Starr	$8.95
Forbidden Quest	Dar Tomlinson	$10.95
Fragment in the Sand	Annetta P. Lee	$8.95
From the Ashes	Kathleen Suzanne	$8.95
	Jeanne Sumerix	
Gentle Yearning	Rochelle Alers	$10.95
Glory of Love	Sinclair LeBeau	$10.95
Hart & Soul	Angie Daniels	$8.95
Heartbeat	Stephanie Bedwell-Grime	$8.95
I'll Be Your Shelter	Giselle Carmichael	$8.95
Illusions	Pamela Leigh Starr	$8.95
Indiscretions	Donna Hill	$8.95
Interlude	Donna Hill	$8.95
Intimate Intentions	Angie Daniels	$8.95
Just an Affair	Eugenia O'Neal	$8.95
Kiss or Keep	Debra Phillips	$8.95
Love Always	Mildred E. Riley	$10.95
Love Unveiled	Gloria Greene	$10.95
Love's Deception	Charlene Berry	$10.95
Mae's Promise	Melody Walcott	$8.95
Meant to Be	Jeanne Sumerix	$8.95
Midnight Clear	Leslie Esdaile	$10.95
(Anthology)	Gwynne Forster	
	Carmen Green	
	Monica Jackson	
Midnight Magic	Gwynne Forster	$8.95
Midnight Peril	Vicki Andrews	$10.95
My Buffalo Soldier	Barbara B. K. Reeves	$8.95
Naked Soul	Gwynne Forster	$8.95
No Regrets	Mildred E. Riley	$8.95
Nowhere to Run	Gay G. Gunn	$10.95

Object of His Desire	A. C. Arthur	$8.95
One Day at a Time	Bella McFarland	$8.95
Passion	T.T. Henderson	$10.95
Past Promises	Jahmel West	$8.95
Path of Fire	T.T. Henderson	$8.95
Picture Perfect	Reon Carter	$8.95
Pride & Joi	Gay G. Gunn	$8.95
Quiet Storm	Donna Hill	$8.95
Reckless Surrender	Rochelle Alers	$8.95
Rendezvous with Fate	Jeanne Sumerix	$8.95
Revelations	Cheris F. Hodges	$8.95
Rivers of the Soul	Leslie Esdaile	$8.95
Rooms of the Heart	Donna Hill	$8.95
Shades of Brown	Denise Becker	$8.95
Shades of Desire	Monica White	$8.95
Sin	Crystal Rhodes	$8.95
So Amazing	Sinclair LeBeau	$8.95
Somebody's Someone	Sinclair LeBeau	$8.95
Someone to Love	Alicia Wiggins	$8.95
Soul to Soul	Donna Hill	$8.95
Still Waters Run Deep	Leslie Esdaile	$8.95
Subtle Secrets	Wanda Y. Thomas	$8.95
Sweet Tomorrows	Kimberly White	$8.95
The Color of Trouble	Dyanne Davis	$8.95
The Price of Love	Sinclair LeBeau	$8.95
The Reluctant Captive	Joyce Jackson	$8.95
The Missing Link	Charlyne Dickerson	$8.95
Three Wishes	Seressia Glass	$8.95
Tomorrow's Promise	Leslie Esdaile	$8.95
Truly Inseperable	Wanda Y. Thomas	$8.95
Twist of Fate	Beverly Clark	$8.95
Unbreak My Heart	Dar Tomlinson	$8.95
Unconditional Love	Alicia Wiggins	$8.95
When Dreams A Float	Dorothy Elizabeth Love	$8.95

Whispers in the Night	Dorothy Elizabeth Love	$8.95
Whispers in the Sand	LaFlorya Gauthier	$10.95
Yesterday is Gone	Beverly Clark	$8.95
Yesterday's Dreams, Tomorrow's Promises	Reon Laudat	$8.95
Your Precious Love	Sinclair LeBeau	$8.95

Order Form

Mail to: Genesis Press, Inc.
P.O. Box 101
Columbus, MS 39703

Name _____
Address _____
City/State _____ Zip _____
Telephone _____

Ship to (if different from above)
Name _____
Address _____
City/State _____ Zip _____
Telephone _____

Credit Card Information
Credit Card # _____ ☐ Visa ☐ Mastercard
Expiration Date (mm/yy) _____ ☐ AmEx ☐ Discover

Qty.	Author	Title	Price	Total

Use this order form, or call 1-888-INDIGO-1	Total for books _____
	Shipping and handling: $5 first two books, $1 each additional book _____
	Total S & H _____
	Total amount enclosed _____
	Mississippi residents add 7% sales tax

Order Form

Mail to: Genesis Press, Inc.
P.O. Box 101
Columbus, MS 39703

Name _____
Address _____
City/State _____ Zip _____
Telephone _____

Ship to (if different from above)
Name _____
Address _____
City/State _____ Zip _____
Telephone _____

Credit Card Information
Credit Card # _____ ☐ Visa   ☐ Mastercard
Expiration Date (mm/yy) _____ ☐ AmEx   ☐ Discover

Qty.	Author	Title	Price	Total

Use this order form, or call 1-888-INDIGO-1	Total for books _____
	Shipping and handling: $5 first two books, $1 each additional book _____
	Total S & H _____
	Total amount enclosed _____

Mississippi residents add 7% sales tax